G4M3

SHATTERED REALITY

By Justin R. Stebbins

Cover design and illustration by Justin R. Stebbins

ISBN 0-9727341-0-4

First published 2006
This Second Edition was edited, revised, and re-published in 2018

Additional copies of this book are available online at
http://www.saber-scorpion.com/g4m3

Published by Justin R. R. Stebbins

P R O L O G U E

It's not real. It's not real.

He had to keep reminding himself of this as the bullets shattered the concrete walls around him, sending splinters flying into his face. He could feel them strike his skin – could feel the dust in his eyes. He had to blink and wipe away the tears in order to see again, at least as much as he could ever see in this dark, war-torn hellscape.

He felt a strange warmth all over the side of his leg. He reached down and felt something wet there. It was blood. He'd been hit, and it was bleeding badly. Suddenly, as the adrenaline ebbed away, the pain hit him like an oncoming train. He had never felt such agony in his entire life – a life spent in Utopia, a perfect world, free of all violence. He had to get back there...

It's not real, he told himself again. The pain is simulated. It's not real.

He heard a boot take a grinding step on the dusty ground nearby. Looking up, he saw one of those rebel guerrilla fighters with the familiar eagle tattoo on one arm. The violent thug spotted his wounded target and lowered his shotgun to fire.

But the wounded man was faster. He still had his pistol ready. The recoil felt so real, and the bang of the gunshot was deafening. He knew the man he'd killed was just a mental projection of a computer program, but he still couldn't look at his face as he toppled to the ground, unmoving.

More Eagles would arrive soon, he knew. He had to move. Lifting himself painfully to his feet, he hobbled toward a doorway, beyond which lay a pitch-dark room. Just dark enough, he hoped...

"Freeze!"

For some reason, he did as commanded. Perhaps it was because he feared the pain of being shot again... or perhaps because he'd spent his whole life in Utopia obediently following orders, so he still did it, even in this game.

He started to raise his hands, but as he did, he also drew out a grenade and armed it. He would take out a few of these damned Eagles before he left the game. Even if it wasn't real…

As he reached for the hidden button that would end the simulation and take him home, he felt bullets strike him in the back – so many bullets. Their impacts sent him stumbling and falling into the dark room ahead, still clutching the armed grenade.

Then, even as the pain overwhelmed him, he felt the familiar sensation of wind blowing around him, which meant the game was ending. He closed his eyes, letting his grenade fall to the ground. He hoped the soldiers would rush into the room after him and find the grenade there, just in time.

Or not. It didn't really matter. None of it was real.

ONE
A PERFECT WORLD

The light from the explosion flooded my living room with its orange glow. I had never seen anything so terrifyingly beautiful. It was like a blooming flower of fire and destruction.

Of course, it was only an image on the holovision. And as soon as it faded, a man stepped into view to replace it. He was old, though his exact age was impossible to determine due to modern cosmetics. Despite his dark black hair and relatively unlined face, he was probably as old as my grandfather. Some wrinkles did appear beside his mouth when he smiled. And on the holovision, Frank Billings was always smiling.

"This is the wave of the future," Frank Billings said, throwing his arms dramatically into the air. "The ability to experience violence first-hand without actually harming a soul. The power to live life to its fullest without disrupting the Order. GAME now has over a million players all over Utopia! All of them have discovered the wonders of the alternate reality, and not one has been taken into custody for a criminal offense. GAME does not provoke violence; it keeps it off the streets and in the virtual world of GAME…"

"I don't know how Grandfather ever put up with him," I said casually, to no one in particular, watching as the G4M3 lettering – spelled with the number four in the place of the A and a three in place of the E – appeared on the screen. Despite its strange spelling, it was simply pronounced 'game'.

My father, who was sitting at the table behind me while eating dinner with Mother, said, "Frank is a fine man. There is nothing wrong with Frank. Your grandfather trusted Frank perhaps more than he trusted me. We wouldn't have been able to keep the G4M3 running were it not for him."

"I know," I answered, stretching myself out on the sofa.

I remember our house perfectly. It was spotless and white, with furniture an eye-calming shade of beige. The sunlight, dim as it was, streamed in through multiple windows that were kept so clean by automatic cleaning devices that there hardly seemed to be glass in them. The glass, I knew, could be tinted automatically, or even turned opaque by the Order whenever they thought it necessary.

The lower floor of the house was split into two main rooms: the kitchen and dining room, and the living room with the couch and holovision. Between them was a small half-wall. The bedrooms lay upstairs. Everything was very open, flat, smooth, white, clean... basically sterile.

Our house was almost exactly like every single other house in the residential area of Utopia. Everyone lived in total equality under the Order. There were no rich, no poor – only citizens, doing their jobs.

No one knew exactly what 'the Order' was, precisely. It was simply a vague idea of a guiding force, a leader, almost a deity, that moved all things according to its will. The Order saw all things at all times, and those who spoke against it or disobeyed its laws were taken away to be reeducated or permanently relocated.

One always felt secure in Utopia, because even if you did not know where you were, or even where you were going, the Order did. The robots that worked for the Order, along with their few human counterparts, were always more than willing to help citizens of Utopia, or to stop them from breaking the law. The Order had legal ownership over everything in Utopia. There was no such thing as private property. The Order owned everything, including the citizens.

Each house in Utopia had the same style of architecture, and each street looked the same. Everyone's clothes looked the same. Everyone's hair had to be styled to a certain standard. Every man had to be clean-shaven. The people were not all exactly alike in manner, but the Order herded them into groups that were similar to one another. There were certain people who thought differently, and they were put in the philosophers' group; there were those who were creative, and they went in the artists' group; but most people just stuck together in the general society, living together, working together, and playing together. Everything in the Order was perfect.

There was only one problem: It got a little bit boring after a while.

That was why it was actually lucky for the Order that my grandfather invented G4M3. It gave people a chance to enter a virtual war-zone and experience violence, chaos, bloodshed, hatred, and destruction. Some people who played G4M3 were revolted by it, and it only deepened their belief in the beauty of the Order's world of Utopia even firmer.

Other people could not get enough of G4M3; it was like a drug, and they kept going back for more. They were known as the Players. The Players were mostly young people who enjoyed the exciting life offered by G4M3, though they were always more than happy to return to the nice, peaceful life afforded by Utopia once a gaming session ended.

"Today is an important day for you, son, and you have to make a decision," my father said as he entered the living room, carefully sipping his tea. "You're old enough to play G4M3 now, but the question is: Do you want to?"

"I don't know how I could stand not to experience my own grandfather's creation at *all*," I said with a little laugh. "Of course I'm gonna play G4M3. I'm officially twenty-one today, so I can finally give it a try."

"I know I can't control you, Kyle," my father said. "You're an adult and free to do what you like. The Order dictates that you must move out on your own this year. You've stayed with us too long anyway, really, son. I fear it comes from a lack of socialization. A certain amount of socialization is necessary for a healthy lifestyle."

"Let's not get back into this conversation, Father..." I said, shaking my head with an exasperated sigh. "I had friends... You remember Billy Byrd, don't you?"

"Yes, but you didn't have any *girl*-friends," he said, smiling the same smile as always.

I frowned ever so slightly as I replied, "I've told you, none of the girls I met in education interested me. They were all exactly the same."

"Perhaps you'll meet a girl more to your liking at the G4M3 facility," my father said. "It's all right, Kyle. I respect your decision. But we should all marry and settle down eventually."

My father was a perfect follower of the Order's rules, though you wouldn't think so by looking at him. He was a tall man, and broad-shouldered, but of an exceedingly mild temperament. He was not as intelligent as Grandfather had been. Whereas Grandfather had spent all his time in computer labs, Father enjoyed recreational activities and sports.

It was a shame that Grandfather had created the G4M3 so late in his life, for he had never truly gotten to enjoy it himself. Especially since, soon after its completion, he'd been struck with a strange disease. It was exceedingly rare for a disease to appear that the Order did not know how to cure immediately... but Grandfather had somehow developed one. No one knew exactly what it was, and his condition had only gotten worse since. He never left the hospital.

Grandfather, Father, and I all shared the same blue eyes, brown hair, and bright smile... except that Grandfather almost never smiled, even before his condition deteriorated. He had always seemed haunted by something, and he'd been abnormally dedicated to his work. I often wondered why he had wanted to work so hard for a living when the Order provided everything that was necessary for life, but there were always some people who lived to work regardless.

Finally, I decided it was time for me to leave. I was eager to experience G4M3 as soon as possible. So, I said goodbye to my father and mother and went outside to catch the bus.

Upon leaving the house, I was greeted by the familiar overcast yellow-grey sky and equally familiar, featureless grey streets. I jogged to the nearest glowing yellow lamppost and pressed the button for the Universal Transport System, or UTS. Within minutes, the UTS bus came rolling up on its track.

The bus was long and sleek, with rows of windows behind which sat placid-faced citizens of Utopia. The robotic driver turned its metallic head in my direction, and blinked his glowing eyes. One of its thin mechanical arms motioned for me to take a seat. I walked up the stairs and sat down in the back. I rode placidly along, waiting patiently at every stop, until I heard the calm voice, which could not be recognized as exactly male or female, announce over the bus speakers: "Next stop… G4M3 Facility."

I felt a little bit nervous. This was it, I thought. I was about to enter the G4M3. I knew that no one ever got hurt in G4M3, but the stories that I had heard of players' experiences were enough to make anyone a little frightened. I stared out the window, watching the identical off-white houses pass by under the pallid yellow sky.

The sky of Utopia was always a strange, sickly color, grey in the upper reaches but changing to a sickly yellow closer to the horizon. The sky was sometimes lighter or darker, but never truly bright and never truly black. The sickly clouds always reflected the ground light from the streetlights right back down into the city. Even the sun seemed to be choking in the smog, so small and dim it appeared. Of course, at that time, it was all I had ever known.

As I watched through the window, we rode by one of the hundreds of statues in Utopia. The Order considered statues to be an improvement on the overall appearance of the streets, so it constructed many of them. The problem was that they all looked the same. They depicted a standard human, carved in a simple way so that he had no real facial features and his gender was not quite certain, though he looked mostly male. He always held in his hands a large hammer.

The plaque at the bottom of each statue proclaimed it to be the Builder, the backbone of Utopia. Every citizen, they said, was a Builder, and Utopia existed because of them and for them. They existed to maintain and improve the city of Utopia, and Utopia existed to make their lives as safe and comfortable as possible.

Suddenly I saw a slightly taller blank white building appear: the G4M3 facility. Frank Billings himself, head of the company, was standing outside the door, smiling and shaking hands. I wondered vaguely why he was there, but then I realized that it was probably because of me.

I watched him for a moment before I exited the tram. He was smiling just like he always did on the holovision. I ignored the voice in the tram that kept insisting I get out, saying that passengers with this stop were to exit immediately, and I kept watching him until the last guest had passed inside.

For a moment I got a glimpse of what I had wanted to see: Frank stopped smiling. He looked twice as old the moment he did so, and his shoulders hunched as if under a burden. He worked hard, I thought, just like Grandfather. Both of them had put a lot of work into developing G4M3 and spreading it across Utopia.

The smile quickly returned to Frank's face as he realized that the tram was still before him, which meant that someone was inside who had chosen the G4M3 facility as their destination. I walked out then, and the doors of the tram shut quickly, almost with an angry note, behind my back. Frank Billings smiled even wider as I drew nearer, striding across the clean, grey sidewalk.

"Kyle Roswell!" he exclaimed joyously at my approach. "So good to see you! I've been waiting for you all day, boy, to introduce you to G4M3 personally! You would not believe all the people I've shaken hands with! I think my hand is beginning to smart. So, how are you?"

I was always uncomfortable around Frank, because I had the feeling that he was still using his holovision voice and tone... instead of being frank with me, so to speak.

"It's good to see you too, Frank," I said.

"Please, call me Uncle Frank," he said, as he shook my hand with a surprisingly strong grip. "I'm sure you already know the rules of G4M3, but I'll go over them again anyway."

"There's no need, Uncle Frank," I said. "I know them well enough. I've been waiting almost at your doorstep for years to play G4M3, asking you all about it..."

"Of course there is still a need, Kyle," he said, his voice suddenly taking on a serious tone. "Protocol is all-important, as the Order always tells us."

"Of course…" I said with an apologetic smile.

Frank smiled back as he shut the door behind us and led me down the white hallways. "That bot at the entrance is my secretary and door greeter. She'll be who you speak to when I'm not around. These computers you see here on the walls, Kyle, are for everyone's use. You can access them to learn about the virtual lifestyles of the artificial men and women that exist in G4M3. The screens will also instruct you in the use of weaponry. As I'm sure you know, there are training robots in that room there to help you in the combat areas as well."

I laughed at his official-sounding tone. "I've trained with them often already, actually. You know that."

"Of course I do, Kyle, I'm just following the protocol. I have to tell you everything, just like the android would do if she were leading you around. Here, step into the elevator."

The hallways on the second floor were all exactly the same as on the first, except that the blank screens on the computers attached to the walls glowed a dark shade of red instead of green. The rows of doors on the stainless white walls were evenly spaced, the exact same distance apart. An android cleaner rolled past us down the corridor, scrubbing the walls to keep them shining and reflective.

"Now these computers on the upper floors," Frank said to me, "are not for use by mere Players. They are for authorized personnel only, as they determine the settings of the G4M3. Here, I will show you to your room."

Frank placed his palm on one of the red computer screens, and it left a glowing red print. The print slowly faded into blue and then lit up green. The door slid open. The room inside contained two tables. One was soft and cushioned – white, as always – with a strange device lying on the corner of it.

Upon the other table lay some dirty clothes, along with one of the assault rifles that I had trained to use in the simulators on the first floor, some armor plating, and a few other weapons. There was even some food there as well.

"This is your standard soldier equipment," Frank said, his strangely pale brown eyes scanning the military gear. "You should already know how to use all of it properly once you're in G4M3. There's some in-game currency there too, so you can buy new items in the game-world. I'll let you suit up in a second. First, I'll go over the basic rules again, as per protocol."

I sighed at this unnecessary delay, but allowed him to continue.

He cleared his throat. "First of all, you are entering a section of the G4M3 world inhabited by three warring factions. These are the Eagles, the Bloodletter Blades, and the Iron Fist. The Iron Fist is the law in the area, and their official name is 'NEWOR,' which stands for New World Order. They are trying to establish law in the region. The Eagles and Bloodletter Blades both want to bring them down, and, along with other small gangs, are always fighting with one another. Your role is to pick a part in the conflict. All of the gangs will be looking for new recruits, and you will come in as a wanderer from the city of Agelles. Remember that name now: *Agelles*. Tell them that you're tough, ready to kick butt, and are looking for work. Be violent and impulsive. Stop *smiling* all the time."

I was surprised to hear these words from this man as he stood there smiling broadly at me. Here in Utopia, politeness was always encouraged, and smiling showed satisfaction and fostered general good feelings. Though most smiles were quite frankly fake, and most people knew them to be so, it was the custom to wear them almost all the time, especially when speaking to someone. But of course, this virtual world would have far different rules, and its people would be programmed with a far different attitude.

Frank stepped over to the bed as he continued: "Now, please lie down and lift up your shirt. I'm going to use this device here to implant a tiny microchip under your skin. It will hurt a bit; consider it a small taste of the pain stimulation you'll experience in G4M3. Though nothing can quite prepare you for the feeling of being shot or stabbed. Sure you're up for it?"

"I'm ready," I said with determination.

Frank paused and stared at me for a moment then, before he said in a much graver tone, "Sure you are. Well, this device that I am about to implant into you will ensure that the pain is nothing too severe... nothing like the real pain that a soldier would feel in the horrors of an actual war."

"I don't like to think of it as real at all," I said.

"It isn't, but I would advise acting like it *is* once you're in G4M3," he continued talking as he lay me down on the white table and picked up the device, which looked like a large white remote control. "The characters in G4M3 consider their world real, since they've been programmed that way, and talking to them otherwise won't get you anywhere. They'll just think you're crazy. That won't help you in G4M3."

Frank pressed one end of his device against my stomach – right inside my navel. Then he pressed a button, and I felt a quick stab of pain. Then nothing. He held the device against me for a moment longer, then drew it away. There was no sign of a wound.

"If you're ever 'killed' in G4M3," Frank went on, "you will be whisked back here, to reality. The simulations are persistent worlds. Do you know what that means? It means that, even though there are usually at least a dozen players in each virtual world, the worlds will continue to be simulated inside the computer servers even if no one is playing there. They 'evolve' on their own, just like real worlds, and the artificial intelligence programs who live there remember each Player.

"Because of this, there's no there's no 'loading your game'. Once you die in a particular G4M3 world server, you cannot return. We here at the facility will offer you a new virtual life in another server, but you can never return to the first. You have one life per world. Those are the rules of G4M3."

I began strapping on my gear with Frank's help. It was very heavy and felt and smelled terrible, but I felt more alive with each piece that was added. The coarse, dirty clothing and armor plating made me feel more like a man somehow, just like the soldiers on the posters in the training rooms.

"If you ever want to leave G4M3, you must run to a very dark room and press a button on the device implanted within you," Frank went on. "The button is in your navel... your bellybutton. Just pinch it. It won't work unless the room is extremely dark – that's what we call a safe zone. You have to reach a safe zone to quit. Those are the rules. We don't want you logging out in mid-combat. Note that any items you pick up in G4M3 are only virtual, so don't expect them to come back with you on the return trip... They feel so real that some players actually expect that."

He chuckled. I loaded my assault rifle and shoved my pistol into its holster. I bared my teeth and scowled at the mirror on one wall, but quickly wiped off the expression so that Frank wouldn't see. I was hoping for intimidating, but it only looked foolish to me. The strong and manly feeling that the armor had instilled in me instantly disappeared. I felt like a sheep in wolf's clothing.

At that point, Frank Billings grabbed me by the shoulders and wheeled me around to face him. Looking into my eyes, he asked, "So, Kyle... are you ready to experience G4M3?"

I nodded quickly – too quickly to appear confident.

Frank gave me a skeptical look, but smiled and said, "You'll learn fast."

With that, he turned and stepped out into the hallway. The door closed behind him. Frank was never one for idle conversation. He was too much of a businessman. My heart really did skip a beat then, as the room suddenly went pitch black. I heard a whirring noise and sat down on one of the tables in the room, my heart beating fast.

After a second or two, I felt a strange sensation, as if the room was filled with a burst of wind as strong as a tornado... and then the table disappeared from under me. My rear end hit the ground hard, and I reached down with my right hand to push myself back up.

Dirt.

The ground was dirty – no, the ground *was* dirt. I could feel it under my fingers. Only then did I realize that my eyes were closed. Looking around me, I saw a most desolate and terrible place... a land

I had never even dreamed of, not even in my nightmares. I took a deep breath and hefted my assault rifle.

I was in the G4M3.

TWO
THE G4M3S BEGIN

All around me, the wind howled over a barren wasteland. Clouds of swirling dust whipped up in patterns of grey-black sand, like ash. The sky above was a dark, reddish haze, with thick, black, smoke-like clouds clogging out any view of the sun. It boiled and churned like lava.

This world, this G4M3, was so much the total opposite of Utopia that at first, I felt completely at a loss. The landscape around me was dreary and desolate. I had seen images of a desert once, on a holovision program about the horrors of the world before it was saved by the Order. But even that desert had looked friendly compared to this one.

The sand was not a pretty shade of gold, but a bleak grey color, reflecting the dreary atmosphere that surrounded and oppressed me. It was, in the purest sense of the word, a wasteland. I coughed. The air smelled of smoke and dust, though it was not much worse than the polluted air of Utopia.

The sunset, the red light of which filtered through the clouds, seemed to be on my right, judging by the shadows. To my left stood a large town… or the ruins of one. The buildings were so dramatically different than those of Utopia that it almost took my breath away.

Each one was a different color and made out of a different material. There were crumbling brick buildings and concrete buildings with gaping black holes blown in the walls. Some looked to be recently constructed, slopped together out of any available materials, many with metal plating all over the lower walls like armor. All of them were filthy and blackened, and in a terrible state of disrepair. Some looked completely abandoned, buildings devoid of living inhabitants, a concept that had never before entered my mind. Others were completely destroyed, with only a few ruined walls standing like graveyard monuments to the structures that had once stood whole.

When Frank Billings had been explaining the rules of G4M3 to me, it had been hard for me to imagine not smiling all the time. Now, in this frighteningly realistic world, it was hard to imagine smiling at all.

It's not real, I kept reminding myself. *It's not real.* Eventually my courage started to return, especially after I readied my assault rifle. Taking a deep breath of the dry, dusty air, I set off into the ruined city.

The streets were mostly deserted, but here and there a few people stood or sat slumped on the sidewalk. Most were clothed in rags so filthy that they blended right in with the landscape. They watched me with eyes sunken into their worn and dirty faces as I passed. They made not a sound.

And all of them were armed. They wore their weapons and ammunition prominently, daring anyone to confront them. Even a child I saw hiding behind his mother had a pistol in his pocket. That was a frightening sight.

At length I heard hushed voices coming from an alley as I passed. They spoke in low, hushed tones, as if talking was illegal, and they were breaking the law. I peered into the alley and found them staring right back at me. Both had long hair and beards, filthy and greasy.

"What do you want, stranger?" grunted one of them, his voice gruff and strangely accented. Both fingered their weapons.

"Hello there," I said cautiously, patting my rifle. "I'm looking for work."

They stared at me, clearly unsure what to think. At first, they looked almost afraid, then slightly amused. Then angry.

"If you want to work," growled the second man, "then go do somethin' useful like join the farmers out in the wastes. No honest work for a man here in the city. Just pointless gang wars."

The first man spat on the ground, mumbling to his friend: "This kid looks eager to join 'em too. Can see the bloodlust in his eyes. Fool boy."

"Get out of here, boy," said the second man, almost with a note of sadness in his voice. "If you want to die so bad, go ask someone else. They'll be happy to help."

I nodded and stepped away from the alley, keeping my eyes on the two men until I had walked out of sight. Even then, I kept glancing over my shoulder as I continued down the street. No one else spoke a word in my vicinity, but in the distance, I could hear echoes of shouting… and gunshots.

I headed in the direction of the sound, half hoping to find some action, and half fearing it. As I walked, I noticed sounds coming from the nearby buildings, but the noises would quickly die as I passed, and if I turned, I saw eyes watching me from cracked doors and windows, and from holes in the walls. This whole city was paranoid; the land of G4M3 knew nothing but war. How had my grandfather created such a terrible place?

At last, I reached the source of the gunshot sounds. Unlike most of the buildings, there was light coming from the windows, which weren't as boarded up as usual. Upon the wall were crude paintings of mugs and bottles and foaming cups. I guessed it was a bar.

As I approached, the door to the bar swung open, and out stepped a man in dented, dark reddish armor, wearing a tattered brown poncho. His face was covered by a full-face helmet with a gas mask, and as he turned his face in my direction, I saw my eyes reflected where his should have been. The man simply nodded, and then he proceeded to walk off.

Since this nod was the closest thing to friendliness that had yet been shown me, I tried to stop the man, saying, "Sir, is anyone around here looking for a mercenary for hire?"

The man stopped and slowly looked back over his shoulder at me, and a filtered voice escaped from his mask: "Go home, kid. This is no place for you."

I heaved a deep breath, getting fed up with the general attitude around here. "Hey! I can take care of myself. There's a scorpion symbol on your armor; are you in one of the gangs? They say the gangs are always looking for new mercs, and they pay well…"

"They say a lot of things," replied the armored man. "Once you join the gang wars, boy, you don't get out alive. Leave the city while you can. Guard a merchant caravan. Go be a farmer. And never look back."

He stared to walk away then. I felt my anger rising. I was tired of these people treating me like a child. I reached for my gun...

And before I could even blink, the red-armored man had wheeled again and pointed his pistol at my face. I froze completely, my weapon barely raised. He twitched his pistol, indicating I should drop my rifle. I considered trying to fight... but then quickly changed my mind and let my gun hit the sidewalk.

The man calmly lowered his pistol. "If I were you," he said, "I'd leave that thing on the ground. Next guy you point it at might not be as friendly as me." Then he looked up and turned his head to one side, staring at the sky, reflected red on his black visor. "Storm's coming..."

I turned to look where he was gazing, but I saw nothing. When I looked back again, the man was gone. All I saw was the dust blowing along the cracked asphalt of the streets where he'd once stood. Then there came a shout from within one of the nearby buildings.

"Raiders!" the voice yelled. "Everyone in!"

The few people still on the streets immediately started to run, ducking into alleys or buildings nearby. I turned to head into the bar, but they slammed the door in my face. I then saw metal panels, covered in graffiti, thrown over the windows. Tiny slits were in each panel, and I wondered vaguely what they had been put there for. Then I heard a terrible, ear-piercing noise that made me drop to the ground and cover my ears. It sounded like the screaming of dozens of men and women combined with the roaring of some strange animal. Looking up, I saw the source of the disturbance.

It was an aircraft. It was sleek and reflective, with wings arched back like a falcon's on the dive, cutting through the black clouds above. Blue fire streaked from the engines. The aircraft in Utopia always slowly drifted miles and miles up in the air, making no noise and attracting little attention. This one was entirely different. I could even see blue fire streaking from the engines.

Reluctantly, I took my hands off my ears. I fumbled with my weapon, as if it could do any good against the flying machine. Then I heard a different, more high-pitched sort of screaming sound. There was a muted boom in the distance, and smoke billowed up from behind some of the nearby buildings. The plane turned and flew off toward the horizon. I saw men and women rushing out of the destroyed buildings, holding weapons of various shapes and sizes.

Armed soldiers appeared, pouring through the alleys on the opposite side of the street. Unlike the civilians, these wore matching uniforms and dark facemasks. They opened fire on the rabble in the street with methodical precision. I turned and banged my fist on the door of the bar, begging the men inside to let me in, but they paid me no heed.

Instead, they started shooting. I saw gun barrels force their way out of the slits in the boarded-up windows, each one spewing fire. I saw one of the street-fighters shot down by a masked soldier. It was a woman. She screamed as she fell, clutching at the wall and slowly sliding down to the earth.

The sight of this woman dying in such a clearly painful way knocked some sense into me. I pulled myself up to my feet and ran for cover. There was a large, metal trash bin in the alley beside me, so I ran and hid behind that.

One of the masked soldiers called out, in a voice amplified by a handheld device: "Bloodletter Blades! Throw your weapons into the street and surrender!"

A voice answered from inside the bar: "Come and get 'em, ironclad scum!"

"We have superior firepower, armor, and discipline," the soldier responded calmly. "You cannot hope to win against us. Surrender now, so that we will not have to kill you."

Instead of replying again, the voice inside the building just shouted, "Fire! Everyone fire!"

Reminding myself with great force of will that this was still only a game, I stood up and raised my assault rifle. I'm still not quite sure why I chose the side I did. Perhaps it was the fact that the soldiers across the street looked so inhuman, wearing their uniforms and facemasks, as opposed to the poor people on my side of the street, who appeared to be destitute men and women merely defending their homes. Perhaps I equated the appearance and words of the opposing soldiers with Utopia and the Order, and my secret, long-buried revulsion for those things made me want to fight them.

Or maybe it was just because I was on *this* side of the street, and the soldiers were over *there*.

Whatever the reason, disobeying the advice of the red-armored man, I aimed and opened fire upon the invading soldiers. I chose as my first target the soldier who had shot down the woman earlier. He was reloading. I took careful aim at his neck, where the armor he was wearing appeared to be the weakest, and I pulled the trigger. Somehow, inside, I knew I would miss. I was too inexperienced, and the soldier was certainly expecting an attack. But he was not expecting one from my direction.

As the flash of the gun lit my vision, the loud crack of the shot echoed in my ears, and the butt of the weapon snapped against my shoulder… blood flew from a wound on the enemy's neck, right where I had been aiming, and the soldier's back hit the wall as he stumbled limply. Just as the rebel woman had done earlier, the soldier slid down the wall and fell to the ground… dead. I stood for a moment in shock, wondering at what had just happened. Then, after hearing my gun go off, the other soldiers seemed to notice me for the first time.

I saw dozens of rifles trained at me, seemingly all at once. Fire erupted from all sides, peppering the ground and the wall behind me with bullet holes. I felt one of my feet blown out from under me as a bullet struck it with incredible force. I fell to the ground and was hit again the chest. The impact of it knocked the wind out of me.

Mostly using my arms, I was able to drag myself back behind cover. Pain shot through my leg and chest. I could never have imagined such agony. Even with the device implanted in me, the pain simulation was terribly real… unbearably real. I thought that I was going to die for certain.

I rolled over in the dirt, coughing, trying to breathe. I knew I was wounded terribly. This game was disgusting, I thought. As I lay there, gasping for breath, I swore that I would never return… if I survived. It was hard to believe, in that moment, that I would, even if I knew it in the back of my mind.

As these thoughts swirled through my head, I saw the tattered wall of the building beside me – the graffiti and the trash – begin to swirl and swim… and then all went dark.

===

When I awoke in the tiny simulation room in the G4M3 facility, it was like waking up from my worst nightmare. I felt like I should be dead, but I was not. In fact, except for the strange feeling in my stomach, I felt perfectly healthy.

I sat up in the bed and stretched. Only then did I realize I was wearing simple, clean white clothes… a button-up shirt and a pair of loose-fitting pants. My military uniform, armor plating, and weapons lay on the table on the other side of the room once again, none the worse for wear. My body was none the worse for wear either; I couldn't feel any wounds on my skin at all.

I blinked, sitting and staring at the wall in shock. Like first waking from a particularly lifelike dream, it was hard to believe that none of it had been real. How could anyone call that a 'game'?

I stood up and stretched. The only other thing in the room was an android worker, who was standing between the two tables. His elongated head and thin metal limbs rotated and whirred as he looked at me, and then, satisfied, he activated his treads and rolled out of the room. Frank Billings stepped right in to replace him. He smiled warmly at me. I didn't return his smile.

"I'm… never doing that again," I said immediately, my voice hoarse.

Frank let out an amused laugh. "That's what they all say. You'll be back, kid."

"I will not..." I insisted, feeling even more sure of myself. "That was terrible."

"Come on," Frank said with another laugh. "The tram's waiting for you."

I followed Frank into the elevator, feeling every sickening lurch that the device made. The world around me seemed so unreal now. It was like my perspectives had switched... The G4M3 felt more like reality than reality did.

I stumbled along until I emerged outside the facility. The clean, perfect streets and the rows of identical buildings at the same time both reassured me and made me feel dizzy. With a great effort, I steadied myself. Frank stepped up behind me and put a reassuring hand on my shoulder.

"You had a bad experience, kid," he said encouragingly. "Most Players do get killed on their first session of G4M3, but not that quickly. You'll do better next time."

"There won't be a next time..." I muttered.

"Kyle, I'm serious," Frank said. "While it's not rare that a Player dies in his first round, it *is* rare that a Player is placed into the middle of a battle and killed right away. I'm sure your next session will be more peaceful, at least at the beginning. And then you can start the combat on your own terms."

Frank spoke of all the shocking warfare as if it were so simple, just a game. Of course, I knew that he was right, but had he ever experienced it? Yes, I knew he had. But it was hard to believe, seeing how lightly he treated it. I nodded to him, but didn't respond otherwise. Then I walked back up the street, called the tram, and began the journey home.

THREE
THE SILENT CREATOR

All night I dreamed of G4M3. I could see the men and women hefting their heavy weapons, their dull eyes filling with determination as the enemy approached. Life for these artificial intelligence units was a constant battle, but they kept it up admirably, along with the thousands of Players who joined the G4M3 every day. I felt like such a coward for trying to run away from it all, for being frightened by a simple game.

As I got out of bed and went downstairs, it struck me yet again just how boring this life was. Every day was exactly the same. Even if one traveled around Utopia and explored the various activities that the Order recommended for a varied and healthy lifestyle, they were all still the same.

One always felt relaxed in Utopia, even when competing in recreational games and activities. This was because, in truth, there was no competition in Utopia. Every person was afforded a healthy lifestyle by the Order. There was no reason to work hard, because everyone was paid the same. There was no reason to play hard, because everyone was a winner.

Not so in G4M3, I thought. In the world of G4M3, every character lived every day fighting for their very lives. Conflict was the essence of survival.

I did not even greet my parents as I descended the stairs and sat down to eat breakfast. It was the same perfectly healthy meal as always. Meals could only be purchased in special packages in Utopia. Each package included all the right nutrients for that meal. There were hundreds of different breakfast, lunch, and dinner packages, along with healthy snacks available at the markets. Each one was different, and yet they were all the same. As I sat and ate, I wondered vaguely where it all came from.

"Is something wrong, Kyle?" my mother asked me with a sympathetic smile.

"I'm just a little... shaken up after playing G4M3, I guess," I replied.

"Then perhaps you'll decide not to play it anymore," my father's voice said from the living room sofa, where he sat watching holovision. "That's what I did."

I gave a slight sigh, put my dishes in the washer, and got up from the table. My father was echoing exactly what I had said upon leaving the G4M3 facility. Did I really want to be just like him? I left the house and went outside with no real destination in mind. The day was dimly sunny, as usual.

The idea of there being any other kind of weather never occurred to me. The Order controlled the weather in Utopia, keeping it comfortably warm, but not hot, at all times. There was no rain or snow. Everything was watered by automated irrigation. They couldn't completely stop the pollution from clogging the air, but at least it didn't completely block the sun. I looked at the sky and saw the anemic little orb glowing warmly overhead. It did little to comfort me.

"Is there a problem, sir?"

I turned to see a patrolling security robot – a Patrolman – staring at me with its emotionless, glowing blue eye. The patrol bots differed from the worker bots in appearance. They were colored a dark metallic blue-grey and were human-sized. They were also stockier than workers, with two large, thick arms, and legs instead of rolling treads. I gazed at the robot blankly for a moment, hardly registering it.

"Are you lost, sir?" it prompted, its single eye flashing along with its deep, monotone voice.

"No..." I responded automatically. "I'm going to... see my grandfather in the retirement home."

"Very well, sir," the robot buzzed, helpfully pressing the tram-summoning button on the lamppost for me with a metal finger. "Your transportation will arrive shortly. Have a pleasant evening."

"And... you as well," I said, forcing a smile.

The robot walked around me and resumed its pre-determined path. A thought surfaced into my head: *Just who controlled those things, anyway?* It wasn't the first time I had wondered. But I shook the question away. I didn't care.

When I spotted the tram sliding down the street, I remembered what I'd told the Patrolman. I was going to see Grandfather Walter at the retirement home. Mechanically, I repeated the instructions to the tram-driver bot as I boarded the vehicle. The other passengers smiled at me as I took my seat.

Staring out the window at nothing in particular, since there was nothing to look at anyway, I wondered what had possessed me to choose that for an answer. Then I realized it... I wanted to ask Grandfather about G4M3. I knew that, due to his disease, he couldn't actually answer, but I wanted to try.

When the tram came to a halt, I bid the pilot bot good day, which was standard etiquette, and then I stepped out onto the sidewalk. The blank, off-white building in front of me was slightly taller than normal: the retirement home. I strode up to the door, which had no button or handle upon its smooth surface, and it slid aside to grant me passage inside.

The interior of the building was a cool, soothing, pale shade of blue. It was a calming place, and very quiet. Few people wandered its halls. I didn't go there often, but I had been a few times before, so I knew where my grandfather's room was.

I got in the elevator and pressed the button. The ride was smooth and noiseless as always. When I found Grandfather Walter's room, I read the computer screen on the wall. It said: *'Walter Roswell – Problem Unknown – Symptoms include memory loss and inability to communicate– Press HERE for Status Report – Press HERE for Diagnostics Checks (Authorized Personnel Only).'* I ignored the sign and pressed the green rectangular button under it. The door slid open.

When I was younger, I used to be terrified of Grandfather Walter. He seemed like a ghoulish creature to my young eyes, always moaning and occasionally slurring out some odd sentence that made little sense. He was old, that much was certain, but unlike most people in Utopia, his age showed clearly on every inch of his body.

I saw him now, lying there under his bed's white sheets, his face turned in my direction, his eyes staring dully at me. His head was completely bald and covered in wrinkles and dark spots. His eyes were a dull blue, with the lids drooping over them, and his mouth hung open slightly. He lay there, still as a cadaver, staring at me, as the door closed behind me.

I walked slowly up to the side of his bed. I saw his head turn and follow my movements, staring at my face with those big, blue eyes… my father's eyes… my eyes. It was unnerving to say the least. I suddenly recalled why I'd been so scared of him as a child. I confess I was a little frightened once again.

"Grandfather?" I said. "It's me, Kyle."

He reached out with claw-like fingers, groping for me. I caught his hand, felt his dry, leathery skin rub against mine. He closed his eyes, and his other hand came around and felt of my hand and arm, patting it softly. I sat down in the chair next to his bed and waited.

"Grandfather?" I repeated. "Walter?"

His only response was a slight moan.

"Grandfather, I want you to tell me about G4M3."

The old man's eyes opened again at this, and rolled around to lock onto mine. He gave another groan and let my hand drop. Then he folded his hands together and placed them on his stomach, looking away.

"Maybe you understood me…" I said.

There was no response. He stared vacantly at the wall, looking dead except for occasionally blinking and licking his almost nonexistent lips. His mouth hung limply open.

"Can't you tell me anything about it? Why did you invent it? How did you do it? How does it work?" I asked the questions as they came to me, not knowing what I had really come to ask.

Walter's head turned back in my direction and his eyes met mine again. The lids seemed to be sagging even more now, and there was a slight wistfulness in his eye that had not been there before, as if some old thoughts were stalking their way out of the dusty corners of his mind and into the light.

I had set some of the gears in his head to turning, I thought. His mouth opened and closed, his flabby skin rippling with every movement, but no sound came out. It was like talking to an animated corpse. He kept blinking, very slowly. I grew impatient.

"Can't you tell me anything?"

He moaned, and at first, I thought it sounded like, "Sooooon… soooooon…" but I convinced myself I was mistaken.

"Please, I want to know," I said, "and Frank Billings doesn't want to tell me."

At this, he gave a loud groan and rolled his head back and forth. One of his hands went up in the air and clenched into a tight fist, and then came back down on the bed with a soft thud. He was growing angry. He didn't like anything being demanded of him.

I suddenly had an idea. I cleared my throat and did my best Frank Billings impersonation, trying to throw a serious note into his usually jovial tone. "Walter… It's me, Frank. I want you to tell me more about G4M3."

My grandfather responded this time… and the reaction was stronger than I had hoped for. His eyes went wide, the wrinkled skin peeling away from them in layers until they bulged. His mouth opened and his jaw shook. I saw his chest rise and fall, and a wheezing noise came from deep in his throat. Then an almost speech-like groaning forced its way out of his gaping mouth. Was he… afraid?

"Noooo… Should not… Caaaan not… nooooo…"

I took a step back, startled. At that same instant, the worker robot that I hadn't even noticed sitting in the corner of the room suddenly came online. Its elongated head rose and its bright blue eyes lit up. With a whirr, its treads propelled it to the side of my grandfather's bed. Before it moved a hand to help Walter, however, it turned his head toward me. I heard the door behind me slide open.

"I am sorry, but you have disturbed our patient. Please leave the room."

"It's okay," I said. "I'm his..."

"Please leave the room," the robot repeated.

I took a step back and nodded. The robot's eyes seemed to glow a little brighter, and his long metal head seemed to rise a little higher on his thin, tube-like neck, but it may have been my imagination.

"Please leave the room," it said insistently, though its tone remained exactly the same.

Once both of my feet were in the hallway outside, the door slid shut in my face, clipping the end of my nose. I rubbed the sore and stared at the door's blank, light-blue surface. My mind filled the blankness with images of G4M3: the wasteland, the dark red and black sky, the rising smoke, the ruined city, the men and women fighting... In that moment, I made up my mind. I was going to play it again.

"I'll be back, Grandfather," I said to the door.

But actually, I never would.

===

The ride through the streets of Utopia was uneventful, as usual, and the pale sun reminded me of my grandfather Walter's clammy skin and dim eyes. When I arrived at the G4M3 facility, Frank Billings was sitting behind the desk at the entrance, his android worker standing idly beside him.

Frank was muttering something to himself... catches of a song I'd never heard before. I tried to listen, but before I could make out what he was saying, he noticed my presence and looked up. As expected, a smile lit his face.

"Back for more, eh, boy?" he chuckled. "I knew you would be. Very few kids your age stop after just the first game, except a few peace-loving oddballs, like your father."

"Hi, Frank," I replied, smiling in return. "How's business?"

"Booming, as usual. If I had a bigger facility, I could entertain even more players, but the Order will only build one little building like this in each community... Oh well. It's all I can handle anyway. Perhaps all that Utopia can handle."

"I went to see Grandfather Walter at the retirement home today," I remarked offhandedly, watching his reaction.

Frank's keen light-brown eyes seemed to turn brighter and sharper as they focused on mine, though his tone was merely one of friendly curiosity as he asked: "So... did he say anything?"

"No," I replied. "He just moaned a lot. He got a little upset when I mentioned you though."

"No doubt," Frank said, his eyes now leaving my face as he walked around the desk to join me. "No doubt about that. I was Walter's business partner, you know. He taught me every trick of the trade. He was as much my father, or perhaps brother, as he is your grandfather. I was the only person he trusted with the knowledge of G4M3's programming."

Frank looked at me as he said this, awaiting a reply.

"I... want to play again," I said reluctantly.

Frank's smile almost took in his ears. "I hoped you were going to say that. Actually, I knew you were. Hah! Come, come - I've left a slot open just for you."

Frank kept talking in a friendly manner about unimportant subjects as we walked down the hallway, and as we rode the elevator up to the second floor. He opened up one of the simulation rooms and nodded to the robot inside. It rolled out past him and continued down the hall.

Then Frank turned to me and said, "Now, you already have the return button implanted in you this time, so there's no need to go through that again. Just press the button in a dark spot when you're done playing. Oh, and try to leave using *it* this time, instead of getting killed, eh?"

I laughed and nodded as I walked into the room and began slipping into my gear. In reality, I had butterflies in my stomach and a knot in my throat. Still, *something* was forcing me to do this again. I couldn't seem to help myself. Despite all its horrors, I wanted to explore this virtual alternate world so badly I could taste it.

As Frank turned away, a thought struck me, and I said quickly, "I just have one more question, Frank."

Frank turned around. "Yes?"

"I was wondering... Some of the characters in G4M3 talk strangely. They speak words I've never heard and pronounce some words incorrectly... Why is that?"

Frank shrugged. "Something Walter programmed them to do. He talked that way himself, you see – had a funny way of speaking."

"Oh..." I replied, nodding, "but why did Walter talk like that?"

Frank turned to look at something on the wall as he replied absently, "Oh, that's just how people talked in the Central District back when he grew up. Fortunately, the Order has corrected that now, with more standardized linguistic education. Anyway, have a good game, Kyle."

Frank flashed another smile and walked away. I prepared myself for the simulation to begin. The door closed in front of me, and the lights went out. I felt that sudden fit of nausea come over me again, and that feeling of being in a windy storm, as the G4M3 activated, and reality slipped away...

F O U R
THE UNREAL WOMAN

When I awoke in the world of G4M3, I looked around with confusion. The world in which I had arrived looked almost completely identical to the location where I had "died" during my last G4M3 session. But Frank had said that I would be playing in a different server now – an entirely different virtual world. Apparently, all the areas in G4M3 looked very similar.

This time, I thought, I would try harder to fit in. So, with a front of quiet confidence, I stepped onto the cracked and broken sidewalk and shouldered my rifle. Sidling along at an easy pace, I tried not to make eye contact with any of the natives, while still keeping an eye on them at the same time. I soon heard the crackle of a fire coming from an alley to my right.

Turning to look, I beheld a young man and woman sitting in front of a garbage can, in which the fire was burning. The man was holding a stick with a dead animal impaled upon it. The creature's corpse was a hideous, filthy thing, with the fur stripped off and the bloody muscles bare. It was a dead rat, huge and deformed. I felt sick.

I moved on. To my surprise, someone bumped into me almost as soon as I turned away from the alley. The cloaked figure tried to make a dash for it, but I instinctively caught his arm. I gave it a wrench and pulled him back to my side, drawing my pistol with my free hand. I shoved the barrel of the sidearm against the man's back, and he ceased struggling. I could hear his rapid breathing. As I stood there with this being's life at my mercy, I silently congratulated myself on my skill.

"I didn't do anything to you, pal," came a low voice from beneath the hood. "I'd let me go, if I were you."

Though the tone of the voice was gruff, it sounded very youthful, and I asked, "Are you… a woman?"

The voice lost its false masculine gruffness in a flash, and the girl asked, "So what if I am?"

The hood flew off as the girl tossed back her head. She turned to glare at me, giving her arm a twist. Seeing her young, feminine features, I immediately let go of her wrist, as if by reflex. She jumped back a step, ready to flee at a moment's notice.

She was quite attractive, I thought, though her dusty face had more lines than I would have expected for her apparent age, and there was a hardness in her green eyes. Her brown hair was pulled back from her face by a dark green bandanna.

"Well, whaddaya want?" she asked. "Shoving a gun in a girl's back is a lousy way to apologize for bumpin' into 'er."

I wasn't sure how to respond to that, so I just asked, "Who are you?"

"What do you care, huh?" she asked suspiciously, looking jumpy and ready to run.

I waved my firearm menacingly, though I had no intention of using it on her. The very idea of her being only an illusion controlled by artificial intelligence had completely fled from my thoughts.

"Don't go anywhere," I said. "Tell me what you know of the factions in this area."

"*Factions?*" she asked, sneering at me. "What's... You mean the gangs?"

"Yes," I replied, still attempting to look capable of violence should she try anything. "I'm looking for work."

"Oh, is that all?" she said with a snort of contempt.

"Yes," I replied, not used to sarcasm. "Any gangs in this area in need of a mercenary?"

She stared at me suspiciously for a moment, licking her lips and thinking, before she finally said, "Maybe. Ever heard of the Eagles?"

I shrugged. "No. I'm from out of town."

She snorted again. "From where? We don't get many newcomers. Come in with a caravan?"

"Yes..." I said slowly. "I'm... from back east."

She nodded. "Alright then. Follow me."

Without another word, she turned about and, pulling her hood over her head again, shuffled off down the sidewalk. I followed, staying close behind her. How she could walk so silently and quickly, and yet look so casual doing it, was beyond me. I had to fairly sprint along to keep up with her, and I caught several wary glances from the rough-looking passers-by.

As I walked, I kept glancing at the men on the street and at the sky, wondering when a gunfight might break out or another bomber plane might come down on our heads. To my surprise, the woman in front of me seemed unconcerned by such matters.

Suddenly, she seemed to disappear. I halted and looked around. All I saw were destroyed buildings under a churning lava-colored sky. It was surprising how different each building could look and still look so very much the same as all the rest. Where had she gone?

I pondered the idea that there might be glitches in the G4M3 systems. Perhaps a bug had caused her to disappear. I mourned the sudden loss of my intriguing companion for only a second before I was interrupted.

"Psst!" I heard someone hiss to my left. "Get in here, waster. What are you, blind?"

I turned and beheld the young woman's green eyes staring at me from under the shadow of a nearby doorway. Her hand appeared in the light and indicated that I should follow her. I stepped through the door.

I almost immediately regretted the decision as I heard a metallic panel slam over the portal behind me, closing off my exit. I heard rapid clicking noises issue from the darkness all around me. Then a light came on, illuminating the room, and I saw at least a dozen guns trained on me. One of them was held by the girl I had met in the street.

Though their outfits and armaments varied, all of the armed men and women had the same tattoo on their arm, depicting an eagle in flight. They all had their right sleeves either rolled up or torn off to show it. These were obviously the Eagles.

"Here's the clueless waster," the girl said with a laugh when she saw me, her gun not budging an inch and her eyes as steady as a snake's. "I took his wallet when I bumped into him, and he didn't even notice."

I patted the back of my pants, and discovered she wasn't lying. I felt color rise into my cheeks.

"Doesn't sound too useful," came the deep, gruff voice of a dark-skinned soldier next to me.

"Doubt he is," said the girl, shaking her head sadly. "But not too dangerous either. We could just take his gear and dump him someplace."

"This is some gratitude for you..." I said, keeping my voice and gaze as steady as I could. "I could have killed you at any time, and this is how you repay me?"

"Like I said: clueless," she remarked to her comrades. Then she turned back to me and said, "You couldn't have killed me, even if you'd tried. And I saw in your eyes weren't gonna try. I bet you've never even shot anyone."

"You're wrong about that," I said, taking a step forward and trying to seem tough. "Anyway, wouldn't it be better to–"

I stopped talking, and moving, in mid-sentence. Because as soon as I moved, the guns around me suddenly jumped into a tighter formation, concentrating on my head.

"No sudden movements," said the girl, her voice suddenly cold as steel.

"He could be a spy," said the dark-skinned soldier.

"It's okay, Don," the girl replied, slowly lowering her rifle. "Look at his eyes; he's too much of a rookie to be a spy."

"What makes you think I'm such a rookie?" I asked somewhat angrily.

She smiled then for the first time, causing my anger to be replaced with shame. "It just shines off you."

"Thanks," I said sarcastically.

Don, as the girl had called him, gave a gruff laugh. "You're right, Sofia. This kid's too green to eat! Hell, let's give 'im a chance. We could use more guns for the raid…"

Sofia looked at me then, long and hard. Her green eyes narrowed, and her face went deadly serious. She was sizing me up, weighing my worth.

"Fine," she said at length. "We'll give him one chance. But only 'cause he's so cute."

She chuckled again, and Don let out a guttural laugh. As Sofia shouldered her rifle, all the men around her followed suit. I took this to mean that she was the leader. Even Don didn't lower his weapon until after her. I was a bit surprised by this.

I was even more surprised when Sofia shook off her cloak, letting it slide to the floor and kicking it into a heap in the corner. Her long, brown hair fell down to her waist in a loose ponytail, and her figure was quite feminine despite her manly attitude. I reminded myself this was only a game.

"Alright, kid," Sofia said, "it looks like you're in the Eagles now, whether you still wanna be or not. My name's Sofia Tyler, and I'm in charge here. You'll take orders from me. We're going to raid a USOW supply depot this afternoon, so you'll get your hands dirty real quick."

"USOW?" I said.

"Where the hell *are* you from?" Don asked incredulously. "Must be from the other side o' the world if you don't know who the USOW are. They're the United States of the World. They're what's left of one o' the big governments that all blew each other to hell in the Great War that ruined everything. Why anyone still fights for 'em after that is beyond me. They don't control much anymore, but they're always tryin' to take back what they lost. We make sure they can't."

Sofia snorted. "Don't listen to all that, kid. Don's an idealist. Truth is, things ain't what they used to be. We Eagles used to be part of a big alliance of rebel gangs who helped take down the USOW. But now that the USOW's broken, so are we. We fight 'em when they show their face, sure, but we spend more time fighting each other, or just trying to survive…"

"Now, don't go an' get all bitter, Sofe," Don scolded. "We still do good work, help people…"

"We try, Don. But half the time we get sold out or stabbed in the back for the trouble. That's why we have to operate from secret hideouts. No good deed goes unpunished."

Later I would reflect on the intricacies of the world my grandfather had created, with all its factions and history. But at the time, I could no longer even force myself to think of it as a game. It was all too real. I was lost in this world, this G4M3, and at least for the time being, I had no desire to leave.

"Time to eat, guys," I heard someone say from across the room.

I looked up to see the man I had seen roasting a rat on a stick in the alley. He had several similar giant rodents now in a sack, and he was displaying them to the other soldiers. Some looked at them eagerly, others turned up their noses, but I got the feeling that they were all going to eat them anyway.

"Why can't we get some fruit from the wasteland farmers? I'm so sick of rotten meat. No offense ta the cook, of course," one soldier whined.

"Suck it up," Don growled. "Those poor waste-farmers need their food more than we do. We *ain't* raiders."

"That's our big ol' angel Don for you," said the man with the rats, laughing. "Well, pass 'em around, boys."

One soldier dragged a large box from a corner of the room into the middle of the floor, and the cook dropped his roasted rats on top of it. Whipping out knives from hidden locations in their clothing, three soldiers began cutting the food apart.

I fought back my nausea as they handed me my own meager portion. I was not all that hungry, and though the food looked reasonably good in small portions, the knowledge of what it actually was turned my stomach. But I was not going to appear squeamish in front of these hardened men and women, so I grabbed a chunk with my bare fingers and forced it into my mouth.

"Tastes like chicken," I joked, trying to provoke a lighthearted conversation.

Instead of laughing, all of the soldiers turned to regard me with wide eyes.

"You've tasted... chicken?" the skinny cook boy asked in a sort of awe.

Sofia's eyes narrowed. "No one's seen a chicken in Saltpit City in a hundred years, nor in any city beyond. Just where the hell *are* you from?"

I licked my lips. "I... It's just a saying, where I come from. A joke. 'Everything tastes like chicken.' It's funny because no one knows what chicken really tasted like."

Everyone in the room either groaned or laughed and turned away, except for the cook, who kept staring at me intently, with wide eyes full of wonder... and disappointment.

He swallowed hard. "Is it jus' a story, really?"

I blew out a sigh. "Afraid so, Jim. Just forget about it."

As we ate, Don walked over and sat down near me. "So, what's your name anyway, rookie?"

I paused a moment, then answered, "Kyle Roswell."

He gave me a hard slap on the back, which nearly knocked the wind out of me. "Welcome to the team, Kyle. Hope you survive the raid!"

Everyone laughed, and after a second I joined in myself. Just then, despite the dark joke and my filthy surroundings... I had never felt so alive, or so welcome.

===

Later that day, the entire squad moved out for the attack. I was surprised by how many Eagles there were in total. I had assumed they were a small gang of a couple dozen, but there were several hundred gathered out in the open wastes. They even had vehicles – rusted-out old trucks, seemingly repaired with junk – and stacks of crates of supplies and weapons.

Sofia climbed up on top of one of these piles to give a speech to her men. I saw two or three other commanders doing the same; apparently, Sofia led some of the Eagles, but not all. She looked impressive in her military gear, with her assault rifle strapped over her shoulder and black cloak blowing in the dusty desert wind.

"Alright, people, listen closely," she said, taking on a more authoritative tone than I had yet heard her use. "The USOW supply depot's on the other side of the Sandpit. Most of the guards have left the base, to reinforce the USOW army at another location. Our objectives are to move in and take as many of their supplies as we can.

"And then we destroy the base. When we leave, I want nothing left of it but ash and rubble. It's too dangerous to hold. Don will take the main force around the outer edge of the Saltpit. Another group will go around the other side. They'll ride our transports until they get close, then attack on foot. Meanwhile, I'll take our trucks directly through the Saltpit. Hopefully, they'll spot my guys before they spot Don's. That'll allow at least half of Don's forces to sneak into base..."

"How are they supposed to sneak into a fortified compound?" asked a soldier in the crowd.

Sofia shrugged. "Blow a hole in the wall, try to bypass a door lock, sweet talk 'em into opening the gates... I don't know; that's their job. Our job is to survive in the Saltpit until they take out the defenses from inside. We have a better likelihood of surviving in the trucks than they do on foot."

"What about that last truck?" asked one soldier, pointing to a large flatbed truck loaded with crates and barrels.

Sofia looked down at her soldiers grimly. "That's our backup plan. It's loaded with explosives, and if it comes to it, we can just drive it into the base's wall. If things go that badly, that last bang should turn the tide in our favor, but it's a waste of a truck and a lot of explosives, and I don't have to tell you how precious those are. Plus, we need a volunteer to drive it. You should be able to bail before it hits the wall, but if you can't rig it to keep going, or if something else happens…"

I stuffed my hands in my pockets and looked around, expecting everyone else to do the same. To my utter astonishment, I saw hands go up in the air. A wave of hands swept through the crowd of soldiers. As I saw that crowd of people willing to sacrifice their lives for this endeavor, I felt a chill run up my spine. Reluctantly, I raised my hand. I felt like I had to. Only then did I remember that this was only a game anyway, and I couldn't actually die.

Sofia nodded and began climbing down from her perch. "All right then. I'll let you draw straws. Meanwhile, I'll load up my three trucks."

I wanted to go with Sofia, but before I could follow her, I felt a hand on my shoulder. I turned to see Don staring at me, stony faced.

"Sorry, but you're comin' with me, boy," he said. "Get ready. I hope you know how to fight, 'cause otherwise you're a dead man – either by their hands, or ours if you run for it."

"I'm ready," I said with as much courage as I could muster.

He grinned at me as he walked off toward the transport's cabin. "Then get in the truck, soldier!"

Don's two groups set off immediately, one going around one edge of the Saltpit and one around the other. We rode in large transport trucks – old, beat up things that raised a terrible racket as they rolled across the desert. The soldiers and I were jostled to and fro in the awkward seats, always bumping into one another.

There were three transports in our group, and each long, green truck stayed a good distance from the other. The vehicles had no armor or protection for the men. The greatest defense they had was the firepower of their occupants, and, thanks to the lack of protection, the men were able to shoot all that they pleased, though hitting something while bouncing around like this seemed impossible.

I remember the feeling of depression I felt when I first glimpsed the Saltpit. The pit itself was huge and stretched out as far as the eye could see into the hazy, polluted air. The bottom of it was smooth and white, covered in a thick layer of salt. It had once been a lake, I later learned, filled with salty water like an ocean. I'd never seen a lake this large, but I'd never actually seen the ocean before either. I imagined that it must have been magnificent once. Now it was a disgusting thing. Only a few pools the size of small ponds remained standing in the bottom of the pit, each a greenish color, with flies swarming around them.

As the city behind us grew more distant, I turned to look at its full skyline for the first time. Only then did I realize how big it was. Its tall, blackened high-rise towers stretching into the air like thin, jagged teeth or the tips of giant spears. The tops of some of the skyscrapers were completely gone, and some had been reduced to a metallic framework, now merely the skeletons of their former selves. One gigantic skyscraper had even toppled over onto its side, struck another, smaller tower, and split in half. Now it leaned there, supported by the smaller tower, ready to fall at any moment.

There was a bleak sort of majesty to the sight. Nothing visibly stirred in the awful, silent ghost city. I imagined how it must have looked once, with windows clean and shining instead of brown and broken. The city must have been amazing – a dazzling array of oddly-placed buildings of various shapes, sizes, and colors that would have put the strictly ordered, simple buildings of Utopia to shame. Even as ruins they dwarfed my home in their terrible, awe-inspiring magnificence.

A few of the other soldiers gazed back at the city as well, but in a different way than I did. They had seen it hundreds of times before, I thought. Most of them, however, were looking elsewhere, thinking only of the battle ahead.

It was impossible to talk as we rode on the noisy transport vehicles, but finally Don turned and shouted through the rear window of the drivers' cabin: "We're comin' up on the base! Everybody get ready to hit the dirt!"

I looked out across the edge of the Saltpit and saw the USOW base. It seemed so insignificant and unimportant compared with the ruined metropolis. It was merely a square box surrounded by fortified walls, with a tower poking out of the top. But it contained life-giving supplies, foods, and other resources so scarce in this wasteland that men and women were willing to kill for them.

As that thought struck me, I noticed Sofia's band of trucks speeding their way over the very middle of the Saltpit floor. I knew that anyone inhabiting the USOW base had surely spotted her, and I was right. A missile, trailing smoke, flew from the upper levels of the base as I watched, headed for the approaching vehicles. The missile was well-aimed, but it had a long way to travel, and the trucks managed to dodge it before it struck the salty floor with a tremendous explosion.

Our transport skidded to a halt, and Don climbed out of the front at the same time that I stepped out the back with the rest of our squad. He looked at Sofia's unit in the pit below with little emotion, every line of his face showing his complete concentration on the task at hand. He commanded the troops to fall in behind him, and so we did.

In single file, we made our way into the sparse brush that grew between the USOW compound and ourselves. All of the plant life in G4M3 was more grey than green and appeared to be quite dead, but the Eagles somehow managed to use it to stay out of visibility. Indeed, as the group slinked into the brush, they disappeared almost entirely. I followed, but felt as if I stood out like a giraffe in a group of creeping tigers.

The harsh staccato of gunfire met our ears as Sofia's group came in range of the USOW defenders' rifles. I heard the guns on the trucks return fire and looked up to see a man fall off the upper edges of the USOW base's wall. We were close now. My heart hammered against my chest. Suddenly, Don gave the order, and we all stood up. In a mad rush, we cleared the distance between the end of the line of shrubbery and the base.

Bullets spattered in the sand around us, kicking up clouds of dust. Some of the soldiers fired back as they ran, but it was wasted effort, since it was impossible to hit anything without stopping, and holding still meant giving yourself away as a target. I believe only three soldiers fell in the charge. It was fast and unexpected, which was a lucky thing for us.

Once the rest of us were close enough to the wall, we stopped to aim our weapons. Some of the sentries were poking out of the windows or atop the wall above, leaning over to aim their weapons down at our positions. Gunfire of varying pitches exploded all around me. I heard men screaming, and saw one fall from the heights above to land with an unnatural thud right beside me.

My heart gave a leap and I bounded back, thus accidentally saving myself from the burst of bullets that peppered the sand where I had just stood. Leveling my rifle, I aimed in the direction from which the barrage had come. I shot three times at the helmeted head in the window above and was rewarded with a splash of blood and a scream.

I felt exhilarated for a moment, almost enough to shout with triumph. It was horrible to feel so excited about killing someone, even in a game, but at the time it just felt natural. There was a muffled boom then – too quiet, I thought, for an explosion. Then I heard screeching and crashing – the collapse of concrete and steel.

"Into the breach, men!" Don yelled with vigor that enlivened all the soldiers who heard him.

Everyone obeyed his command immediately, some before he'd even issued it. The soldiers pushed their way past each other and through the shattered walls, into the dusty courtyard of the USOW base. Gunfire erupted inside, and the rapid pace of the Eagles slowed to a crawl as they had to step over the bodies of their fallen vanguard upon entering the breach.

Slowly, we crawled in, helping each other take down the guards on the walls. Luckily, the USOW forces decided to retreat within the base then, allowing us a mostly clear passage. Don slipped in right beside me as the rest of the group opened fire on any enemy they saw – even some that looked dead.

"Team two," I heard Don bark into his communicator, "have you breached the wall yet?"

"Negative!" came the response. "It's rainin' hellfire over here! We might have to fall back!"

"Negative!" Don commanded. "We're inside. We'll try to draw their fire. Come around to our side and get in!"

"Yes, Sir…" the soldier had time to say before Don switched his communicator to a different frequency.

"Sofia?" Don said, and I was surprised to hear his voice lose its optimistic enthusiasm all of a sudden. "This is Don. We're inside. Lots more resistance than we thought. Might end up with heavy losses. Sure we're still up to it?"

The roar of combustion engines came back over the communicator along with Sofia's voice. "Keep going! We can't stop now!"

Don switched off the communicator and looked daggers at me, bellowing: "What is this, your break time, soldier!? Get to work! Get in there and fight!"

I scurried off into the courtyard and dropped behind the nearest cover, firing as I went. The soldiers on the walls had returned now, with reinforcements, which put us in a bad spot: surrounded in the low ground. The blood rushed in my veins. I had never felt such excitement and invigoration, nor such fear. My hands were shaking. The men around me were soldiers, but I had never even been in a fight before – not really. I wished I was riding with Sofia in the trucks outside.

I don't know how long the battle lasted, but to me it seemed like days. The sky grew dark overhead, and blood was spilled every moment. We had breached the wall, but the defenders still held the inner fort, and they held it well. They knew we were here now, and they were ready. They wouldn't let a man of us get close to the main building.

I lost track of Don during the fighting, and the soldier I was holed up with in the pit we were using for cover was none too talkative. So, I had no idea what had become of Sofia or even how well the battle was going overall. No orders came over the communicator either. I felt that I was worrying needlessly, as the soldier beside me seemed almost calm.

At long last, I heard Don's voice break through a bout of static from the communicator: "Move in, everyone! Now's the time!"

It was amazing to see the soldiers emerge from their hiding places. They seemed to just crawl out of the woodwork, rushing in on the central fortress with a collective cry. I hadn't even realized there were this many left. I felt pulled by the rushing tide of people like a magnet. I followed them into battle and fired as they fired, though I couldn't even see the enemy. Only a few stray shots were fired at us, as I recall. The USOW defenders must have retreated into the fortress.

I followed the crowd, which seemed smaller when packed together, probably consisting of only about twenty men. We went around the side of the fort until we came upon a blown-open door. The edges of the metal door were melted, glowing orange. The first soldiers to enter stepped carefully over the hot steel, moving cautiously, rifles raised. I heard the clatter of feet down the hallway inside, and then gunfire erupted.

The line moved, and I soon found myself stepping into the halls of the USOW base. Don was right beside me, having somehow ended up at the entrance at nearly the same time as me. I fought back revulsion as we stepped over the strewn, bloody corpses of our fallen comrades and enemies. The differences between the two were in uniform only. The enemy had a stricter dress code, each of them wearing the same blue and black uniform with the same silvery armor plating, but the dead men's contorted faces and blank, staring eyes were still just as human. It was lucky that most of the enemy wore tinted facemasks on their helmets. Don didn't even look down as he moved cautiously through the tunnels.

"Is that all of them?" I asked in a whisper.

Don turned to glare at me for speaking out of line. Then his head snapped back around, and his gun came up. An enemy soldier leaned out from behind a door down the hall and took aim. But Don was quicker, and he laid the enemy soldier down with a single shot to the head.

I fumbled with my own rifle as more soldiers came pouring from the other doors in the hall. Bullets whizzed past my ear, and one or two struck Don directly in the chest. He was knocked to the ground by the impact of the bullets. He did not get back up.

My bravery fell with him. Seized by panic, I ran. I ran to the first open door that led to what looked like a good hiding place, and I slipped inside.

But I wasn't alone. There was a USOW soldier in the room, reloading his rifle. For a second we stood and stared at one another, but I soon caught sight of his hand moving toward his sidearm. With lightning quickness and precision that surprised me, I fired a burst of ammunition into his chest. He shook for a moment, and then fell over without a sound. I looked quickly away and slid to the far corner of the room, awaiting the arrival of more hostiles... and tried not to look at my latest kill.

I recall sitting in a backwards metal chair with my gun propped up on the upper edge of the back, staring fixedly at the open door. Minutes dragged by, and I saw no one. I could hear gunfire echoing through the building, filling me with ever-growing fear and anticipation. Yet I didn't use my implant to end the simulation; I was determined to see this to its end.

After what seemed an eternity, I saw an enemy soldier's silhouette appear in the entrance. My twitchy trigger finger was at last appeased, and the man was dead before he ever even knew what hit him. I heard his armored body hit the floor.

To my astonishment, Sofia Tyler herself was next to burst through the opening, leaping over the corpse like a cat. As soon as she was inside, she slammed the door shut behind her. Then she staggered and leaned against the wall, panting, and began reloading her assault rifle. Seeing the body of the man I had killed earlier, she gave him a kick to make sure he was dead, then spat upon his corpse.

"Sofia," I said, rising from my hiding spot. "It's me, Kyle!"

She was startled for a moment, but quickly regained her composure. "Kyle! I wondered if I'd ever see you again. Give me a minute to catch my breath... I see you've managed to pull your weight, after all."

Sofia hefted her assault rifle and, indicating with a jerk of her head that I should follow her, moved to open the door. It didn't budge. She rattled the handle a few times before she was convinced that it was locked. Then she took a step back and fired at it with her rifle. The bullets had little effect upon the strong metal surface, and posed more danger to us as ricochets that it did to the handle. She kicked at the door frantically, growling with frightening ferocity. Then she took a step back and landed in the nearest chair, exasperated. There was no other way out of the room. The walls were made of concrete, and there were no windows.

She looked at me and gave a wry smile. "Looks like we're stuck. Got your radio? Mine was destroyed."

I reached for the one on my belt, but found it was gone. "I... don't have mine either. I don't know what happened to it... I must have lost it."

Sofia cursed and slammed her fist upon the table. The sounds of battle, though muffled, could still be heard coming from all sides, including above and below. Sofia looked anxious to resume the fight. I was nothing of the sort.

She turned to look at me and smiled. "I guess we're stuck here with each other for a while."

"I guess so," I replied, swallowing hard.

Being around women in general never made me nervous, but Sofia was entirely different: the complete opposite of every woman I'd ever known. Actually, she was the opposite of every man I'd ever known too. They all seemed effeminate compared to her; myself included.

"You're kinda cute when you're scared witless," she joked, obviously reading me like an open book.

I blinked at her and tried to look incredulous. "I'm not afraid!"

She laughed. "Sure you are... I can see it in your eyes. They're not a soldier's eyes. What were you before you grabbed a gun and decided to try killing? A farm-boy? Scribe, maybe? You seem smart... You're thinking about all this bloodshed, I bet."

"Aren't you? You look like you're thinking too…"

She just shrugged. Her smile then faded, and she averted her gaze. Crossing her arms on the table before her, she lay her head down and gazed at the blank, filthy wall.

"Did anyone ever tell you that you have beautiful eyes?" I said on a whim.

She nodded grimly. "Yes. Of course."

"Really?"

"They're all dead now," she said with a shrug.

"Oh…" I said quietly. "Sorry."

"Come over here and sit beside me," she said, though in a disinterested voice, still staring at the wall, her head resting on her arms.

"I thought you said you weren't afraid?" I asked, half-teasingly, as I slid my chair closer.

She sat up and looked daggers at me. "No. I just figured that you'll probably be dead too by tomorrow, so…"

When she mentioned my death, I suddenly recalled that this was all only a simulation… a game. It seemed that only the mention of my death ever made me recall that this wasn't real. I looked at her, saw the pain hidden behind her jaded eyes, and choked. How could this woman not be real? She seemed more real than anyone I'd ever known.

"Sofia…" I said.

"Shhh…" she said, shaking her head and leaning back in her chair. "Just sit and rest, okay? We can talk later, if we survive."

I nodded. She slid down into a resting position and looked up at the ceiling. I wondered if she was trying to follow the events around us merely by the sound, or if she was thinking of something else entirely. The din of battle was growing quieter overhead. I hadn't realized how tired I truly was due to the excitement of warfare, but sleep crept upon me and took me by surprise. I was soon lost to its dark but peaceful embrace.

FIVE
A GRIP ON UNREALITY

When I awoke the morning after the intense battle for the USOW supply base, I was startled to find myself back in a simulation room of the G4M3 facility in Utopia. My stomach was aching. I wondered briefly if it was the cooked rat I'd eaten, but then I remembered it hadn't been real. I could almost still taste it…

I reached under my coarse white shirt and scratched my chest. I was clean and fresh, and an unmarked uniform lay on the table across the room. This was odd, I thought, since I had let it become stained with blood the previous day. But that was in G4M3, I reminded myself. I was obviously still not thinking clearly. But I knew one thing: I hadn't died. So, what had happened?

I was startled for the second time that morning when Frank Billings stepped into the room, his teeth shining at me. "I always say you should play on weekends. You spent most of the day in G4M3 this time, boy. You're lucky it's your day off, or you would have missed work."

"I don't have a job…" I answered absentmindedly. "I haven't selected a new one yet."

"You should," Frank replied. "Better than letting the Order pick one for you."

I nodded, changing the subject. "What… Why did I come back? I didn't die or activate the return device…"

"You must have fallen asleep then," Frank replied with a laugh. "Everyone has to sleep, and when you fall asleep in a suitably dark area, G4M3 boots you out. Don't worry… you can resume your life in the world you left… tomorrow, or whenever you like."

I hesitated. "There was… a girl… Will… Will she still be there?"

"Maybe," he replied, tapping his chin. "Like I told you, G4M3 is a persistent world. There are dozens of other players in the same server as you, so we can't 'pause' the action. The world keeps going even when you leave."

I scratched my head. "You mean she'll... wake up with me gone?"

Frank smiled sympathetically. "Yes, yes, Kyle. She will. She might even be dead by the time you get back. But don't worry about it. There are more female characters in G4M3, and you're better off meeting a real woman anyway."

I felt my stomach tighten inside me, but I didn't feel like mulling over the information at that moment. I may have fallen asleep in G4M3, but in this world I was still thoroughly exhausted. So, I pulled myself up from my bed and walked out of the room, pulling on my jacket as I went. I didn't even say goodbye to Frank, nor did he say a word to me.

Like an automaton, I walked out of the G4M3 facility and into the transport cab, telling the driver to take me home. My parents were gone when I got there, so I went straight up to my room. When I threw myself in bed, I could still hear the sounds of warfare all around me... but they were only in my mind. It seemed that I could no longer discern reality from fantasy. My brain was flooded with conflicting thoughts, but sleep soon overrode them, and I blacked out once again.

===

That night, I dreamed about Sofia. She was unlike anyone I had ever met. Sure, she was attractive, but I had met plenty of pretty girls in Utopia – some downright beautiful. But they had all been exactly the same – practically carbon copies of each other – all boring. By comparison, the depth and intensity of Sofia was almost overwhelming...

I couldn't believe it: I was falling in love... with a girl who wasn't even real. I felt like an utter fool. What kind of dork falls in love with a fictional woman?

She wasn't the only thing I dreamed about. I saw Don too, bellowing out orders in the heat of battle. I saw him get shot down in front of me, over and over again. I felt the impact of bullets striking my armor, heard the sound of screaming, smelled the stench of Saltpit City…

I woke up with a headache. I ached all over, in fact. It felt almost disappointing to wake up at home: the blank white walls around me were comforting and sickening at the same time. I went about my morning routine robotically, methodically. My mind swam in another world as my body carried me downstairs.

"Good morning, Kyle," my father said from the sofa, where he was watching the morning news on the holovision, as usual.

"Good morning, Kyle," Mother said from the kitchen as she cooked.

"Good morning…" I said, trying to sound casual, though I felt like I was walking in a dream.

The smell of food floated in from the kitchen. It was the smell of a healthy breakfast, far different from the smell of cooked rat. I sat down and slowly ate my meal. It wasn't very appetizing, somehow, but I was starving, so I shoveled it in. Father came in and sat down, talking to Mother about today's news as he ate. I listened to him but didn't make reply. The news bored me – just the usual local events. Nothing ever really happened in Utopia.

"Old Joe Williams died today," he said with the slightest note of concern. "You remember Joe, don't you? His store will be under new management now."

"What a shame," said my mother. "Joe wasn't really that old. I wonder why he died…"

"It is a shame," my father agreed, "but he'd been unhappy for years now; no one knew why. Might be better this way…"

I gave a sigh, pushed away from the table, and stood up. "I think I'm going to go downtown for a while…"

"All right," Father said, starting a little as if he'd just noticed me. "Have fun."

"Bye, Kyle," Mother said.

I got up and almost ran out of the room. I stepped outside and took a deep breath of the stale air, walking along the rows of identical homes. I didn't really know where I was going. I was trying to get a firm grip on reality again. When I'd awakened after the battle in G4M3 to find myself back in Utopia, I had sworn that I would return to G4M3 and find Sofia again as soon as possible. But now I wasn't sure if I should go back; it was doing things to my mind.

As I wandered along the sidewalk, lost in thought, the sun rising behind me, I was interrupted by the deep metallic monotone of a patrol bot: "Excuse me, sir. Are you lost?"

"No," I said automatically.

"May I ask where you are going?" the robot inquired, its blue eye blinking at me. "Perhaps I may be able to help you."

I paused for a moment, curiosity getting the better of me, and said, "I'm just out for a walk."

"You should visit the park, sir," the robot piped. "It's the perfect place to enjoy the beauty of nature's order."

"I think I'll just wander the sidewalk for a bit, thanks," I said, changing direction and walking past the robot.

"One moment, please," it said, its tone changing slightly. "You are Kyle Roswell?"

The bot put this as more of a statement than a question, as if it already knew, so I hesitated before nodding in the affirmative.

"I have a message for you from the retirement home, Kyle Roswell. I have just received information that your grandfather, Walter Roswell, has regretfully passed away." The bot's voice was emotionless. "His body ceased functioning exactly three minutes and fifteen point two seconds ago, and medics were unable to revive him."

I stared at the android's blinking lights in wonder. I had never truly known Grandfather, but his death startled me. I felt as if I had lost a potential friend and source of information, though he truly could have been neither in his condition. He was probably better off this way, but it was strange that he should die at that moment. I had been entertaining the notion of visiting him again to see if he could tell me anything more about G4M3.

"That's terrible," I said. "Have you told my father?"

"He will be informed soon," the patrol bot answered.

"I'll visit him after you've told him then," I said with a sigh. "I think I'll go to the G4M3 facility."

"Very well, sir." It walked to the nearest lamppost and pressed the button. "Your transportation will arrive shortly."

I watched the robot stalk off down the sidewalk. The patrol robots were perfectly friendly and very helpful, but I always felt an aura of menace emanating from them. The fact that they always knew just who you were, just where you lived, and just about everything else about you, made them more than a little unnerving. They appeared unarmed, but their thick limbs looked very powerful.

The tram arrived quickly, and I stepped on board. The robot pilot greeted me with the usual "good morning." I ignored it at first, but as I ascended the ramp leading inside, the bot repeated it: "good morning." I looked up. The robot's elongated head was staring directly at me, its blue lights glowing softly.

"Good morning," I answered it.

As soon as I responded, its head swiveled around to face forward, and I heard the doors close behind me. Once I was seated, the tram began to move. I almost fell asleep while watching the identical buildings slide past the window, listening to the passengers talk, smelling the perfumed air, and feeling the cold hard metal of the wall against my arms and the plastic of the chair on my back.

I didn't have enough time to completely doze off, however, before we arrived at the G4M3 facility. I left quickly and walked up to the door. Peering in, I saw Frank's robotic assistant sitting behind his desk. Frank himself was nowhere to be seen.

"Good morning, Mr. Roswell," it piped amiably as I entered.

"Good morning," I responded, with little enthusiasm. "Where's Frank Billings?"

"He is in his office, Mister Roswell. He has given me permission to let you in, if you wish to speak with him."

"I do," I said.

"Very well, sir. Step back here."

With that, the little robot opened the glass door beside its desk and allowed me into its cubicle. The computers around me blinked and glowed, streams of data flowing over their screens at a mind-boggling rate. I could not read any of them.

There was a door on the wall marked 'Commander's Room.' The bot raised its arm, and a long stick of metal slid out of the its finger into a port under the control panel. A green handprint then appeared on the screen, as if someone had placed their hand there, confirming their identity. Then the door slid open and allowed me to enter.

As soon as I was inside, the robot shut the door behind me. Frank's office was a very dark place. None of the lights were on, and the only sources of illumination were his computer screen and holographic projection panel. I watched as a glowing green hologram of the Builder statue rotated slowly above Frank's dark wooden desk.

Frank Billings sat in his chair, his elbows on the desk's polished surface, his eyes staring at the holographic statue and looking very sullen. Then he noticed me, and his face broke into the usual smile, a smile of complete openness and friendliness. I wondered if my sessions of G4M3 had changed my outlook on life, for I seemed to detect something… different… in Frank's smile, much as I had felt about the patrol bot when it had questioned me. Perhaps it was just because the room was so dark.

"Kyle!" he shouted in his all-too-friendly manner, which seemed somewhat out of place. "Great to see you again!"

"Why's it so dark in here?" I asked.

"Oh, don't worry about that. I just get tired of so many artificial lights all the time," he said. "You know, the lights in the hallway, the sun, they're all so *yellow*. Like a disease… But enough about that. Are you here for another game?"

I shook my head. "Frank, have you heard? Walter's dead."

His face suddenly became serious. "Is that so? That's really too bad. He was the best kind of guy: friendly, smart, hard-working… Still, I guess he's better off now than he was in that terrible condition. Well, so much for the G4M3 session today…"

"Actually, I want to enter G4M3 again, Frank," I blurted out. "I can't help it."

"You don't *enter* G4M3, Kyle. You play it. But do you really think you should do it right now? Your grandfather just died... Don't you think you should go be with your family?"

"Father doesn't have to know where I've been," I argued.

Frank looked hard at me and said, "Listen, Kyle: I know that you're really obsessed with G4M3 right now, but... You don't want to deviate too far from the norm. It isn't... healthy. It's expected that you go see your parents when a tragedy such as this occurs. I don't want to get my company in trouble."

I looked at him where he sat behind his chair, illuminated in the green light of the hologram of the Builder.

But I really, really wanted to get back into the G4M3. "I didn't even know Walter very well, Frank. We can just say I didn't learn about his death until after the G4M3 session. Who cares what I do with my own time?"

"The Order cares, Kyle..." Frank replied gravely, rising from his chair. "Do you think they monitor your every movement because they don't care what you do?"

I blinked at him. "What?"

He looked so strange standing up like that, with the green light illuminating his face from below. His face's lines and wrinkles were more noticeable, and the shadows cast over his features were long and sinister.

"I used to work for the Order, Kyle," Frank said. "I know how they work. That's one reason your grandfather hired me. If you keep letting G4M3 rule your life, you could get in trouble."

"I thought you said your *company* could get in trouble."

"Don't turn this around, Kyle. I'm trying to help you. Both of us would be better off if you just stopped playing G4M3, at least for a while."

I closed my eyes and sighed, thinking for a moment before asking, "So you won't let me... play, then?"

"No," Frank replied with finality. "Not right now. This is for both our sakes, Kyle. You'll thank me someday."

"Don't talk down to me, Frank," I said angrily, surprising myself. "I'm not a boy anymore."

Frank looked hard at me then for a moment, but after a moment of thought he broke out in a smile and nodded. "I know, son, I know. I'm sorry, Kyle, really. But you can't play G4M3 today, at least. Maybe tomorrow, all right?"

"Fine," I said with a long sigh. "I think you're being paranoid, but fine. Goodbye, Frank."

"You'll understand one day, Kyle. Come on."

He smiled at me as he got up and walked around his desk, placing his hand on the palm-reading panel next to his door. The green light of the panel lit his face up eerily again. I wondered vaguely if his pearly white teeth were fake, if his smile was fake.

He motioned for me to leave. "Now go home, Kyle, and try not to think about G4M3. I have work to do, so I'll see you around."

When the door closed behind me, I looked up at the sickly yellow-tinted sky and tried to imagine it black and red, awful and oppressive, like the virtual sky in G4M3. It was hard, very hard. I could hardly remember. It was as if I was losing my grip on... unreality. Then I shook my head and decided to try my best to just forget about G4M3 entirely. Frank was probably right. That would be best for everyone.

===

I spent several days after that with my family. They were mostly unaffected by the loss of Walter. Father had been close to him, but he showed only a little emotion. He knew, like everyone, that Walter was better off now than he'd been while alive.

The next three or four days of Utopian life allowed me to adjust and get things in perspective once again. I convinced myself that G4M3 was only a game, that the men and women fighting and dying were not real, and that Sofia was only an artificial intelligence program.

So, I decided to get out and meet real people. It was frightening to rediscover how similar they all were, smiling and naïve. Everyone in Utopia was like this. Everyone was exactly the same.

I even went to the Artisans' Circle and wandered its gallery, looking for those interested in new ideas and imagination. But all of the art was meaningless – just vague shapes of color and form, or random objects, meant to convey thoughts and emotions rather than images, or to make some kind of statement. But to me, all of the thoughts and statements seemed as simplistic as the art. I felt nothing. Somehow, even as each piece tried to look different, they all looked the same: downright sterile.

I wandered on. The more people I met, the more my grip on reality began to slip once again. I felt the urge to return to the intense realism of unreality, of G4M3. I wanted to leave behind these robotic, mass-produced citizens and return to a world of more lively and unique individuals, like Sofia.

I choked on the stale air of Utopia more than ever. I was suffocating in this huge prison of a city. I once took a ride as far as I could go in the transport bus, but I never saw anything new. I kept waiting for the city to end, but it never did. Eventually, the driver bot just forced me to leave, saying that it had reached its destination limit. I just told it to take me back home.

As the days went by, I longed for escape. So it was that, around four days after the death of my grandfather, I once again found myself in the blank yellow-white halls of the G4M3 facility.

"Greetings, Kyle Roswell," said the robot greeter. "It has been exactly 4 days, 6 hours, and 12.2 seconds since you last visited us. Master Billings wanted to know when you returned, but sadly he is away. Can I help you with something in his absence?"

I shook my head at the little robot and said, "You don't need to tell Frank I've been here."

"Oh, but I must, sir. He has given me specific orders to inform him of your return. I am sorry if this displeases you in any way. Can I help you with something in his absence?"

This time I nodded and replied, "Can you start up a G4M3 session for me? Can you restore my previous world?"

"Of course, sir!" the bot squeaked. "Proceed upstairs and enter the third room on your right, room number 5. Your G4M3 session will begin as soon as you are ready."

"Thanks," I said, walking off toward the elevator.

"Have a pleasant game, sir!" it said cheerfully as I left.

I grew lost in thought as I rode the elevator, and I will confess that I was nervous at the thought of returning to the war-torn Saltpit City. I wondered if I was doing the right thing. At the same time, however, I was eager to see Sofia again.

I'm not sure which of these two anticipations made my hands shake while I was suiting up. The robot at the door waited for me to confirm that I was ready before activating the simulation. I felt the now-familiar sensation of the wind blowing around me. My heart beat faster as the world went black... and then I opened my eyes to the world of G4M3.

SIX
THE THOUSAND YEARS WAR

The G4M3 began in exactly the same location as last time. I was back in the blackened, crumbling streets of Saltpit City. On my right stood the familiar building with the metallic panels welded to its dilapidated walls: the Eagles' hideout. With only a moment's hesitation, I headed off toward it.

I paid no heed to the few people wandering the streets, and they ignored me as well. When I got to the door of my destination, I paused. I had to alert them to my presence. A stranger suddenly barging in with no warning would probably be greeted with gunfire. So, with little idea what to do, I knocked on the simple wooden door. The men on the street turned to look at me. I shot them a glance. They turned away again immediately.

"Who goes there?" came a surly voice from inside the building.

"It's me... Kyle Roswell," I said.

"Kyle Roswell? Sofia said to let you in if you came back. Stand up to the door."

A slot opened up near the top of the door and two eyes peered out. Then the door swung wide open. There was a gun pointed straight at me. The man wielding it waved me in with the barrel. I entered slowly, and the guard slammed the door shut behind me.

"Sofia!" the guard called out. "Kyle's back!"

There was a moment of silence, and then I heard the rumble of several sets of feet coming from the floor above. Sofia herself soon appeared atop the staircase. She leaped over the railing and landed softly on the wooden floor. Her face showed surprise and concern as she approached, but these emotions were quickly replaced by anger.

"Where in the hell have you been, Kyle?" she growled. "Where did you go? What happened?"

I wasn't a great liar by any means, and the story I hastily concocted was very unconvincing: "I... I was captured."

"What!?" Sofia asked incredulously. "How?"

"I don't know!" I replied, trying to use outrage as a defense. "One minute I was asleep in that room with you, and the next minute I woke up in a USOW holding cell, okay? I barely managed to escape! I got lucky when they were trying to transport me and got attacked. What about you? How'd you get out of that room?"

"I heard gunfire outside," Sofia said, so coldly that I couldn't tell if she believed me or not, "and when I woke up, you were gone. Some Eagles were fighting USOW soldiers outside the door. They won, and then cut through the door lock with a blow-torch."

One of the Eagles laughed and glared at me. "You mean the USOW busted into a dark room, found the leader of the Saltpit City Eagles and a total rookie asleep inside, and they took *you* captive instead of Sofia?"

"You'll have to tell me all about it," Sofia said in an authoritative tone. "Follow me upstairs."

I glared at the soldier who had made the remark about my story, but he ignored me and said to Sofia, "I'll be going out for a while. Permission to leave, Commander?"

"See you around, Webb," Sofia said dismissively as she ascended the creaking wooden staircase.

The building that the Eagles were using as a base was definitely not originally built for such a purpose. It was made entirely of wood, which was not in good condition. The Eagles had reinforced it with metal in several places. Perhaps, I thought, this rather large building had actually once been someone's house.

Sofia led me up the creaking stairs into a small room with rather luxurious furnishings, at least for the world of G4M3. It had a long, wooden table and two sofas with faded, cracked red cushions. The walls were relatively clean, and electric lights illuminated the room. There were no windows, however; only slits in the walls, from which to fire guns.

Sofia threw herself down on one of the sofas and adopted a reclined position. I sat down in the opposite chair and looked across the low table at her. She put her feet up on it and reached under it with one arm. Drawing out two cups and a large bottle, she set them down on the table and began pouring.

"Congratulations," she said. "You're the only member of the Eagles that's ever been captured by the USOW and escaped on his own. Here, have a glass. I don't have the slightest clue what this stuff is, since the label's long gone, but it hasn't killed me yet."

I took a sip of the clear fluid and immediately coughed and sputtered. It tasted terrible – like drinking some kind of toxic chemical. But I cleared my throat, swallowed some more, and gave a teary-eyed smile.

"Thanks," I said hoarsely.

She gave a mirthless laugh. "You're such an idiot. I don't believe that 'captured' story for a second, and no one else does either. Why would they grab you and just leave me there? I'm giving you a chance to tell me the truth here. *One* chance. Because I like you."

I swallowed hard, then decided to use an old tactic I'd read about in a book once: telling the truth but not the whole truth, so you technically weren't lying. "Listen… I know it doesn't make any sense. I was afraid to even come back here and tell you what happened, because I knew you wouldn't believe it. But I swear to you, this is the truth: I fell asleep next to you, and when I woke up, I was in a completely different place. Here one minute, gone the next. Like magic."

She stared at me for a long minute then, her green eyes narrow, as she swirled her drink around in its glass. "Hmm. I guess it's possible they could only take one of us and didn't know who I was. Maybe thought they could come back for me later. Weird though…"

"So how did the battle go?" I asked, eager to change the subject. "How did everything turn out?"

"It was pretty much over when I got out of the room. We raided the place for supplies, dragged out our wounded, and blew the base to hell."

"So, everything went perfectly? Why are you still holed up here then? I thought we were going to move to some other base after the battle."

"I thought we might as well keep a footing in Saltpit City," she answered, taking a swallow of her drink. "But it's a good thing we did stay here, since you wouldn't have known the way to the cave…"

I was reluctant to ask the question that was foremost in my mind – the chief question that made this entire G4M3 a little hard to believe – but finally I threw aside caution and spat it out: "One thing I don't understand, Sofia… Why, if you're… I mean, the people of this city seem to be intelligent. So why do you keep *fighting?* What are you fighting about?"

She looked at me like I had lost my mind. "One day you're gonna tell me where you're from, Kyle Roswell. Because I've never seen a place on this blasted earth where people *aren't* fighting."

"But… imagine if there could be such a place, I mean. Imagine if all the gangs and factions could make peace, create a city where no one fought…"

She snorted. "Sure, I can imagine that. But only if one side won, and made all the others their slaves. That's the kind of 'peace' the USOW want: the peace of a prison camp."

Not an entirely inaccurate description of Utopia, I thought. "But… How long have you been fighting?"

"Who knows?" Sofia shrugged. "More than a hundred years. Maybe a thousand."

I stared at her in amazement. "A thousand… But why? Why the endless war? What are you fighting about?"

"Territory. Food. Survival. And mutual hatred." She threw back the last of her glass of drink.

"But what started it all?" I asked.

"Nuclear warfare," she answered immediately.

"Over what?"

"I…" her voice trailed off. She looked far away for a moment. I suddenly remembered that she was an AI. Perhaps I had just posed an unanswerable question to her. Perhaps I had locked up her programming.

I blinked, realizing the truth. "You don't even remember... You've been fighting for so long that you've forgotten why it all started in the first place. You just keep butchering each other for the same piece of rock, again and again. You've never known anything else; there's never been anything else..."

She stood up angrily, nearly knocking over the table. "We *did* fight for a cause, Kyle! We fought for the *world* – not just the rock, but for the people on it! Because there *was* something before this: there was the USOW, and other big governments too. They ruled the world with their iron fists, ruined it for everyone, and then tried to make a new peace from the rubble. But we wouldn't have it! We gave up peace in exchange for *freedom*. And I'd do it all again."

I fell silent then, unable to really retort. Could I really say that I hadn't thought the same thing about the Order? That maybe it would be worth destroying the peace of Utopia if it meant we could live in freedom?

Had Grandfather programmed these thought patterns into G4M3, I wondered? Perhaps he'd had his own misgivings about the Order, expressing those through his creation. It certainly sounded that way, judging by how Sofia was talking. Her speech was much clearer now, without so much slang. It sounded more like an educated Utopian.

"But enough about that," she said at length. "I know how you feel, Kyle. We all feel like that once in a while. But we're soldiers, not philosophers. So... Now, tell me about your own experiences. Tell me about this USOW base you woke up in."

I swallowed again, looking around and trying to think fast. "Well... the base was very... clean."

"Cleaner than this roach-hole?" she prompted.

I nodded. "Yes. And they had pretty good food, even for a prisoner like me – so good I had a mind to stay for a while just to eat it."

She laughed. "Can't blame you for that."

I took another swallow from my glass. I was stalling for time while I tried to make up a believable story about my escape. Luckily for me, in a way at least, my tale spinning was interrupted by a cry from downstairs.

"Sofia! Enemy forces are headed this way! USOW tanks are headed down the street toward us!"

Before the soldier was half done, Sofia was already up and loading her rifle. "Get ready, Kyle. Everyone assume defensive positions! Get to your post and fortify the base! Cover all sides! And call for reinforcements!"

After issuing her orders, Sofia ran to one of the slits in the wall and peered through. I followed her example. Sure enough, there was a huge armored vehicle riding along the road. Its turret creaked and clanked as it rotated toward our building. The gun rose into the air until it was pointed almost at my face.

In the schools of Utopia, they had taught a class about the horrors of war and how they had been finally eradicated thanks to the wisdom and kindness of the Order. In that class, I had learned of several foolish battles in which many hundreds of men had died pointlessly. Those images are what allowed me to identify the vehicle I now saw as an armored battle tank, a machine of war.

Running alongside the tank were a squad of infantrymen like the ones we had fought in the USOW base, though these were wearing desert camouflage instead of blue and black uniforms under their armor. They came marching out of the gloomy haze down the street and turned their helmeted faces toward us. Their visors glinted, and I saw the red targeting lights on their guns as they aimed at the building. Sofia slid around to put her back against the wall as they opened fire.

"They're retaliating after our strike on their base," Sofia said. "We'll show 'em how to defend properly!"

With that, she rushed out of the room. I barely had time to follow. She issued orders to her soldiers as we ran down the stairs. They were already firing through the slits in the windows at the enemy soldiers. Several were readying anti-tank missiles and preparing to make their way to the third floor, where the biggest windows were. The sounds of gunfire assaulted my ears. Then there was a deafening blast, a loud, whistling whirr, and I heard the walls on one of the floors above cave in.

"The tank's firing!" a soldier cried.

"They're coming in!" came another shout.

Wanting to take part in the fight, I ran to the nearest slit window and poked my gun barrel through. When I looked outside, I saw several soldiers flying up into the air, up toward the opening that had been blown in the wall above. Fires were spurting out of their backs and lifting them up to the sky. I had never seen anything like it, but I fired at one anyway. The man screamed and lost control of his flight. He slammed into the wall of the building and tumbled to the ground.

"They're usin' jetpacks!" came a shout from downstairs. "Comin' in the third floor!"

I heard loud boots on the stairs outside. Sofia fired at the door before it even swung open. Then it did swing wide, and a dead USOW soldier fell through.

We ran out into the hall, joining a few Eagles there, fighting their way to the staircase. The lead man was peppered with bullets and fell back on his followers, creating a domino effect until the third man threw his falling allies out of his way and began firing. Then the enemy came in full force. They cut down most of the men on the stairs, and Sofia ordered the rest to retreat. The USOW obviously had us outnumbered.

"Get out of the building!" she commanded. "Take the back exit!"

The soldiers began streaming out of the room through a door in the back, which I hadn't even noticed. Sofia went with them. I was left in the room with just a few defenders.

I was about to follow them when I heard one of the enemy soldiers shout: "Kyle Roswell!"

Without thinking, I froze and turned to look. The soldier on the stairs was pointing at me, his helmet gone. It was one of the Eagles –

the one who had left earlier, called Webb. But now he was wearing USOW armor. I scowled at him and leveled my rifle. He ducked behind cover just in time, but I managed to take out his comrade.

I stared stupidly and watched the man clutch at the wound I had made in his throat, which was spraying blood. I listened in horror as he let out a gurgling scream and fell back against the wall. *Why do I always have to hit them in the neck?* I thought.

This delay cost me my escape. They were upon me then, in the blink of an eye. I scrambled for the exit, but tripped and fell. I felt something heavy hit the back of my skull. There was a second of intense pain, and I felt my weapon torn from my grasp. A boot was placed on my back. My hands were grabbed and bound.

"Doctor Matthew Noble wants to have a chat with you, kid," said the USOW soldier who was tying me up. "You're the *lucky* one."

"What?" I blurted, turning my head to get my face off the ground. "Why?"

"Hell if I know!" retorted the soldier, heaving me up onto my feet. "He said that he wanted to know more about you and where you're from. But if you want to argue about it, I'm warning you… it won't take much to convince me to just shoot you."

I was about to respond to this comment when the door through which the others had escaped burst open once again. Several of the Eagles entered the room and began firing. Sofia was there, leading them. They moved slowly and professionally through the room, walking in formation and firing at each of the hostiles.

Sofia raised her rifle to shoot the man holding me, but he heaved me up off the floor and used me as a human shield. I quickly wrapped my foot around behind his and gave it a jerk. We both toppled backwards onto the floor. The soldier landed on his back with me on top of him, which knocked the wind out of him completely. Then I rolled out of the way and saw Sofia fire a round of ammunition into his prone form.

But the room was rapidly filling with more enemies, and my hands were bound. I couldn't get up, and I knew Sofia could not pause to help me. The base would soon be overrun.

"Go!" I yelled. "Get out of here! Save yourself!"

Sofia saw the wisdom in my advice as a grenade landed in the middle of the room, spewing smoke. She ordered the Eagles to get out, and they obeyed quickly, heading out the back door. I scrambled to my feet, my vision blurry as the room filled with the grey-white gas. I tried to run for the back door, but instead ran straight for a boarded-up window.

My shoulder slammed hard against the wood planking. The boards splintered and broke, and I fell screaming down to the street, landing on my back. I saw the red and black clouds swirling above me like a smoky, hellish abyss. I tried to rise, but I was out of breath, gasping for air.

I felt a pair of men grab me by the shoulders and heave me up onto my feet. Seeing quickly that they were USOW, I struggled in vain to escape.

"Put him in here! We're leaving!" I heard someone shout.

I felt myself lifted bodily off the ground and hurled into a small square space. My back hit the metal walls hard, knocking the wind out of me again. Looking around, I realized that I had been tossed into the trunk of a vehicle, perhaps a storage compartment on the USOW tank. The soldiers outside started to shut me in…

"Wait!" I cried.

There was a loud thump, cutting off my voice, and then the world went black. For a second, all I could hear was my own breathing, but this was soon replaced by the deafening roaring and clanking of the tank as it began to move. I felt the floor beneath me vibrate.

I had been captured. They were taking me to their base. I had lied earlier about being captured, but now that I was actually faced with the prospect, it seemed much more daunting. Hadn't Sofia said that no one had ever escaped from a USOW prison before? I imagined the tortures they might inflict upon me before I was allowed to 'die' and return to Utopia, but then a thought struck me: The trunk they had placed me in was perfectly dark.

I sat for a minute, feeling the cold metal wall with my arms, wondering if I should really leave again. Perhaps, I thought, I should keep playing until I discovered what this 'Doctor Matthew Noble' wanted with me. But eventually I began to get nervous and to feel a little claustrophobic. I managed to get my hands free, and, reaching up under my shirt, I pressed the tiny button in my navel. I felt wind blowing around me again as the simulation deactivated...

===

I could not tell how much time had passed between the moment I pressed the button to end the simulation, with the tank's engine roaring and clattering in my ears, and the moment I awoke in the empty white room of the G4M3 facility, with only the lights above my head buzzing almost imperceptibly. As usual, the robot worker had changed me into my normal civilian clothing, and I awoke lying on the bed. The change of setting was so sudden that I just lay there for a while, trying to convince myself of where I was. When I started looking around the room, I noticed Frank Billings standing beside my bed. He looked even older than ever. It looked like he was letting his hair turn grey.

"Frank?" I said.

"Rough game?" he asked, his smile appearing again. "You didn't stay in there long, I'm told."

"I... was captured by the enemy," I said, sitting up.

He looked at me quizzically. "Captured? Not killed? So, you just pressed the button to escape?"

"Yes..." I answered slowly. "Does that mean I'm not allowed to go back to that world?"

Frank smiled and shook his head. "No, no. Not at all. I'm just surprised that any of the factions would want to take you alive."

"The soldiers said they were taking me in for questioning."

Frank nodded. "I see. Knew something they wanted, did you? Hah! Looks like you're making yourself important in this little world of yours!"

"No…" I said slowly, recalling what the USOW soldier had said. "They didn't want to know about the Eagles' base. They wanted to know about me and… where I was from… I think."

Frank looked vaguely concerned, which surprised me a little. "Really? Well now… Which faction wanted to know this?"

"The USOW – the United States of the World, or something like that… and a man, a character in G4M3 named Matthew Noble."

Frank stared at me for a moment. It felt like he was scrutinizing me. I stood up and stared right back at him. Then suddenly his smile appeared once again.

"Matthew Noble!" he exclaimed, giving a short laugh. "My, you *have* gotten important! You're about to face your first boss! Surprised it's so soon."

"Boss?" I asked, scratching my neck. I didn't feel quite right.

"Bosses are the main enemies in G4M3," Frank explained. "Every Player who gets good enough at the game to survive for a while in one world will eventually face a boss."

"But I've hardly done anything…"

"You've survived two battles, Kyle!" Frank laughed. "But Doctor Noble is just your first boss. You'll probably face more, if you live in this world long enough."

I blinked. This explanation sounded much too artificial. It made the world I had grown to love as much as fear sound too much like… a game. I had come to care about the characters there, and here was Frank Billings speaking as if it were all just a joke. He spoke as if there was hidden order behind even the chaos in G4M3. It seemed so impossible… I had to force myself to remember that he was right.

"Is there a… final boss?" I asked. "Can you… beat… or *win* G4M3?"

Frank paused before responding. "In a way, I suppose… It… G4M3 is open-ended, meaning you can still play after you win. But the likelihood of you actually *beating* G4M3…"

"No one's ever done it before?" I asked.

Frank shook his head. "They say it's impossible."

"So, do I have to... take out Matthew Noble to continue?"

"Yes," Frank said gravely. "You have to kill him."

My eyes narrowed. "Then I will."

I expected Frank to smile or laugh, but he only nodded. "We'll see... But not today. For now, you should go home and rest. I never allow more than one session a day, Kyle."

"Alright, Frank," I said, shaking his hand. "This is quite a place, Frank. I don't know what I would do without G4M3 now."

Frank sighed. "Neither do I."

Again, I had expected him to be amused, so I asked, "Frank... is something wrong?"

He shook his head and stepped out of the room. "Nothing, Kyle. Nothing's wrong."

I stopped him by placing a hand on his arm. "Frank, is it something about the Order? Last time I wanted to play, you said something about the Order... Are they trying to shut down G4M3?"

When he looked at me then, Frank's face showed more grave seriousness than I had ever seen before. "Kyle, I don't think it's wise to talk about the Order. They... could be listening."

"They always are, aren't they?"

Frank looked up and down the hallway. "Not here."

"What? You mean there are no monitoring devices in the G4M3 facility?"

"I know too much about the Order, Kyle. I know more than anyone was meant to know. I used to work for them, and no one who works for them is ever intended to *not* work for them. I've been to the poor sectors, beyond Utopia – the ones no one's allowed to see. I've watched as the Order put its accursed implants into every innocent newborn child, keep track of them... to change them from humans into robots... just like all the rest of them..."

His eyes had glazed over while saying this, as if he were back there, seeing it all again. I felt a sick feeling deep in my stomach. My mind reeled.

"You're talking crazy talk," I said, forcing a laugh. "You're joking, right?"

"It's getting dark, Kyle," Frank said loudly, as if he had not meant to say what he had just told me. "You should go."

"I want to know more about the Order…" I said.

"No," he replied. "You don't. The more you know about the Order, the less happy you'll be. The Order doesn't want you to know about it – about how the sausages are made."

"Sausages?"

He gave a mirthless chuckle. "All the food you eat, really. It's all the same. And believe me, you wouldn't want to know what it's made of."

"No…" I said, shaking my head. "What do you mean, Frank?"

"Go, Kyle!" he burst out, almost angrily. "Get out of here! You can come back later if you want to play G4M3 some more. For now… just go. Leave me alone for a while… No, I'm never alone. Like the Order tells us, we are never alone."

Without another word, I walked off down the hall. I pressed the button to call the elevator up, but, before I stepped inside, I turned back around toward Frank.

"Frank…" I said. "What, exactly, *is* the Order?"

Frank turned to look at me from across the hall. His stare was blank and zombie-like. He looked old, I thought – older than ever before. I had seen that look once before… when I was getting off the tram before my first session of G4M3. I had even seen that look in my grandfather's eyes, I thought. It was like a great weight was on their shoulders, as if they were carrying a burden of knowledge so that the rest of us would remain happily ignorant… and they resented us for it.

"No one knows," he said. "Not anymore."

Before I could say more, the elevator doors shut in my face, and I felt myself drop down. I hadn't even realized I had backed into the lift. In a way, I was glad I had.

I left the G4M3 facility in a daze, and not for the first time. It seemed that was always how I felt after a session of G4M3. I wondered if all the other thousands of Players felt this way. Or was I unique, perhaps because I knew Frank Billings so closely, thanks to

Grandfather? Or was I unique at all? After all, everyone was equal under the Order. But Frank had said that I was important now in the world of G4M3...

It was a sad fate, and highly ironic, that I was important there... while here in the real world, I was absolutely no one.

S E V E N
ORDER TO THE MADNESS

I woke up that night with a splitting headache, and my stomach felt like it was rising up into my throat. The entire world swam as I got up out of bed and stumbled across the room. I leaned over the sink, feeling like I was drowning in air, and threw up. Then I stumbled backwards and fell into a sitting position on the toilet, groaning.

My head throbbed. I wondered vaguely if all of this was some side-effect of the gas from the grenade that USOW soldier had thrown, or perhaps the drink Sofia had given me. I grabbed the nearest drugs off the counter and read the labels, looking for anything that could cure this ailment. To this day, I don't know what I took, but those Utopian wonder-drugs did the trick. I sat for while on the edge of the bed, still feeling groggy, but I felt better when I went downstairs. I decided not to tell Mother and Father about the incident.

"Good morning, son," Father said, sitting on our soft sofa and watching the news on holovision, as usual – no, as *always*.

The sick feeling returned to me a little, but I suppressed it. "Good morning, Father, Mother…"

Utopian life was even more boring than usual after my last G4M3 session. The world seemed even less alive. As I sat and ate breakfast, I thought about what Frank Billings had said to me about the Order. Visions entered my head as I looked at my food: visions of workers slaving away to make it, and to support our healthy lifestyles.

"I went to visit Joe's old store," Father said, as he sat down to eat, "and the fellow who took it over seems very nice."

"Really?" Mother replied. "I'm glad. I'm sorry Joe is gone, but it will be nice to have his store back up and running."

"Joe was always a bit of an oddball, anyway. Always joking about the Order's robots, telling stories about them to scare little children. I didn't like it."

"He was only playing around," Mother said.

"You shouldn't play around about the Order, dear," Father replied gravely.

It was appalling how I could no longer stand to be around my parents. They were so simpleminded, and so cheerfully compliant with every dictate of the Order. I wondered what had *really* happened to Joe Williams.

Before I knew it, I heard myself saying, "Maybe that's what happened to him."

"Kyle?" Mother asked, almost in disbelief.

I looked down at my food, scooping up some more with my fork. "Maybe the robots, the Order, got tired of his jokes and put an end to them."

"He just got sick, Kyle," Father said, smiling. "A disease is not a robot. The Order tried to help him, even after he had ridiculed them. The Order cares for us all."

"But they failed, didn't they?" I went on. "Just like they failed with Walter."

Father's eyes widened. Mother started and gasped. "Kyle!"

Father took a disciplinary tone and said, "Your grandfather greatly helped the Order, Kyle. He believed in it as strongly as I do. He never teased boys about the robots being 'bad cops' like Joe did. Now cease this talk before it gets you in trouble."

"Before I end up like Joe?" I asked.

"Kyle," my mother said, sounding terrified, "please, tell us, what's wrong with you? You've been acting so strange…"

"And you missed two days of work," Father said. "Remember that job you signed up for?"

"No…" I said, blinking in confusion. "I never signed up for a job…"

"The letters we've been getting say differently," Father said.

I picked up the piece of paper he handed to me. It said that I had missed two days of work – that I had a job at a building nearby. I didn't recognize the address. I had never been there. I folded the letter neatly and placed it in my pocket.

Father nodded. "There, see? You did get a job, and you should be working at it."

"But it's not just that," Mother said. "You seem so up-tight and thoughtful all the time. Is it G4M3, or are you going through puberty all over again?" She gave a fake laugh.

Father joined in the sickeningly false laughter. "Well, dear, some people never do get through puberty completely."

"Did you ever play G4M3, Mother?" I asked, changing the subject.

"Yes, I did," she answered. "I liked it much better than your father did, in fact, but he got me off of it, and all for the better. This life is much better than any... false life in G4M3."

Was that a very slight longing to return that I detected in her voice, or was it my imagination?

"It's not good to miss work, son," Father said to me, leaning forward and looking me in the eyes, in that fatherly sort of way, "and it is not good to joke about the Order."

I stifled my anger and disappointment with my parents and managed to calmly say, "Yes, Father."

"We only want what's best for you," Mother said.

I looked at them and imagined a pair of silvery Utopian robots sitting in their places, their friendly blue eyes glowing at me.

"Good morning," I said, half to myself.

"Are you leaving?" Mother asked.

I took a deep, calming breath and answered her, "Just let me get some fresh air..."

"Okay, Kyle..." Mother said with a sigh.

"Just don't miss work again," Father added.

I walked out the door and shut it behind me. Going to work was the last thing on my mind. Had my father signed me up for that job? Or Frank? Or the Order? For my own sake, or the greater benefit of society? At this point, I didn't care about all that. Society and its precious Order would do fine without me. I was going back to G4M3.

===

"I knew you'd be back, Kyle," Frank said as I entered the G4M3 facility. He was not smiling now. I couldn't tell whether he was pleased or disappointed.

"It's good to see you again, Frank," I said.

To see Frank there, speaking honestly, without that gleaming smile plastered on his face, actually comforted me. I felt that Frank was a close friend now, a companion who shared his secrets with me about the Order. He was the only real person in Utopia who cared as little for the Order as I did, I thought. Yet both of us saw that it was necessary. I appreciated Frank then more than I ever had before, or ever would again.

"I assume you want to play G4M3 then, Kyle?" he asked, in a hopeless tone. "I suggested to you once that it might not be a good idea, but if you're really going to try to kill this Dr. Noble fellow, then maybe you should go ahead and play."

"Not yet," I answered. "I wanted you to tell me more about the Order…"

He heaved a great sigh. "No, Kyle. It's no use. You're better off forgetting everything you heard me say. I think a G4M3 session might help that."

"I don't see how…" I replied. "But I don't want to forget, anyway. I want to know more."

"Listen to me, Kyle!" Frank snapped. "I understand how you feel. I felt the same way as you when I found out the truth behind the Order. But there's no changing it. It is best to forget about it and keep on living. In a way, the Order is the culmination of the works and hopes and dreams of all mankind. They got what they wanted – what they deserved. You'll learn to do as I've done, and just live here under the Order, and do what you can to get ahead in the system. And I think a G4M3 session will help clear your thoughts… Killing your first boss will boost your self-confidence. Just don't get caught by him again!"

"Frank, I'm not looking to try to bring about some kind of reform... I just want to know the truth."

"Maybe after your G4M3 session, okay, Kyle?" Frank insisted. "I thought you wanted to fight Matthew Noble! Isn't that what you came here for?"

"I... I guess so," I answered. "It's just so hard to pretend that Saltpit City is fake, and *this* world is real. At times, it's hard to tell the difference between reality... and a game..."

"So, forget there is a difference..." Frank muttered. "Pretend G4M3 is real, if that's what you want. It certainly seems real enough, doesn't it? So live there for a while, and forget about Utopia and the Order. Use it as an escape, and then go back to living here when it's over. Follow the rules, then break them in the G4M3. I've done that, for years. That's my advice to you, as a friend."

"As a friend..." I muttered, feeling somewhat better, if only because of Frank's choice of words. "All right, Frank. Fire up G4M3."

When we arrived on the second floor, I was surprised to see a man lying in the hallway, his back against the wall, moaning loudly. He was dressed in the same kind of blank white suit that I always woke up wearing after a G4M3 session.

Frank ran forward and knelt beside the man and demanded almost angrily, "Who are you? What's wrong?"

"Calm down, Frank!" I said. "Give the man some air..."

Frank turned to glare at me, but then he said, "Right, right... Okay, sir, please tell us what's wrong so that we can help. Come now."

The man turned his head toward us. His eyes were red and bloodshot, and his mouth hung open.

"Drugs..." he groaned. "The drugs... in... that game..."

"Oh, come off it, man," Frank snarled. "G4M3 isn't real, you fool, and now that you're back in the real world the drugs can't affect you."

"Frank..." I began.

Frank looked back at me, shaking his head. "He's hallucinating. This has been happening lately. He needs a strong hand to snap him out of it. Medics! Come take this man to the medical room!"

Two little robots came wheeling around the hall immediately. They rolled up on either side of the moaning man and grabbed hold of his arms and legs. Then they lifted him up and scurried off with him, his head dangling, still groaning.

"Poor fool..." Frank muttered, looking at mé and rolling his eyes. "We've been having some problems with the system lately, in all honesty... I think it's the implant."

"Frank..." I began again, "there's something I need to tell you."

"I know, I know," he said, his familiar smile suddenly returning. "Let me guess, you felt sick after playing G4M3 too, right? Well, you're lucky, Kyle. We've just finished the new version of the transceiver, and you'll be the first one to get it."

"Transceiver?" I asked. "You mean the return button?"

He laughed. "Yes, of course, the return button. Shut the door. Now, come lie down on this table. There we are. This won't hurt a bit."

Again I stripped off my jacket and shirt and lay down upon the soft white bed in the simulation room. Frank fetched the implanter device and pressed it against my navel, first removing the old button and then replacing it with the new. It took less than a minute, and I felt nothing.

"That should do it..." he said.

"So that'll fix the sickness?" I asked. "And the hallucinations?"

"Yes," he said, smiling at me. "The devices regulate a lot of effects G4M3 has upon the body, including pain simulation. Unfortunately, it can sometimes cause a bit of a stomachache. But this new one is vastly improved; it's done great in testing... Now get suited up and ready to go. I'm going to go check on that other player."

"All right..." I replied reluctantly. "But there's one more thing, Frank..."

"Yes?"

"I think..." I could hardly get this out, "that I'm... in love with one of the girls in G4M3."

Frank looked at me very seriously. "Kyle, don't do it. It won't work."

I interrupted him, "Is there any way that you could... I don't know... save her? Make sure she doesn't get killed?"

"No, Kyle, there isn't," Frank replied. "Your grandfather knew a lot more than me about the programming of G4M3... I'm afraid I couldn't alter it without his help. And it's made to run so that the world keeps going after you've left. I can't change that, Kyle. Besides, it's better if she does die..."

"Don't say that, Frank," I groaned. "I knew you were going to say it, but..."

"So that you can live a life with a *real* woman," he finished. "Now... just get ready."

Frank waved goodbye to me and rushed out of the room, closing the door behind him. I strapped into my military outfit again and checked my weapons carefully. All was the same as usual. It seemed suddenly almost silly to escape to this unreality again, especially after what Frank had said about the Order and about Sofia... but I couldn't help feeling a rush of adrenaline.

"Are you ready?" the robot outside asked through the speakers in the room.

"Yes," I said.

The room began to swirl...

===

I was back in the world of G4M3. The shattered streets of Saltpit City loomed before me, the crumbling buildings standing out against the terrible red and black sky. If Utopia was Heaven, I thought, then surely G4M3 was Hell. And if the unseen force governing Utopia was the Order, then the force governing G4M3 was Chaos.

As I walked down the dreary streets, the dust blowing in my face, heading for the Eagles' base, I suddenly recalled that it would no longer be there. Then another realization struck me: the streets of

Saltpit City were completely deserted. I felt this to be a foreboding omen of some kind. Though the streets were always silent, and the citizens were often quite hard to spot, there were usually at least a few present. I felt lonely, standing there with the wind whistling forlornly in my ears, the sand and ash blowing through the deserted streets. But I also felt... calm.

As I looked around, one man suddenly became visible: an old man, hobbling toward me on the sidewalk. He was dressed in rags from head to toe, with a large sign hanging from a rope around his neck. The sign said, in remarkably clear lettering: 'THE END IS NIGH.' Only his scraggly grey beard was visible – his dark hood completely overshadowed the rest of his face. No matter how hard I peered into that shadow, I could see nothing but empty blackness.

As he drew closer, the old man suddenly stopped and looked at the sky, which still failed to dispel the shadow that his hood cast over his features. "Dark, dark. Red and black."

I was disappointed to find that my only companion in Saltpit City that day would be a madman preaching about the end of the world, so I said impatiently, "Yes, the sky's red and black here. What of it?"

The old man wheezed. "This is the land of the dead."

I turned to walk away, but the old man stopped me with a look and said, "Red and black, blue and white. Inverted. Law and order, chaos and destruction."

I blinked. "Are you talking about the past? How old are you? Do you... remember when the sky was blue and white here?"

He shook his old grey head, causing his hood to fold back and forth. "What is nature? Is it chaos? Is it order?"

For some reason, though logic demanded that I simply walk away, I felt inclined to answer the old madman's question: "Nature is entropic. It begets chaos."

The old man shook his head slowly. "No. Nature is balance, order out of chaos. Balance is all. Nature is all, in this world – in all worlds. There will come a time of balance. There will come a time..."

"What are you raving about?" I asked agitatedly, looking up and down the street and feeling suddenly naked and uncomfortable. I wished someone else would show up.

The old man's voice took on a deadly serious tone: "The time will come... and you should not be here when it does."

I felt a chill run down my spine, for there was certainly something disturbing about this raving madman. His arms and hands were hidden in the folds of his robe, or possibly behind his sign. In fact, it was impossible to see any of his limbs in the folds of that massive, filthy pile of rags, and his mouth was entirely covered by his beard. Was there even a man under there?

"Explain yourself!" I demanded.

The old man laughed, a wheezing laugh like the whistling wind, and gestured out at the desert, saying, "The scorched plains. The cursed city. A land of deadly, fighting demons. A land of twisted, conniving devils. There must come balance. Balance, in all things."

"You..." I breathed, "Are you talking about... Utopia? Who... are you?"

He turned away and gazed out across the black wasteland. I turned and did the same. It was certainly an awful, desolate place. Everything looked exactly the same, but slightly different – as if there had once been trees, valleys, mountains, and lakes, but all had been reduced to ash.

I heard the old man's unsettling voice behind me: "Dead on the outside or dead on the inside. Light versus dark. But not for long. There *will* come a day of balance. There *cannot* be two worlds. There *cannot* be two skies!"

Without even meaning to do so, I looked up at the sky. The black clouds twisted and boiled, and the red behind them suddenly glowed like crimson fire. It was the sun. I was looking upon the sun of the world of G4M3 for the first time. It was huge and red, like a great red eye, glowing dimly, unable to pierce the clouds of smoke or to lift the eternal gloom of G4M3.

I felt small, under that sky, under that sun, in that great expanse of ash and dust. I felt very small and insignificant. I drew my eyes from the spectacle with a shudder and turned back to where the old man was standing. But he was gone. All that was left was a stray piece of trash, blowing in the biting, stinging, sandy wind, rolling down the abandoned streets of Saltpit City.

Had the old man even been there in the first place, or had he been a hallucination, like Frank had talked about? I shook my head. It was getting harder and harder to tell what was real these days.

Unconsciously, I readied my rifle and slipped into the shadows. Perhaps it was best, I thought, to take a less direct route to the Eagles' base. I should not walk the street. Of course, the Eagles themselves were now located in some caves hidden far out in the desert wastes… but I had no idea how to get there, and I thought that their base might be the best place to search for a clue.

My objective was to find Sofia and convince her and the Eagles to help me defeat Matthew Noble. I didn't know where to look for him, but I doubted that would be a problem, since he seemed to know where to look for me.

I walked into the dark alley between two buildings and looked around. The rotting corpse of a human being lay seated against one wall. It was hard to tell what it might have looked like in life. Now it was food for the insects that crawled upon it. I felt sick as I passed by, and I had to hold my breath, for the stench made my head swim.

With little idea what I was doing, and truly just to get away from the carcass, I grabbed the iron rungs of a nearby ladder and started climbing. I did it as quietly as I possibly could; some inner warning, some sixth sense, told me to do so. It turned out I was right, because I quickly spotted a pair of snipers on the building's roof.

I slipped up onto the roof in a crouched position, as silently as possible. There were no other snipers in sight, on this or any other building, and these two had their backs to me. But these snipers wore USOW uniforms. Were they looking for me? It was a miracle they hadn't noticed me before. Perhaps they were watching farther out, and I had spawned into G4M3 too close for them to see.

Silently praising my good fortune, I slinked my way toward the nearest of the snipers. My heart beat hard against my chest. The man never turned around, but he did freeze up for a second, as if he had heard something. That was when I leaped, drawing my knife, and grabbed him around the throat with one arm. His hands flailed about madly, his long rifle swinging like an axe. I kicked up with my knee, and it struck the man on the elbow, causing him to drop his rifle. Hearing the commotion, the other sniper turned and raised his own gun. But by then I had my knife against my captive's throat.

"Drop the gun," I hissed, "or your partner gets it!"

The man didn't move, but I heard a slight sound come from behind his visor: a voice saying, "This is Charlie Four, I've found the target…"

I swore silently to myself, then started muttering, "It's only a game… It's only a game…"

In one swift movement, I slit my captive's throat and then drew my pistol from its holster. My remaining enemy and I both fired at the same moment. Unluckily for him, his shot hit the helmet of his partner as he dropped. Luckily for me, my shot was much truer. It went right into the soldier's heart, sending out a terrible gush of blood. He dropped down next to his partner, dead.

I grabbed one of their sniper rifles and raised its scope to my eye. Dropping onto one knee, I surveyed the streets and buildings. Sure enough, there was a contingent of soldiers running directly toward me. Taking careful aim, just like in the training sims, I shot the leader of the group in the head. The others scattered like rats into the nearest cracks.

I had by now lost all thought of the evils of killing fellow humans. This was a game, and I was playing it. And I was winning. I ran along the roof and jumped the gap between two buildings, landing on some scaffolding on the next rooftop. It was exhilarating, and I paused for a moment to catch my breath.

Then I ran on, ready to do the same with the next alley, since the first leap had been so successful. Unfortunately, the next building in the row was nothing but a square of crumbling brick walls. This was probably for the best, I thought as I climbed down the ladder into the alley. I didn't want to be caught in the open with more snipers potentially watching.

A black alley cat darted into the shadows as I touched the ground. I drew my pistol, but saw nothing. The best way to pass by the crumbling building before me, I thought, was to go directly through it. I wound my way through the maze of ruined brick walls, looking at the personal articles lying about. There was even a child's toy, hidden in the ashes. This had once been a house, probably burned to the ground by street gangs. G4M3 was a harsh world for the children and the elderly, and I had seen few of either kind.

As I was thinking this, I suddenly caught movement out of the corner of my eye and stopped. There was a red dot moving along the wall to my right. It was one of those red targeting devices that many USOW infantry had attached to their guns. I slipped behind the nearest cover and waited, watching the tiny red dot move.

When it disappeared, I turned to peek around the wall. There were three soldiers approaching. I grabbed the strap of my assault rifle and slid it off my shoulder. As the armored soldiers approached, I sized them up and prepared to kill. It was not so hard anymore, though I was still thankful that the USOW soldiers wore masks.

"Come out, kid!" one of them cried out. "We want you alive!"

I fumbled with my gun, trying to get the grenade launcher open. Finally, I succeeded in getting a grenade loaded. I felt a surge of adrenaline, and a smile played across my lips. It scares me now, thinking that I had felt that way. But at the time, I was eager and confident.

"Take this!" I shouted, launching my missile.

The grenade sang as it flew through the air and landed in the midst of the soldiers. There was a cloud of dust, a loud boom, and bodies flew through the air. I fired at them with my rifle to make sure they didn't get up. Then I ran, leaping over one of them in my flight, toward the ruins of the Eagles' base.

The building was a skeleton of its former self. It had been almost destroyed during the USOW siege, and I now saw that someone had put it to the torch afterwards – whether Sofia or the USOW I didn't know.

Not putting too much thought on the subject, I stepped through the doorway. The room was dark, so I turned on my helmet's flashlight. I cursed myself for not having taken a pair of night-vision goggles from one of the USOW soldiers, but I felt it unwise to go back for one now.

I began ascending the blackened staircase with caution. One of the stairs broke under my boot, but I quickly regained footing and continued. Then I stopped. I had heard something… a sound coming from the nearest room: the room in which I had talked with Sofia about being 'captured' by the USOW. I wondered who was in there. Probably not the Eagles; it was more likely to be a squad of USOW soldiers waiting to make my lie to Sofia into a reality, by capturing me for real.

I crouched down as I stepped into the hall. Approaching the door cautiously, I peered carefully inside through the crack. I was rewarded with a bullet whizzing right past my face. I drew back just in time, with a nick on the cheek to show for it.

Thinking of the success I'd had with the previous use of explosives, I tore a grenade off my belt and pulled the pin. I could hear the sounds of footsteps approaching the door. I held the grenade in my hand for a split second before chucking it into the room and then throwing myself onto the floor. There was a loud explosion and the sound of splintering wood, and then I heard the screams and moans of several soldiers.

I decided it was best to vacate the premises. Unfortunately, when I approached the staircase to head back down, I spotted several more enemies coming up toward me. I opened fire with my rifle and felled the first one, but the others soon returned fire, and I was forced to retreat. But that exit was cut off too… There was another contingent of soldiers in the hallway now.

I raised my rifle, ready to fight to the death… but then a thought struck me. This was a game, I kept telling myself, but if I died in this world, then I would never be able to return to it. The Eagles that I felt such kinship with; Sofia Tyler whom I felt especially fond of; and even my unseen nemesis, Matthew Noble, would be lost to me forever. No, I could not die.

I lowered my rifle. "I surrender!"

The soldiers were quick to accept it. One of them came up behind me, tying up my wrists, while another took all of my weapons. Then a third took off my helmet and threw a bag over my head. All went black.

EIGHT
THE FIRST BOSS

The USOW soldiers carried me, bound and blindfolded, out of the old Eagles base and threw me into the back of a truck. It was a long, dark ride. I could hear the roar of the truck's engine and feel it jostling beneath me, but I had no idea where we were headed, and after a few hours, I lost all track of time.

Finally, the truck skidded to a halt. Someone grabbed me, and I felt a needle sink into my arm. The bag was removed from my head, but the world was hazy. I started to lose all feeling, and my vision swam. I drifted almost out of consciousness, into a dreamlike state.

When I fully awoke again, I thought at first that I was back in the G4M3 facility. The room was mostly clean and white, but the lights overhead were different. The room was lit by a single old-fashioned light bulb, dangling by a wire in the center of the ceiling. And I lay upon a hard, brown cushion instead of a soft, white one.

I tried to rise but found that there were strong leather straps over my wrists, ankles, and waist. I raised my head and looked around. There were two men in lab coats fiddling with tools in metal trays on a desk. Their faces were obscured by surgeons' masks, but I saw that one was bald and the other had thick grey hair.

The bald man turned his head and noticed me, speaking in a gruff voice with an accent I had never heard: "He's awake, Doctor."

"Good," the grey-haired man said. "It is time for more... experiments."

"How are you feeling?" the bald man asked me. "Stomach feel okay?"

I looked down at my torso. There was a bandage over my stomach, and I could feel a sharp pain near my navel.

"What... did you... do?" I asked through gritted teeth.

"I removed that thing in your stomach," the grey-haired doctor answered.

I squinted at him in confusion for a moment, but then the truth hit me... very hard. My eyes went wide. He must have removed my... Was that even possible? What was going on? I felt my heart beating against my chest. My breathing quickened. I was panicking.

"Wha–" I began.

"Yes," the doctor interrupted. "I suppose it would be fair play to let you ask your questions first. Go ahead, though I will decide whether or not I answer them."

"Okay..." I said, taking deep breaths to calm myself. "Who... are you?"

"Don't you already know the answer to that? Surely my men told you?" the doctor didn't turn to look at me as he said this. He was leaning over his table and inspecting the device he had taken from my abdomen. He nudged his colleague and whispered something to him.

"You're... Matthew Noble?" I asked.

"*Doctor* Matthew Noble," he corrected dryly.

"*Doctor* Noble," I said slowly, "can you please... please tell me what is going on."

"I see you *do* have manners," the doctor said, with a small chuckle. "I believe my assertions were correct then: you *must* be from another world."

"I never disbelieved you, Doctor Noble," said the bald man.

"Of course not, Sergei," said Dr. Noble in his soft, muffled voice. "Now, young man, will you please introduce yourself in return?"

"I'm... Kyle Johnson," I lied cautiously.

"Well, Mister Johnson..." he said respectfully, "where are you from?"

"I'm from... Danver," I answered, recalling the name of a city I had overheard two men talking about on the street.

Dr. Noble laughed aloud. "Oh my, that's a good one! You pronounce every word you say correctly, but you mispronounce the name of the city that you're from? Come now, I know you're from another world. Now tell me about it."

"Another... world?" I asked stupidly, even though the truth was now apparent.

"Yes. The one we saw with the camera: the peaceful city of which we only saw a brief glimpse."

I gasped, and the word involuntarily escaped my lips, "Utopia…"

Matthew Noble gave a soft laugh. "Yes, that's a perfect name for it, in a way. Sir Thomas More, correct? But you claim this one is real. What's it like?"

"This can't be happening. You aren't supposed to know about Utopia, are you? You're not even real…"

Doctor Noble turned to look in my eyes for the first time. His eyes were blue, peaceful and calm. "Not real? What do you mean?"

"This is just… a game," I said.

Doctor Noble shook his head. He removed the white mask from his mouth. He had a grey beard that matched his hair, and his face was visibly worn from time's passing. He seemed sad… but determined. I could not estimate his age, being from a world where most men and women usually looked a good decade or two younger than they really were. Perhaps he was in his fifties or sixties.

"A game?" he said. "My God… what have they been telling you? No, this is far from a game. This is reality, but on a different plane from the one you're used to. This world – our world – lies parallel with your own. This city is near your own city of Utopia, but on another dimension. Or at least that's my theory. I could be wrong though. It could be a time change; Utopia could be our future, or this place could be Utopia's future."

"So you're saying… you're real?" It was too much to take in all in a second.

"We are both as real as can be, Mister Johnson," he replied, nodding to his colleague, Sergei. "It's been a long time since my old Globejumper team found your dimension. We were searching hard for another world, a better world. It was our only hope."

I lay my head down and closed my eyes. "Why?"

"You've seen the streets of Saltpit City, Mr. Johnson," he said grimly. "Our world is destroyed, ruined, forsaken by God. The very idea of attempting to 'repair' this place is out of the question. It is no longer possible. The only way to save our people is to escape. We've tried many different ways. With the first Project Exodus, we tried to evacuate as many of our countrymen as we could to our station on Mars, to terraform it."

My mind was whirling. I refused to believe he was telling the truth. Perhaps this was all part of the game? Maybe he was programmed to tell players this, to scare them? He was a boss enemy, after all...

"But the terraforming suffered many problems and eventually broke down," Doctor Noble went on, "and our colonies on the Moon and Mars allied against us, trying to keep us off their lands to keep themselves out of our war. Then the USOW and the NAE, feeling betrayed, began attacking them. Now both the moon and Mars are as hellish as this planet."

"In Utopia, Mars is a mining colony..." I muttered. "It's operated by robots. I've read about it..."

Matthew Noble nodded again. "See? Our worlds are almost exactly the same, yet entirely different. At one point, the USOW tried to manufacture an army of robots to bring the continent back under their control, but the machines went haywire and began attacking their owners. Some say stray robots still wander the wastes, hostile to everyone they encounter."

"Amazing... In your world, everything went wrong."

"And in yours, it all went right."

I shook my head. "From a certain point of view, maybe..."

"I'm sure you take it all for granted, Mr. Johnson," sighed Matthew Noble, "but we saw the beauty of your world as soon as we found it. We had finally connected to another plane of reality, and the portal device was working. First, we sent in a camera, setting it to take pictures for us. When it returned, we saw glimpses of your city."

"But... if the machine worked, why didn't you use it?"

Matthew Noble's gaze dropped to the floor. "A great tragedy happened. After the completion of G3, the third Globejumper machine, we were prepared to send the first team to Utopia, and to begin the next Project Exodus. But when we came back to our science facility the next morning, it was destroyed. All our data was gone, all our work was lost. And the man who had the only backup copies of our records had disappeared, along with his all-important disks. It was hard to recover from that setback, but we had no choice. We started all over. We had to, for the people of our world."

I could hardly listen to Dr. Noble talk anymore. The truth of his words was just starting to sink in. This place was real. Sofia was real. Don was real. Matthew Noble was real. All the men and women I had fought alongside, and the ones I had fought against and killed… had all been *real*.

My thoughts escaped my lips in a gasping whisper – a disbelieving, distraught wheeze that spoke of my great desire to deny the truth of everything Dr. Noble had said: "This is impossible!"

Dr. Noble shook his head. "Oh, but it's true. Now, Mr. Johnson, could you be so kind as to tell me what this device we found in your body is used for? The X-ray picked it up, but I'm beginning to wonder if removing it was the right thing to do. It seems… useless. Perhaps your technology is just far beyond ours…"

"It's my… return home button," I replied.

No, I remembered suddenly: *it's a transceiver*. Just before I had entered the world of G4M3, Frank had referred to it as a transceiver. He'd acted like it was a mistake, but I knew now that must be its true name. But what was its true function?

"Yes, so this device can somehow transport you from dimension to dimension… fascinating. And so small, too."

I opened my eyes and turned my head over to see Matthew and his assistant, Sergei, peering at the view screen on a strange device. Sergei had his hands stuck inside the machine, and he was using them to control mechanical arms to manipulate the components of my tiny transceiver. They were looking at a magnified view of the device on the screen. Suddenly a realization struck me.

"I need that… to get home!" I gasped.

"It won't help you any," Sergei said with a laugh that to me seemed cold and heartless. "It is empty."

"Empty?" I echoed.

"I see…" Dr. Noble said in a low voice. "Strange…"

Sergei shook his head. "There is nothing in this machine. The pod contains no electronics – just an empty pocket of space. The button is attached to nothing. It does nothing."

I blinked. "Frank…"

"What?" Matthew Noble asked, perking up.

"He replaced my transceiver after I saw a man sick in the hallway. The man said he had taken some drugs in G4M3, and that was what made him sick. But Frank said it was the devices, so he replaced mine. But…"

Matthew Noble heaved a great sigh. "Sounds like this 'Frank' must not have wanted you to get home. In that case, the device is no use to us."

"This can't be happening," I groaned.

"Who is Frank, and why would he not want you to return to Utopia?" Sergei asked.

It took me a moment to gather my wits enough to answer, but they waited patiently. "Frank is the manager of the G4M3 facility – the place that I go to… to come here. He runs the game. And I don't know why he wouldn't want me to come back. He's always been like an uncle to me!"

Dr. Noble took a deep breath. "Well, there is still…"

His speech was interrupted by a deep rumble from outside, causing the whole room to shake. Sergei cursed, and Dr. Noble began quickly gathering up as much of his equipment as he could. I knew what was happening. This USOW facility was under attack. I hoped beyond hope that the attackers were the Eagles.

"What of the captive, Dr. Noble?" Sergei asked his superior.

"We have to take him with us," Matthew answered. "He's our only clue… Roll his bed out here."

Sergei moved to the foot of my bed and began wheeling it off behind Dr. Noble as he ran out the door. The halls sped by on either side of me, and lights passed by overhead. Where Dr. Noble's surgical room had been Utopian in its sterile clean whiteness, these halls looked much more like something from the world of G4M3 – ancient and ruined. They looked to be made of stone, and they had clearly not been cleaned in a long time. Mildew grew in the cracks between the slabs, and I saw a lizard-like creature slither into a crevice as I watched. Suddenly another rumble shook the halls, and dust fell from the ceiling.

The doctor cursed again, still softly and with no real anger, as if he felt sad and disappointed instead of resentful. "It's those rebels. Don't they understand they'll be stopping their own saviors?"

"Of course not, Doctor," Sergei said, with considerably more passion, pushing my stretcher now even faster. "They are fools. Blind and prejudiced fools."

As the two doctors ran, wheeling me down the halls, I heard gunfire coming from below. Then a nearby door opened, and my rolling bed struck it, jolting me to a stop and sending Sergei off his feet. The two scientists drew pistols from their lab coats, but the intruders turned out to be their own men.

"Sirs, we need to get you out of here," said the armored USOW soldier, as I craned my head around to look at him.

Doctor Noble shook his head. "We must take this young man with us. He may be our only chance to save our people."

"All right, Doctor," the soldier replied. "Follow us."

We turned off into an elevator. The group of four soldiers, two scientists, and me on my bed almost took up the entire lift. I felt it start to move. Then, without warning, the lights went out, and the elevator came to a halt.

"No..." Matthew said, sounding more than a little afraid now. "They've cut the power."

"How close are we?" Sergei asked. "Could we detach the elevator from the cables somehow and fall the rest of the way?"

"Are you insane?" one of the soldiers exclaimed. "We're stuck, and thank God for that! They can't get to us, and we can't get to them."

Matthew Noble stood up on one of the railings and opened the elevator's maintenance hatch. I heard him gasp and hurry back down. From my position, I could see what he was alarmed about. There were soldiers sliding down the elevator cables toward us, and they weren't wearing USOW uniforms.

Dr. Noble slammed the hatch shut. "They're coming."

"Get under the table, Doctors!" one of the soldiers ordered.

The maintenance hatch swung open as Matthew and Sergei dove for cover under my table. Bullets flew and pinged about the room. I saw a dead body fall from the maintenance hatch, right past my head, and then Matthew rolled me out of the way of the hatch. He was just in time.

More soldiers dropped inside, these alive and with rifles at the ready. I felt like a sitting duck in the firefight, but since the quarters were extremely close, it was over very quickly. In less than a second, all that remained of the fighters on both sides were a pair locked in hand-to-hand combat on the floor.

I turned my head to watch the soldiers' struggles, but my attention was distracted by a loud, reverberating creaking noise. It sounded like a metal cable vibrating and echoing in the shaft overhead – a loud twanging bouncing off the walls in the long, dark tunnel. I looked up, and at that moment something on the top of the elevator gave way. Either the cable or the pulley device broke loose, and the elevator dropped like a rock.

We fell for hardly a fraction of a second before we hit the bottom. My bed was knocked on its side, so that I hung in a sickening sideways position by my shackles. The two soldiers were still fighting, now right in front of me. The USOW man was on top, holding a knife, trying to jab it into his assailant's chest. The other man had a hold on the USOW soldier's wrists and was trying with all his might to shove the dagger away.

This second soldier was clothed in a dirty green outfit seemingly constructed out of whatever was available. He was heavily armed, however, so I knew he was a rebel of one faction or another. I looked for the tell-tale Eagles tattoo, but the man's sleeve was rolled down.

As the two of them fought like this, I heard a shuffling sound from behind me. I soon saw Sergei dart out from behind my bed, dragging the unconscious Dr. Matthew Noble along with him. Seeing that the fall had dislodged the elevator doors, leaving a small opening, Sergei turned sideways and squeezed through. But he could not get Dr. Noble out. I heard him curse under his breath yet again.

As soon as my eyes turned back to the fighting soldiers, the battle was resolved. In one quick and skillful shove, the unknown soldier rolled over so that he was now lying atop the USOW guard. He put a hand under the man's knife and forced it upwards, jabbing it into the USOW man's chin. There was a gush of blood and the dying soldier let go of his knife. His assailant forced the weapon farther down into his throat until there was no life left in him. Then the unidentified attacker stood up and wiped his bloody fingers on the sheets of my bed. His eyes were closed tight. He looked sick.

Just then, Dr. Noble woke up. I heard Sergei whisper something to him, and he began squeezing through the door. The soldier beside me shouted for them to stop, but then Dr. Noble slipped through, and both scientists took off down the hall, their shoes squeaking on the slick floor as they ran. The soldier tried to follow them, but he couldn't squeeze through the aperture with all of his gear on. He cursed.

"Hey, over here!" I called out.

He turned and looked down at me. He was an ugly man, I thought. There was a scar running down the length of his face, and his eyes were dark and sunken. He had seen a lot of battle. He smelled like sweat and blood; but then, the whole elevator smelled that way now.

He asked in a gruff voice, "Who are you? A prisoner?"

I nodded. "Kyle Roswell... Who are you?"

The man rolled up his shirtsleeve, revealing a tattoo depicting a flying bird of prey. "Well, ain't you a lucky one? I'm with the Eagles."

I smiled. "Is Sofia here with you?"

"Commander Tyler?" he asked. "No, she ain't leadin' this attack. Don is."

"Don's alive!?" I gasped.

"He wondered if you knew. It'll take more than a couple bullets to put big Don in the dirt. He told us to keep an eye out for you. I think you might-a been this mission's secret objective. Apparently, you know somethin' that the USOW wanna know… and anything they wanna know is somethin' we *don't* want 'em to know. You know?" He grinned hideously.

I nodded. "Whatever. Just get me out of here. Any chance you could get me off this bed?"

The soldier pried open what was left of the elevator doors until he had a hole large enough for my bed to fit through. As he wheeled me off down the hall, he said, "You just hold on, okay?"

Luckily, the Eagle knew his way out of the base. We rendezvoused with another group of Eagles, and they were as ready to leave as I was. They wheeled me off down another maze of tunnels, and finally out through the entrance doors. The sun shone brightly overhead, but there was a dark black cloud looming on the horizon ahead, casting a shadow over the Saltpit. I felt the hot wind blowing against my face, and I saw the jagged skyline of Saltpit City in the distance.

"Well, well, well," said a familiar deep, throaty voice, "if it ain't the wonder kid."

I tilted my head to see Don approaching, a bright smile across his dark face. But the smile disappeared quickly. I heard him whisper some orders to his men.

"Can I, uh, get out of this bed now?" I asked.

"Don't think so," replied Don. "You're easier to carry around this way, and there's less chance you'll just up and disappear. That seems to happen with you, doesn't it? Put 'im in the truck, boys."

Before I could even protest, I felt my bed lifted off the ground and thrust into the back of a transport truck. The doors closed behind me, enveloping me in almost total darkness. I felt deep disappointment that the Eagles were showing me such distrust, but perhaps I'd earned it. I just hoped Sofia didn't share their feelings…

Sofia, I thought. *She's real.* It was too much to take in…

As we rode off down the streets and into the desert, I had time to think about everything. Back when I had first started playing G4M3,

I'd found it hard to accept the fact that it wasn't real. Now I had evidence that it actually *was*, and I found it hard to believe that it *could* be. It was as if everything I'd ever known was wrong.

My whole world had been turned upside-down. I almost entertained the idea that *Utopia* might be the fantasy world. But as I bounced along in that old-fashioned vehicle, the guns and equipment rattling all around me, I began to force myself to believe that what Matthew Noble had said was simply not true. He had been programmed to say that. My grandfather had programmed him that way, to lie. That had to be the truth. Yes… it had to be.

"Ambush!" Don roared.

Gunfire split the air outside, and the vehicle came to a screeching halt. The doors to the back swung wide before me, flooding the area with sunlight. I squinted and watched as one of the men released me from my manacles. I rubbed my sore wrists. Don appeared and grabbed me by the shirt, hauling me down out of the vehicle.

"You don't get a gun," he said. "Just keep your head down and stay alive. If you try to run, I'll shoot you. Just like I promised before."

I shook my head frantically. "Don, I'm not a traitor!"

"No," he said, his face like stone, "you're a prisoner. Scott, watch him!"

I took the situation in at a glance. Our transport truck had passed through the desert for a few miles before dropping into an almost invisible ditch along the side of a mesa. The ditch was big enough and low enough for a truck to pass through without being seen from the regular desert surface.

The soldier Don had called Scott half dragged me up the hillside, to the edge of the trench, though he pushed my head down when I tried to peek out across the desert. I only got a glimpse of the world above, but it was enough to see USOW transports advancing on our position, dropping off soldiers. Then I curled up in the dirt and plugged up my ears to block out the ear-splitting sounds of gunfire.

Now that I was in the heat of battle, with death so close, my earlier determination to deny that this world was real started to waver. I rolled up my shirt and felt of my stomach, sticking my fingers between the bandages there. The cut that Dr. Noble had made burned painfully when I touched it, and I sucked in my breath through my teeth. I was not used to physical hardship.

And the device really was gone. They had taken it, and they said it wouldn't work anyway! I was trapped in this horrible, hellish world, and it was *real!* Then, to add to my suffering, the soldier beside me got shot. He screamed and fell to the ground, clutching his shoulder.

I saw images of death around me – bullets spattering into the earth, Eagles taking hits and bleeding. We were outnumbered, and our cover would not hold for long. I realized then that, if I died... it would be the end.

In a moment of panic, I stood up to jump back into the trench below, beside the transport vehicle. But as soon as I stood, two bullets hit me. One lodged in my shoulder and the other in my back. I let out a cry and fell, rolling through the dirt, back to the bottom of the trench. My bandages came loose, and the wound in my stomach ripped, staining them red.

Spitting out dust, I crawled under the truck and pulled myself up on the other side. I was finding it hard to breathe. I coughed, and blood sprayed out, all over my hand. My body was wracked with pain. I curled up to hide... to die.

But I wasn't alone; there was another man hiding there too. And I recognized him.

"Billy... Byrd?" I gasped.

The man looked up at me, and his eyes went wide. It was him! It was my friend from the school in Utopia! He was here with me, thinking that he was innocently playing a game. He groaned. I saw that he was wounded mortally, as I probably was too. Soon I would just die, but he would return to Utopia.

But how could he die and *not* die? Perhaps it *was* all just a game. Maybe Matthew Noble really had been wrong. But where was my device then?

Suddenly it struck me: *the device*. It was the transceiver device that transported the players back to Utopia when they were critically injured. In Utopia, they could receive the most advanced treatment, practically restoring them to life after death. Soon my friend would be back home, and I would be stuck here in purgatory to rot for the rest of my mortal life!

I have since made thousands of excuses to myself about what I did that day, at that moment. I could blame any number of things for what I did: I was stuck in a world of horror, where everyone seemed out to get me now, even the Eagles. I was wounded – possibly mortally – and in pain such as I had never experienced. My stomach, shoulder, and chest hurt so badly that it nearly blinded me.

No human can know how they will react when they are driven to the bitter edge, until they actually get there. There had been days when I thought I hated life, but at that moment, all I could think was how much I desperately wanted to live. And there was my salvation right in front of me. And yet, no matter how many excuses I make, I can never forgive myself for the act.

But it was me or him.

I saw that Billy's wound was in his stomach, near the area where his transceiver would be implanted. He was reaching for the wound even now, groping for the device that would take him home. I got down on my knees and grabbed his wrists. He struggled, trying to move his arms down to the transceiver. I could see that the pain of his wounds was making him frantic. I wondered vaguely if he recognized me – if he had figured out all of this was real – or if he just wanted to save his progress in G4M3.

"Billy," I said, "wait! You have to..."

I had hoped his name would rouse his attention, but he barely seemed to notice. He was frantic. He started kicking me, though this obviously caused him great pain, as he cried out terribly. Still his hands clutched tightly on mine. I forced them away from the transceiver. We were *both* frantic now.

Without even thinking about what I was doing, I reached into the wound in Billy's stomach, right under his navel. I felt the device immediately, but I was careful not to press the button. I curled my finger around the edge of the tiny pod, and I jerked it out.

Billy let out a terrible cry of pain and stiffened. His grip on my hands loosened, and his kicking ceased. His eyes looked at me one last time, and then his head fell back onto the dirt. His chest stopped rising and falling. He was dead. It hit me like a battering ram right in the face: he was dead. He was not my enemy; he was actually my friend... but I had killed him. I had *murdered* him.

I hadn't meant to. Why hadn't he listened? Why hadn't he answered me? It wasn't my fault!

These thoughts and more rushed through my mind, until I was distracted by another fit of bloody coughing. My bandages were soaked completely red. I looked at the device in my bloody fingers. I had to use it quickly.

Holding my breath and clenching my teeth tight together, I forced the pod into the wound in my stomach, hoping it would detect its new host. Then I crawled into the shadow of the transport vehicle nearby, and I pressed the button.

To my incredible relief, I felt the wind rushing around me, and saw the world go black...

N I N E
PUTTING IT FRANKLY

I did not want to dispel the blackness, so I kept my eyes shut tight, even when I regained consciousness. But I heard the gentle buzzing of the electric lights overhead, and I knew that I was back in the G4M3 facility, in Utopia. I hoped beyond hope that somehow, *somehow*, everything that had transpired earlier had *not* been real.

It was with great reluctance that I got up off the bed. The room was so quiet, so clean... I felt sicker than ever. I approached the door with thoughts of a comfortable bed and forgetful sleep in mind... but the door did not open. I pushed on it and pressed my hand against the panel on the wall.

"What?" I asked aloud. "Hello? What's going on? Open this door!"

It was the voice of Frank Billings that answered me over the room's speakers: "Kyle? Are you all right?"

"Open this door, Frank!" I raged. "Now!"

"Kyle..." said the voice. "Please, calm yourself. What's wrong with you?"

"I... You lied to me! You told me... And you trapped me in there! You left me stuck in G4M3!"

"What? Why on earth would I do that?" answered the kindly voice, the voice of a friend, the voice of Uncle Frank. "I would never leave *anyone* stuck in there, Kyle. It would be a fate worse than death."

"You lied to me! You're *still* lying! You told me it wasn't real!"

"Kyle, listen to me. I would do nothing to harm you. If I told you a few lies, it was for your own good."

His words hit harder than I had expected. Inside, I had hoped he would say that G4M3 wasn't real, that Dr. Noble had been lying, that it was all just part of the game... but his words now confirmed my greatest fears. I fell back onto the bed and stared blankly at the ceiling. As I lay there, the door opened, and Frank Billings stepped in, his usual jovial smile replaced by a deep and thoughtful frown.

"I'm sorry you had to find out the truth, Kyle," he said. "I know how it hurts you."

My voice was filled with bitterness, at myself as much as him. "You... cannot *possibly* know. I... *killed* them, Frank... I killed *many* of them."

I thought about the people I had killed: the soldiers, the snipers, and everyone else. I recalled the way it had felt – the victorious joy I had felt after killing most of them. It all came back to me now. And Billy Byrd... I felt a knot rise into my throat, but I did not cry. Not just then.

"I know, Kyle, I know..." Frank replied to me, nodding. "But that's the way their world works. If you hadn't killed them, someone else would have. Even scientists like Matthew Noble."

"I didn't kill Noble!" I blurted out.

Frank looked sharply at me. "Why... Why don't you tell it all from the beginning, Kyle?"

I had to take several deep breaths before I could continue. Frank sat smiling sympathetically, like a knowing and caring father. Again, I had the feeling he was infinitely wiser than I, and that he was glad to share the burden of his knowledge with another.

Finally, I found the strength to tell my story. "I was captured by Matthew Noble's forces. They took me to a USOW base and... studied me. He took out my ret-... my transceiver, Frank! He told me that it didn't even work anyway – there was nothing inside!"

Frank bit his lip. "I'm sorry, Kyle. It's a failsafe, for our own protection. If a device is ever removed from the host body, after a small space of time, it self-destructs, leaving only the shell behind. Your transceiver did indeed work, but only until Doctor Noble removed it from your body. Then it self-destructed."

This truly gave me a pause for thought. His story fit. I didn't know why I hadn't thought of that before.

"Frank," I said, "just tell me the truth. The whole truth, about G4M3. I want... I *need* to know."

Frank closed his eyes for a moment before replying, in a gravely serious tone, "Very well. G4M3 was invented, as you know, by your grandfather, Walter Roswell. He was working in one of the Order's scientific laboratories at the time, when he discovered the link to an alternate dimension: the world you know as G4M3. After much trial and error, he finally invented a portal device that could carry a living being from one plane of reality to another. Now, normally, this information would have fallen into the hands of the Order, and your grandfather would probably have been... silenced."

"Silenced?" I echoed, rubbing my neck.

"Yes," Frank said, smiling sadly and nodding. "The Order gets rid of anyone who it thinks it has to, for its own preservation. It gets rid of the malformed, such as children with birth defects. It gets rid of the old and sickly. It gets rid of the injured who cannot be cured. And it gets rid of those who... think differently..."

I remembered the story that my father had told, about the storekeeper Joe Williams. I remembered other stories I'd heard, of people simply disappearing. I stared at Frank in horror.

"Yes," he went on. "The Order does its best to help all humans live a life of peace, comfort, and happiness. They keep the elderly alive for as long as they can still think or move. But once the elderly are no longer functional, no longer able to work in any way, it gets rid of them too."

"What about Walter?" I asked. "Why didn't it get rid of him?"

"I don't know exactly," he answered, shrugging. "Sometimes it... preserves the physically and even mentally useless, when it thinks it can get more out of them. Perhaps the Order thought they could learn secrets from him, or perhaps it just wanted to study the strange disease that had struck him. I doubt the Order would have kept him around for long after they learned the truth behind G4M3 though, because, above all else, the Order silences those who know too much."

"What about you?"

He smiled a strange smile that I had never seen before. "I can be trusted."

I prompted him to continue his story. "So why wasn't Walter... silenced?"

"Because he hid his knowledge from them. He was very good at that, your grandfather was. He told them... the Order... that he was going to change careers. He outlined his new business as an 'arcade' of games. He hired me, one of his co-workers back at the Order's lab, to help him construct robots to staff the building. I was the only one he ever told the secret of G4M3."

"But what is the secret of G4M3, Frank? How does it all work?"

He took a deep breath before beginning. "Well, Kyle, it's nothing but a portal. The device implanted inside each Player is like a dimensional anchor. It has two locations programmed into it: one on this plane, and another in the world of G4M3. When the 'simulation' is activated, the device transports you and your gear to the anchor in G4M3. It's linked with your bio-matrix and with special transceivers built into each piece of your gear. The gear we give you looks, to the device, like an extension of your body. If you are wounded in G4M3, the device senses the injuries to your bio-matrix and transports you home if the injuries are life-threatening, along with any gear that is near enough to you."

"But... my gear is always in good condition when I come back, even if it got bloodied during battle..."

"That's because it's not the same gear. It's a new set. Your old gear is stripped from you and disposed of. Once, we had a player come back with a live grenade in his hand... That wasn't pretty. Destroyed the whole room, the player, a medical robot. That's why we stopped giving Players grenades that would count as part of their bio-matrix."

He cleared his throat and went on: "Anyway, the transceiver device only works in darkness. This is simply so that no inhabitant of the G4M3 world will see your dead body disappear before their very eyes. The transceiver also detects life forms in the area and only transports a critically injured body out of a hostile environment once it can be fairly sure that... no one is looking."

I shook my head. "But wouldn't the injured Player die in that amount of time, if his corpse was forced to lie in the blasted desert until nightfall?"

"You'd be surprised what you can live through..." Frank muttered. "You'd also be surprised at the power of medical technology here in Utopia. We can practically bring people back from the dead. Once they arrive here in the facility, our medical staff is at hand, with the most advanced technology at their disposal. We can replace lost limbs and heal wounds so that it looks like nothing ever happened at all. Even I don't know how it all works. A lot of it involves cloning and such..."

I rubbed my fully-healed shoulder and interrupted him. "Isn't that a bit... wasteful, of the Order's resources? All for a 'game' to distract people?"

Frank nodded. "But isn't it worth it? People have to be distracted, Kyle, or they think too long and hard about the life they're living. They start getting antsy, wanting to shake things up – to *change* things. Or just to fight, even without a cause. It's in our blood. But we can't have that."

I swallowed. "You mentioned you've had players die though... What happens when a Player dies? Doesn't the Order punish you for something like that?"

"We can make excuses..." Walter said, a bit regretfully, his eyes downcast. "I have connections within the Order. They can cover up any... accidents that occur. Of course, they're very rare. We've only had nine as long as we have been operational. That isn't counting your own."

"My own?"

Frank's voice dropped low, and he leaned over to look at me. "Kyle... What happened to William Byrd? *He* was supposed to return to this room, not you. That's why you were locked in here when you arrived."

"I..." I swallowed back my fear and sickness and answered, "I guess I... killed him."

Frank nodded understandingly, which only made me feel worse. "You killed him and took his transceiver to return here… It's a sad twist of fate, Kyle, but it's all you could do. No one can blame you. You only did what anyone else would have done. Normally it wouldn't even have happened. We try to insert Players into G4M3 at strategic points across the globe, so that they never actually meet each other. I don't know how you two managed to do it. I guess he was just in the wrong place at the wrong time."

I looked away, unable to speak. Billy Byrd had been one of the only friends I'd ever had in Utopia. We hadn't spoken to one another in years, but I'd always hoped I would meet him again. And now he was gone. I hadn't truly killed him; the bullet of a USOW soldier had done that… but I had kept him from returning to Utopia to be healed, which would have happened the instant he died. So, I had still killed him as effectively as if I had strangled him with my own hands.

When I tried to remember the moment I had ripped the transceiver from his wound, I could hardly recall it. It was just a blur – a frightened instant of sudden action brought about by pure survival instinct – a flash in time. I almost wished I had never found him. He was gone now, and it was all because of me… and I would have to live with that for the rest of my life. Why had I ever started playing this infernal game?

After allowing me a moment of silence, Frank licked his lips. "Kyle… can you tell me what Doctor Matthew Noble wanted from you?"

I wiped my eyes on my sleeve and looked up, though my voice cracked when I spoke. "He… wanted my transceiver. He asked me questions about Utopia – said that he'd discovered Utopia while he and a team of scientists were looking for another dimension."

Frank nodded. "So, he wanted your transceiver to…?"

"To create a portal device that would transport as many people as possible from G4M3 to Utopia."

Frank's eyes went wide. "No…"

"He wanted to save as many of his people as he could. I don't blame him at all. G4M3 is a horrible place. I almost wanted to help him."

Frank suddenly grabbed me by the shoulders and forced me to look at him. "Kyle, listen to me. We cannot let this happen. We *cannot* let Matthew Noble succeed in his plan!"

I stared back at him with confusion and a bit of disgust. "Why not?"

"Think about it for a moment, Kyle!" he exclaimed. "You know what the people of G4M3 are like! They're uneducated, backwards, and violent! If that mad scientist somehow found a way to transport a large number of them here… it could mean the end of everything we've worked for!"

"How could he possibly transport enough here to make a difference?" I asked.

"Once he finds out how my transceivers work, he can transport hundreds or thousands! You know not, Kyle, the chaos that even one man can cause… the changes that can be made by a single person."

"Good!" I spat out. "Maybe this pristine little world needs to be disillusioned!"

"Kyle, don't speak like that!" Frank shouted. "You don't know what you're saying! Humanity has worked for *millennia* to bring about the state in which Utopia now lives. Think of your parents! Would they survive in the world of G4M3, or any world like it? Do you hold no love for your people, Kyle – your world?"

"I… don't know…" I groaned, rubbing my temples.

"Kyle, I want to show you something," Frank said in a most confidential manner. "Come with me."

I followed him out to the elevator. "Where are we going?"

Frank ran his fingers along the elevator buttons. But instead of selecting one of the facility's floors, he pressed his thumb against the black panel at the top of the row. When he drew his finger away, it left behind a glowing green fingerprint.

"I'm taking you to the roof of the G4M3 facility," he said. "It's one of the taller buildings in Utopia, and you'll be able to see most of this residential sector from up on top."

I sucked in my breath. "The city must be huge. I never even knew there was anything beyond it…"

"There's actually not much to see," Frank replied, a little grimly.

After passing by the many floors of the G4M3 facility, the elevator came to a halt. The indicator overhead displayed the word 'ROOF'. When the doors opened, I felt a cool breeze rush over me. Stepping out onto the concrete roof, I beheld a sight that took my breath away. I would never forget it; the image is burned into my mind to this day.

It was Utopia.

For miles and miles stretched an endless sea of small, square, off-white roofs. They all looked exactly the same: simple, flat squares with very little room between, even for the streets. All of them were shining and clean, reflecting the setting sun almost blindingly into my eyes. The only thing breaking this monotony was the occasional large patch of neatly-ordered rows of trees: the parks.

When I turned around, I thought I could vaguely see the shadows of much taller buildings far away on the horizon… but it might have been an illusion. I actually couldn't see very far in the hazy Utopian air, but that only added to the impression that the houses went on forever.

"It's… huge," I said, at a loss for words.

"I suppose that's one way to put it…" Frank Billings replied. "And this is all the creation of the Order. It is essential for the Order to exist, or all of this would cease to be. This peace and happiness depends upon the Order, and, whether we like it or not, we must… well, we must do what we can to ensure the Order's survival."

"I don't know…" I said.

"Kyle, try to imagine this city looking like the ones in the world of G4M3. Look at what lies before you and imagine it decimated, ruined. Because that's what will happen if you allow Matthew Noble to portal in the violent citizens of G4M3. The Order will become Chaos, and bloodshed shall reign, and *all* of this will crumble. Your parents will be killed, and, if not killed, they will live a life of their worst nightmares: *G4M3 turned real.* Would you ruin all of these millions of happy lives? For what purpose? What gives you that right?"

I swallowed hard, for this speech had a great effect on me. "But what about Sofia, and the other people in G4M3? Don't they deserve a chance to live like this?"

"They *can't*," Frank answered. "It's sad but true. They could never fit in here. And most wouldn't want to. This Sofia – these Eagles – they're rebels. They would rebel against the Order just like they've rebelled against their own governments. You think they would bow down to our laws to keep the peace?"

I remembered then what Sofia had said to me: "I ask you which is better… to die in battle and slip into the unknown, or to die a different death, and live a life without freedom?"

"No…" I muttered. "No, they wouldn't."

He walked over and put a comforting hand on my shoulder. "I'm old, son. I'm no fighter. Do what I cannot. Go into G4M3, find Matthew Noble, and stop him. Save our world! Only you can do this. You'll be a hero, Kyle…"

I looked back at him with a stony face. "A hero? Right. For one world. And a villain for the other. But no need to preach any more – I'll do it. I have to. Send me back, and I'll do it."

"I only wish I could go with you…" Frank said, smiling sadly.

I wondered if Frank suspected the truth: that, more than anything, I just wanted to return to G4M3 and find Sofia. I did not want to go back to my small, lonely house in that sea of mundane similarity I had just viewed, where every day was a nightmarish repeat of the last. Living in Utopia, I would have ample time to think about the things I had done – the atrocities I had committed…

On the other hand, in G4M3, I had at least a chance of finding Sofia again. *She was real!* Now that I knew this for certain, I *had* to see her again – to hear her, feel her, and know she was alive. I knew I was being young and foolish, but I couldn't help it: she was almost all I could think about. I hadn't been sure if I would ever see her again – if

Frank would ever let me use the device again. But now that he was inviting me to do it, I couldn't just say no.

I followed Frank Billings down the elevator, into the hall, and right back into the 'simulation' room. I was about to suit up for the trip, but he stopped me, laughing. He told me to lie down on the surgery table. I had forgotten my transceiver was gone.

"Now, Kyle," Frank said as he retrieved his implant device, "I'm going to be outfitting you with a special version of the transceiver – my own *personal* version. It works like the normal kind, but with one difference: if you hold the button down for three seconds instead of just pushing it, it will turn the transceiver *off*. If you need to turn it on again, just repeat the same action."

"Why would I want to turn it off?" I asked.

"This isn't going to be an easy mission, Kyle. You might end up having to remain in G4M3 for an extended period of time. During that time, you may need rest. So now you can turn off your transceiver and go to sleep. As long as the transceiver is off, you'll remain in the world of G4M3 – in Saltpit City. If it's on, you'll reappear in Utopia. Do you understand?"

"I understand, Frank."

"Good. Because I don't want you to ever tell anyone else about this. Never tell anyone that you have this very special implant, and never tell anyone the secret behind G4M3."

"Are you sure they shouldn't know the truth?" I asked.

Frank frowned at me. "The truth, Kyle Roswell, is a dangerous thing."

"Okay," I said quickly, not wanting to enter into another argument – eager to get back to the world of G4M3. "Okay, just give me the new transceiver."

Frank pressed his device to my abdomen and inserted the implant. Then he left the room without a word, only nodding at me as he went. I nodded back and started suiting up. Once I was done, I said out loud:

"Do it."

Frank's voice answered over the speakers: "Oh, and Kyle... do try to finish your task this time."

I opened my mouth to respond to this statement, which I found offensive coming from a man who was *not* about to embark into a world of constant war on an almost impossible mission. But before I could speak, the room suddenly went dark, and I felt the all-too-familiar sensation of wind blowing all around me. This time I knew what it really was: the feeling of my body slipping through space and time, into the world of shadow…

TEN
FOOLS RUSH IN

The ground rose up to meet me, and my face landed in the dirt. I was surrounded by the red, grey, and black gloom of G4M3. I had emerged once again in the streets of Saltpit City. There were the crumbling buildings and silent pedestrians, all returned to their old posts, and there was what was left of the Eagles' base in this area.

Mentally, I made a list of objectives: I had to locate the Eagles' desert base, and I had to find a vehicle that could take me there... but not necessarily in that order. I had no idea where I could find a vehicle, but I was not about to enter the Eagles' old base again.

I decided to try my luck asking one of the citizens. I strode confidently up to a pair of men standing against the wall of an old building with boards over the windows. One man nodded to me as I approached. I noticed that the other man looked to be asleep. Both of them were attired in long trench coats with rags tied around their heads. They were probably armed, I knew. Everyone in G4M3 was armed, even the children.

"Hey, traveler," said the one who had nodded to me, in a hoarse voice. "Just a bit o' cash and you can board up here for the night. It's well-guarded, and quiet too."

As he jerked his head to indicate the ruin behind him, I shook my head. "No thanks, but I'll pay you well enough if you can give me some information..."

The man nodded slowly and replied, "Information don't come cheap. Depends on what you wanna know. Shoot."

"The Eagles," I said, pointing to the old Eagles' base. "I need to contact 'em. Know where they are?"

He sneered and shrugged. "Nobody knows where the Eagles hide out. If I knew that, I could sell the info for a lot more than you can pay..."

"Fine," I said. "I have another question."

"Shoot," he prompted, "but make it quick."

"I want a vehicle – a ride. Do you know where I can get one?"

The man laughed out loud, and his friend joined in. "Kid, you must be swimmin' in cash, if you think you can pay for the location of the Eagles *and* a slaggin' automobile. But I tell you what: I do know a guy who was tryin' to fix up an old truck; he might'a got it workin'. Since he ain't paid his rent, I'll sell him out to you. Just go past the old buildin' you pointed out, headin' toward the Saltpit, until you see a rusted shack with some green paint still clingin' to the walls. There's a tall rock near it that hides a secret door leadin' to his garage."

I turned my back on the man while I counted out some money. I didn't know whether the amount that Frank had given me was a small fortune or a regular amount in this world, but I didn't want this man to see it regardless. So, I took out fifty dollars and stuffed the rest in my pocket. Turning back around, I shoved it in my informant's hands. It disappeared almost instantly into his trench coat.

"Many thanks," he said. "If you see Rusty there, feel free to shoot 'im for me. Then you can have his room, if you come back this way."

I walked off in the direction he had indicated, carefully glancing behind me on occasion to make sure I wasn't being followed. The shack he mentioned turned out to be all the way near the edge of the Saltpit. The edge of the pit was lined with a hedge of sharp, twisted black brambles. I had to force my way through them carefully, and my suit got ripped in several places.

When I emerged from the brush, I slipped and fell, sliding down the side of the pit. I started rolling, tasting dust and salt, until my back hit the hard floor with a thud. I blinked and saw the black clouds floating eerily across the red sky overhead.

I put my hands on the cracked, dry earth and pushed myself back up. The Saltpit looked far deeper from down here. It looked like an empty ocean, but the bottom was almost completely flat. For a moment, I let my mind slip back to what I imagined as happier times: when the pit was full of shining water and birds sang in the air overhead. But maybe it had never actually looked like that. I would never know.

I turned and scanned the ridge for the rock that my informant had mentioned. There were plenty of rocks, but an especially tall one stood out. I made my way in that direction. It was a treacherous hike, with the ground crumbling out from under my feet wherever I stepped. I was somewhat surprised that the 'hotel manager' had been telling the truth: nestled just behind the rock was a small metal door built into the side of the Saltpit. I jumped down into the little crevice where it was located and shoved it open immediately.

A shower of sand entered the room along with me. It was pitch dark inside, but I had brought night vision goggles from Utopia this time. As I slid the devices over my eyes, the world was bathed in an alien green light. I was in a garage full of trucks, but most of them had been completely stripped of all useful parts, leaving little more than metal skeletons.

But sure enough, one had been repaired, at least mostly. One of the large military trucks was covered in a cobbled-together patchwork of armor plating, with new wheels, and an engine visible under the open hood. I approached cautiously, scanning the area for any sign of the man who had repaired the vehicle. Try as I might, I couldn't stop my footsteps from echoing noisily in the vast, open garage.

I approached the truck, but froze in my tracks halfway there... because a gun barrel suddenly appeared beside my head. *God, I hope Frank gave me a real transceiver this time*, I thought. I knew I was about to die again.

Then the man stepped further into the light... and I saw a familiar tattoo on his arm.

"H-hey," I stammered, "I'm with the Eagles too!"

A sandy-haired young man emerged from the darkness to squint at me. He had a stubble of a beard, and his face was lined from a life in the desert. But his expression showed that he recognized me... and wasn't sure how to react.

"No, you're not," he said. "You're Kyle Roswell. I'm Scott. I was with the squad that hauled your ass out of that USOW base yesterday. You frickin' disappeared on us."

"Not by choice," I said. "I wanted to help, I swear, but Don wouldn't give me a gun. How'd the battle go?"

Scott grunted and lowered his rifle, though he kept it at the ready. "We had to retreat. The USOW made it into the trench and started slaughterin' us. Don had us look everywhere for your sorry ass, but we found nothin', so we left without you. So, tell me: where the hell *were* you, and why should I trust you?"

I must have been getting better at lying, because my reply came surprisingly naturally: "I didn't have a gun, remember? And I got hit! So I was frickin' *hiding!* I crawled in a dark hole and stayed there. The USOW were on top of me before you were, so I couldn't come out. I just waited 'til everyone was gone."

"So, you walked all the way back to the Saltpit, same as me? Damn, I guess you're tougher than you look. Fine; I guess I'll believe you. Don't have much choice anyway – Sofia still wants you alive, an' I think Don does too. He ordered us to split up after our retreat, an' I ended up stranded here. Been tryin' to find a truck ever since, to get back to the base."

"That's where I'm headed too," I said.

"You're one lucky fool then. Lucky to be so important no one wants you dead, and lucky you found me before I left. Someone must be lookin' out for you. Hop in, and let's go."

Honestly, our coincidental meeting surprised me too. I found my mind wandering back to the idea of this all being a simulation, with scripted events that were supposed to happen. Perhaps I was meant to find Scott, so that I could reunite with the Eagles and face down Dr. Noble. But this wasn't a game. It was all real. Wasn't it?

I climbed into the vehicle beside him and looked around as he tried to crank up the engine. "How do we get out of here? This place is sealed up tight."

"See that wall?" he asked, nodding ahead of us. "It's wood, and it's rotten. I've checked the other side, and there ain't much sand. See, the reason I figure no one ever stole these old trucks is 'cause they thought there was no way out with the entrance blocked."

"But you found one?" I asked.

With a wheeze and a clunk, the motor finally started, and Scott turned to me with a grin and said, "Brace yourself."

Before I could comply, he slammed on the accelerator and headed straight for the wooden wall. We crashed through with a terrific splintering of wood and a waterfall of sand over the windshield. But we were on the other side and out in the Saltpit before the avalanche could engulf us.

From there, it was a surprisingly smooth ride. We glided over the hard, salty floor of the Saltpit until we found a low enough slope on the edge to drive up and out. Then we were off into the desert. I just hoped Scott knew where he was going, because the wasteland all looked the same to me: a flat grey landscape overshadowed by black clouds hanging in a red-tinted sky. Gradually, I gathered that we were headed toward a mesa on the horizon.

I was correct. There was a small opening at the foot of the plateau, and there we entered. The doors opened for us, leading into a garage not unlike the one we had just left... except much larger. It was filled with the trucks that Sofia had led on the first USOW base attack. There were also three transport trucks, a rusty old tank, and even some sort of aircraft. This last vehicle hung from the ceiling, attached to a pair of supports and surrounded by walkways and platforms. The far wall of the base was perforated with windows and doors. I'd never suspected that the Eagles owned such a vast complex.

The floor was bustling with a motley crew of Eagle soldiers. Scott asked one of them where we could find Sofia, and he led us up the stairs at the back of the hangar and into the underground base's tunnels. They were much like the tunnels of the USOW base where I'd met Dr. Noble, but they were smaller and actually a little cleaner.

Our guide led us directly to Sofia's personal quarters. He knocked and announced it was me. The door swung open immediately. There was Sofia, glaring at me with those fiery green eyes. She looked furious. I felt my heart sink.

"You two get out of here," Sofia said to Scott and the other Eagle. "Leave this idiot to me."

They hurriedly obeyed her, leaving the two of us alone. I swallowed hard. I was overjoyed to see her alive, but terrified that she no longer trusted me. We had gotten along so well before. If only I had known it was real from the start…

Then Sofia broke out in a smile. "Kyle… It's damn good to see you alive."

My boyish grin of utter joy must have looked incredibly foolish. "Even better to see *you* alive. You have no idea."

"You thought I was dead? Ha! Fat chance."

Not dead, I thought, but not alive either. But now I know I was wrong. Wasn't I?

She waved me into her quarters, then shut the door behind me. The room wasn't quite as nice as her office in the old Saltpit City base, but at least she had her own bed and bathroom. I sat down on the corner of the bed and breathed a deep sigh of relief.

Sofia smiled knowingly and sat down in a metal chair nearby. "Feels nice to take a load off, doesn't it? Sorry I can't offer you a drink this time. They don't keep much here at the main base."

"I had no idea the Eagles' operation was so big…" I said.

She sighed then, as she reached back behind her head and unfastened her ponytail, shaking her dark brown hair loose. "It's bigger than I'd like, honestly. I preferred just being in charge of the Saltpit City outfit. I'm no good at fighting for a cause – not like Don. He told me how he saved you and then lost you. I was mad at him for that last part, but I guess I'll have to apologize and thank him now. He's one of the best, Don. Don't know why they haven't promoted him above me yet…"

I was barely listening while she talked about Don and the Eagles; I was just staring at her, watching the way she moved, the way she talked, the way she kept absently rubbing a scar on her cheek that somehow, I thought, made her look even better.

She caught me watching her and put her hands under her legs. "Kyle... I get the feeling you're not here to join the cause either, not really. You're here for some other reason, aren't you?"

The words came easily: "I'm here to fight for whatever cause you fight for, Sofia – or none at all, if that's your choice. As long as I'm fighting by your side."

Her mouth fell open, and she gave a sheepish laugh, looking away. Then she blew out a sigh and licked her lips. I watched the way her chest rose and fell as she breathed. *There is no way this woman isn't real*, I thought. *She's more real than I am.*

At agonizing length, she finally looked back at me and said, "You're not the first guy to fall in love with me, you know."

I swallowed again. "I don't doubt it. A woman like you... Half the Eagles are probably in love with you. N-not that you've *been* with half the Eagles, I mean – but I'm sure they love you as their commander. Well, more than that, really, but... you know what I mean. How could they not...? I mean, yes, I'm sure there have been others."

I stuffed my hands in my pockets and tried to stop making a fool of myself. Sofia gave a surprisingly girlish giggle at my antics. Then she quickly returned to her old self, with that sad look in her eyes. She stood up and walked closer, looking down into my eyes.

"Kyle, tell me how old you think I am."

I stared back into her fiery green orbs. Sofia was undoubtedly an attractive woman, with elegant, angular features and dark, flowing hair, but hers was not entirely a soft, feminine beauty. She was a hard woman – a survivor. Everything about her spoke of life experience far beyond my own.

The best reply I could manage was: "I'd say you're about... twenty... something?"

She laughed. "You'd be wrong. I'm seventeen."

"Seventeen?" I echoed, staring at her incredulously.

She shrugged. "Possibly eighteen. I'm not sure *exactly*. My father was one of the leaders of the Eagles in their glory days. He taught me how to fight, and by eleven I was riding into battle with him, though I stayed back from most of the fighting. I think one reason he took me out to the field so early was because my mother died suddenly, and there was no one to take care of me anymore. My father was killed in battle when I was thirteen, and I started leading his old squad at just fourteen. By sixteen, I was put in command of the Eastern Saltpit City Eagles. It was a great honor, but I didn't think I was ready. Now I know I wasn't…"

"You did fine," I said. "You did all you could have done."

"I didn't figure out Webb was a spy," she said, "and that cost me my base. But you're right; I'm not blaming myself. I'm just saying I wasn't ready…"

A thought crossed my mind, and I gave voice to it: "Did you have any… education, as a child? Reading, writing? You speak so well, compared to some others around here…"

She laughed again. "Yeah… My mother taught me how to read while my father taught me the art of war. Books were always a pretty rare thing in Saltpit City, but Mother collected 'em. She taught me to read, write, and talk well. It felt useless at the time, and I usually revert to slang around the boys. But not with you – with you, I try harder. That's one reason I like you, Kyle. You're not as backwards as the rest. You're different… something about you is just… *different*."

"Hah," I laughed. "You have no idea."

Sofia sat down beside me on the edge of the bed. "I'd like to find out. Where were you educated? Maybe you can teach me a few things…"

I grinned. "They had a school where I grew up… a good one. I'd love to teach you. But most of what I know came from books. There's a lot you could teach me too…"

She smiled slyly, and then she leaned over and put her arms around my neck, whispering into my ear: "Maybe we could teach each other."

I could feel her breath against my neck. It sent chills all over me. Her skin was surprisingly smooth. Both her skin and her breath were warm. All doubts about the reality of this world disappeared from my mind forever. Sofia was real, and alive, and she was right here.

"I swore I'd never do this again..." she whispered.

And with that, we kissed. I felt her lips against mine, and I felt her fingers grip the skin on the back of my neck. It was the first time I had ever kissed a woman like that. In Utopia, such physical displays of love were not permitted in public areas. But I wasn't thinking about Utopia at all in that moment. I wasn't thinking about anything except me, and her, and right here, and right now...

===

That night, I switched off my transceiver the way Frank had shown me and spent the night in the Eagles' base. As I lay in bed, when I had time to think, I considered what Frank had sent me to do. Sofia had led such a hard life... Did I truly want to condemn all the people of G4M3 to such terrible existences? What was so evil about what Dr. Noble was doing anyway? Could his people really ruin *all* of Utopia? I doubted it...

When I awoke the next morning, I was relieved to find myself still in the world of G4M3. Frank's new transceiver had worked, or rather not worked, perfectly. Sofia was still fast asleep beside me. I felt her hair against my arm, her skin against mine. As I looked at her lying there, more at peace while asleep than at any other time, her eyes blinked open, and she looked around the room.

"Morning already?" she asked.

I nodded. "Yes, if you can call it that."

She sat up, yawned, and stretched, throwing the hair back out of her face. "Yeah... Mornings are the same as nights here I suppose."

"I had a good night though," I said with a smile.

Sofia gave one of her sardonic chuckles as she began suiting up in her combat gear. "Well, don't get your hopes up about the day being the same way."

I sighed. "Work to be done?"

She nodded. "Plenty of work to be done around here... always. We're planning a raid on a recently-discovered USOW science facility today. They're supposedly designing some secret weapon there. This whole war with the USOW... it's really getting out of hand. Wish I could just go back to running my little hideout in Saltpit City again..."

"Science facility..." I murmured. "That has to be him."

"Who?"

"The one who captured me: Dr. Matthew Noble."

"I think I heard someone mention that name..." Sofia said with surprise. "I'll go check on it. You stay here."

And with that, she abruptly left the room. I sat down on the bed and scratched the back of my neck. Earlier, I had been about to tell Sofia the truth and give up on Frank's mad quest. But now that a path lay so easily open to me, I thought, shouldn't I take it? The Eagles were going to try either way. I remembered what Frank had said about saving Utopia...

"To save my world..." I said aloud to myself, trying to fortify my determination, "To save my world, I have to help Frank Billings doom another one."

===

I raised the electronic binoculars to my eyes. I looked at the Saltpit behind me, large and low, flat and white, and then panned my view across the horizon, staring at the phantom black spires of Saltpit City. We were leaving that war-torn home away from home, heading to the secret USOW base nestled somewhere in the mountains ahead. Dr. Noble was building a secret weapon that would give the USOW an advantage in the never-ending war, so we had to stop him. Then the pointless struggle would go on. Unless...

"What are you thinking?" I heard Sofia ask behind me.

I sat back down and put away the binoculars. Both of us were seated in the back of one of the Eagles' transport vehicles. This was the most heavily armed and armored of them, with a canvas cover

over the back, so it was used for the mobile command base. It was full of radios, charts and maps, and even some sensor equipment to detect enemy activity nearby. Sofia was seated comfortably among all this junk, and I was there with her, looking out at the horizon. Don was in the front seat, beside the driver. He had said little to me since we started off.

"I was just thinking about life… and death," I answered her, for those really were my thoughts at the time, as my mind recalled the faces of the fellow beings I had ignorantly ended the lives of. "I still dream about the people I've killed."

To my surprise, Sofia reached up and slapped me across the face. "Sorry, Kyle, but you've got to cut that crap out right now if you're gonna survive this. Focus on the mission and nothing but the mission. Got it?"

I tried to resist rubbing my sore cheek. "Right… I mean, yes, Commander."

Don's deep voice echoed from the front of the truck: "Remind me why he's in the command vehicle again?"

"Because the USOW scientist, Dr. Noble, wants him for some reason," Sofia replied. "And because he was captured by them once and knows something about what they're up to. *And because I said so*, okay, Don?"

"Understood, Commander," Don said stoically, without turning to look at us. "We're coming up on the mountains now."

"Head through the valley," Sofia ordered. "Take route one, and let the other squads split off down different paths. We know where we'll all end up."

The information the Eagles had somehow acquired had been correct: the USOW base was indeed there, nestled between the cliffs that rose on either side of us. It was built into the rocky side of a low mountain, making it all but invisible from beyond this valley.

Don reached out the window and lowered a pair of metal armor plates over the truck's windshield, with only a narrow slit in each one enabling the driver and passenger to see. Almost as soon as they were down, a pair of loud 'CLANG's reverberated through them.

"Sniper fire," Don said. "That was quick. Thought we were still too far out…"

"Don't slow down," Sofia told the driver. "Armor One, this is Sofia. Check the cliff faces for snipers. Eliminate if you can."

After a few minutes, I heard an earsplitting blast come from the convoy behind us – from one of the battle tanks. I wanted to see what was going on, but I couldn't get the right angle to look out of the narrow slits in the thick armor; they were almost impossible to see through, except from head-on.

Sofia was barking orders into the communicator: "We've reached the base. Transports, move in and drop off all squads."

"What about us?" I asked.

In reply, she picked up my rifle and shoved it into my hands. "We're goin' in. I don't lead from the back. Come on!"

Hefting my gun and taking a deep breath, I followed her. This USOW facility turned out to be the finest I had yet seen. Hidden from the air beneath some overhanging rock, the outer courtyard was paved in concrete, and the buildings were clean, with rows of perfect windows. The guards were firing from these windows and from behind lines of barricades. The place was well-defended – almost impregnable. I wondered how we could ever possibly slip inside.

"Are you sure we can do this?" I asked Sofia as we joined our soldiers in the fight.

"It seems a real waste to ruin such a nice building…" Sofia muttered, and then she drew a device from the pouch at her side.

"What's that?" I asked.

"A megaphone," she answered. "Might as well *try* to avoid a fight…"

I was surprised at this desire for a peaceful resolution. Somewhere in the back of my head, I was still thinking of this as a game, where violence was inevitable, because violence was the point. I was happy to be wrong; I just hoped Sofia's plan would work and not get her picked off by a sniper.

"Just… keep your head down, okay?" I said.

She crouched beside the truck and shouted into the megaphone: "USOW soldiers, hold fire! We wish to parley! All men, hold fire!"

The shooting ceased. I stood there aghast. It was amazing to see so many people killing each other at the orders of their commanders, but it was twice as amazing to see them all suddenly stop. They were like pawns, I thought… pawns in a game.

A magnified voice suddenly answered Sofia from behind the enemy lines: "I will speak with you! Bring forth your leader!"

Sofia looked back at me with a cocked eyebrow. "Who is this guy? 'Bring forth your leader'? Who does he think he is?"

"We will allow a party of three to enter our compound," the voice went on. "I promise you will come to no harm."

Suddenly I recognized the voice. "It's him. It's Matthew Noble."

She nodded. "Well then, Kyle… This is your chance to end this conflict without killing him."

"I… guess so," I said. This was a startling turn of events. I had thought a fight was inevitable. I reminded myself that Dr. Noble only wanted to help the people of his world.

"Come on," Sofia commanded, stepping out from behind our cover.

As I strode forward, feeling brave, it seemed to me that the mouth of the giant cave-like hole in which the USOW facility was built yawned yet wider to accept my passage… just before swallowing me whole.

E L E V E N
BETWEEN TWO EVILS

Sofia called Don to join us as we entered the USOW base. I could see they were nervous – even Don, indomitable as he was. They were unused to the harsh glare of the lights overhead and the clean, off-white walls and spotless rows of windows, even as they reflected the dismal red and black sky of G4M3. But I was very, very familiar with them.

Yes, it had to be: Matthew Noble had based the design of this facility off the photos he had seen of Utopia. He obviously viewed Utopia as a dreamland, a wonderful place. It was a fine fantasy, I thought, but still a fantasy. He did not know the Order. Perhaps that was one way I could deter him from his goal: to tell him the truth. I would try my best, at least.

"What do you think, Don?" Sofia asked. "Could we make peace with the USOW?"

"Maybe now they're ready to treat us as equals," Don said, "instead o' subjects. That would mean… we won."

Sofia snorted. "Still the optimist, huh Don? Don't get your hopes up. Not sure if this Dr. Noble has that much authority anyway. Keep your eyes peeled for anything suspicious."

"Stay frosty, yeah…" Don muttered. "Always, Commander."

As a team of armored USOW soldiers escorted us through the halls, I peered through every open door we passed. I saw mostly computer rooms and laboratories. This place was a scientific building, not a fortress. I was even gladder, now, that we were trying to settle things peacefully.

"Through here," one of the guards said.

A pair of doors to our right opened wide. There, at the end of a long, shining table, sat Doctor Matthew Noble. To his left sat Sergei, his bald colleague. To Matthew's right sat another scientist I had never seen. Four guards stood watch over the meeting, one at each corner. I saw Sofia eyeing them carefully, obviously planning an escape, should one become necessary. The other Eagle soldier was doing the same. In this world of chaos, they trusted no one and anticipated treachery at every turn. I didn't blame them, but I hoped it would not come to that.

"Please, take a seat," Dr. Noble said, smiling amiably.

We slowly and carefully sat down in the chairs opposite his. Don was looking very twitchy, while Sofia now seemed outwardly calm and in control. Guess that's how she earned her rank, I thought.

"Now, introductions..." Dr. Noble said – somewhat nervously, I thought. "I am Doctor Matthew Noble, head of the G4 project and lead scientist for the United States of the World. These are my associates, Doctor Sergei Ivanovich and Doctor Simon Land. We've met Kyle Johnson..."

I nodded, ignoring the sidelong glance that Sofia shot in my direction. "That's one way to put it," I said sarcastically. "Let me introduce *my* associates: Sofia Tyler, commander of the Saltpit City Eagles, and Don..."

"Donald Stone," Don cut in, "second in command."

Sofia spoke up: "So what's this about, Doctor? Is the USOW finally trying to make peace with the Eagles, or did you call us in here for your own reasons?"

"Straight to business then?" Dr. Noble cleared his throat. "I should have expected that from the Eagles. I don't mean that as an insult – I do not hate you, like some in my organization do. We're all stuck together in this world of war. The constant conflict is as much our fault as yours."

Sofia didn't seem to believe him. "So, what do you want with Kyle? Why do you keep coming after him?"

Before Dr. Noble could answer, I spoke up myself: "I think I know, Sofia. I... didn't tell you, and I'm sorry, but I was afraid you wouldn't believe me."

Sofia looked at first betrayed, and then absolutely furious, and I wasn't sure which was worse. "*What?* I thought you trusted... Kyle, if you had some intelligence that could affect the mission–"

"*I'm from another world!*" I interrupted, too loudly.

She looked at me like I was either crazy or an idiot. "You mean... the station on Mars?"

"No," I replied, "not another planet... an entirely different universe – an alternate reality."

Sofia shot a look at Dr. Noble, who nodded and said, "He's not joking. Our scientists worked for years on the idea that we could transport the people of Earth to another planet, and when that failed, we tried another dimension instead – another plane of reality. We managed to send a camera into one such world, and it returned showing images beyond our wildest dreams: glimpses of a perfect city, with bright, shining streets and happy citizens... with a bright sky and..."

Here I interrupted: "I'm from that world, Sofia: a world called Utopia. And I'm here to disillusion you, Dr. Noble. You do not know what my world is truly like. There is peace in Utopia, but at a terrible cost. I don't even know how to explain it to someone who's never had to live it..."

Nevertheless, I tried my best. I tried to explain to Dr. Noble how everything in Utopia was ruled by the Order – an unseen hand with an all-seeing eye, which took not only the freedom of the people but also their souls. I told him how everyone had to conform to the Order's ideals, and those who betrayed any thought to the contrary were made to simply disappear, as were the infirm and the elderly. I explained all of this and more. They listened intently... but I could still see the determination in their eyes.

At length, Sofia, still staring at me in utter astonishment, interrupted me to ask: "So... *they* brought you here? The USOW took you from this... Utopia?"

I took a deep breath before replying, "No. It's much worse than that. I came here using a device in my own world. In my world, people pay money to be transported here for short periods of time. But they don't know that. They're told that this world isn't real – that it's all just a game, a simulation. They come here for entertainment, to relieve stress… by randomly picking a side in your war and joining in the fighting.”

“My God…” Dr. Noble muttered.

“Impossible…” breathed Sergei.

Don looked disgusted. “What in the hell…”

Sofia said nothing. She just stared at me.

“It’s terrible, I know!” I said. “I know that now… but I had no idea at first. It was supposed to just be a game…”

“Lord, forgive them…” Dr. Noble muttered, “for they know not what they do…”

There was a moment of tense silence. No one spoke or even looked at one another. They were all deep in thought. Dr. Noble seemed genuinely disturbed, and I hoped that I had successfully put an end to his plans to move G4M3’s populace to Utopia. When I turned to Sofia, she quickly looked away. I blew out a sigh.

Matthew Noble looked up and said, “Kyle, do you mean… your people discovered our world *first*?”

I sighed again. “The machine known as G4M3 – the facility that transports us here to your world – was invented by my grandfather, Walter Roswell.”

Sergei’s mouth slowly opened, and he turned to look significantly at Dr. Noble. Matthew Noble put his hand on his forehead and blinked, staring off into space, his face a mask of pure astonishment. The third scientist looked ready to faint. I looked at them all in confusion.

“*What*?” I demanded.

Matthew Noble squinted at me, studying my features, and said, “So your name is… Kyle Roswell? Not Kyle Johnson?”

I nodded. “Yes. I lied when we first met. I didn’t know what you wanted me for…”

“Do you know who your grandfather *was*?” Sergei asked almost accusingly, his accent strangely grating on my nerves.

“Why don’t you just *tell* me?” I insisted.

“He doesn’t know…” Matthew Noble muttered. “Kyle, your grandfather was the *head* of our G3 project! He worked with my own father on the original research team. He was still part of the team when I joined... and that was when the tragedy happened. Kyle... your grandfather was the man who disappeared with our only backup copy of the original research data. He and his wife and child disappeared, and then the G3 facility was destroyed by a bomb. In one flash, we lost everything we had worked so hard for."

"And now," Sergei put in. "You are trying to tell us that he did not die in the explosion... He actually transported himself and his family to Utopia?"

Slowly, Dr. Noble said, "Kyle... the name of your father was John Roswell, correct? And your grandmother was named Harriet. Those were the names of Walter's family."

Slowly, reluctantly, I nodded. "So it's true. I can't believe it... No one ever told me."

"I can't believe it either..." Dr. Noble said, somewhat to himself. "But in a way, I can. Walter never was very enthusiastic about our ideas. He thought it was a waste of time to even try to save the people of this world."

"I read his report," said Sergei. "He claimed that 'we would just be giving them another battlefield to decimate.' He had lost all hope for humanity."

"I can hardly blame him, but I can't believe he would betray everything we worked for, destroy everything..." Dr. Noble sighed. "But clearly, he must have. He fled to Utopia himself, and made sure no one could follow him."

"And that's not even the worst of it," said Sergei. "Running away, I can almost forgive, but to then make this... G4M3, and send people here to fight and die, while telling them all it's not real? Walter was not just a coward – he was *evil*."

I felt lost and confused in this new flood of information. It seemed that every time I thought I had the truth in my grasp, another bombshell would drop and turn my ideas upside-down. So, my father and his parents were born here, in this world? This meant that I was half-Utopian and half a native of G4M3. I had thought before, when we were attacking Matthew Noble's scientific facility, that I was saving my people and my world. But they were *both* my worlds. What did it matter anyway? Did I have the right to determine the fate of *any* world?

But Dr. Matthew Noble had already made up his mind, and he now stood and spoke it aloud: "Kyle Roswell, we have to take your transceiver. We are going to make that portal device. We are going to finish the G4 project at long last... and save our people."

"Wait!" I shouted. "Didn't you hear everything I said? Utopia isn't a paradise; it's a prison! And if you go there, you'll destroy everything anyway! The Order won't let you just move in – it will defend itself. And then you'll fight back, and Utopia and its people will pay the price!"

I looked at Sofia for support, but she was as torn as I was. I could see it in her eyes. She wanted to save her people just as badly as Dr. Noble and his colleagues. I knew that she could never live under the restrictive conditions imposed by the Order... but the idea of a world of peace could not be refused easily. I looked imploringly at her, hoping that she would side with me.

To my surprise, it was Don who said, "I hate to say it, but Kyle's right. This is *wrong*. We can't just destroy this other world the way we destroyed ours."

But as I watched Sofia, I saw her face harden. I braced myself for what she was about to say. But it still hit me like a wall of bricks.

"Why not?" she said.

"Commander–" Don tried to argue, but Sofia cut him off.

She turned and looked him in the eyes. "Think about it, Don! Think about the world Kyle described. Does that sound like a life worth living to you? To me it sounds like everything you've always lived to fight against! Don't you fight for freedom, Don? This Order *deserves* to be destroyed. And then maybe we can work with the people in Utopia to build a world better than *either* of these!"

Her words swayed him instantly; I could see it in his eyes. I knew Don was an idealist, but the core of his ideals was a love of freedom. But as for me, I still wasn't sure...

"All we need is your transceiver, Kyle," Matthew Noble said, walking slowly around the table toward me. "Once we've used it to build the portal machine, we can use the machine to send you back to Utopia, if that's what you would like."

"I… don't know…" I said, rising from my chair and backing away from all of them. "I can't let you have it… It's my duty to stop you!"

"It *was* your duty," Dr. Noble corrected. "It doesn't have to be anymore."

Sofia rose from her seat, but then she wheeled on Dr. Noble. "Now, hold on! It's Kyle's choice!" She turned back to me. "Kyle… I don't want to force you to do anything you don't believe is right. But deep down, you must know that *this* is right."

"Our world is dying!" exclaimed Sergei, calling attention to himself. "You have seen our fading sun, our blasted earth and sky… Within a few generations, this planet may not even be able to sustain life."

This gave me new pause for thought, and I had to wipe nervous sweat off my brow. "I… I just don't know…"

That was when everything went south. I must have touched the bottom of my shirt, giving the impression that I was reaching for my escape button. Perhaps, subconsciously, I had been doing exactly that. But it was enough to send the USOW scientists into a panic. I saw the kindness in Sergei's eyes disappear, and he drew his gun.

"Don't touch that implant!" Sergei exclaimed, aiming the weapon at my leg.

In the blink of an eye, Sofia was on her feet, with her rifle leveled straight at Sergei's bald head. "Drop that pistol, Doctor!"

Don was right beside her in an instant, his own weapon raised. The two USOW guards at the far side of the room also joined in, backing up Sergei, their rifles trained on Sofia and Don, while the scientist's gun was still locked on me.

Dr. Noble flew into a panic, drawing his own pistol but pointing it only toward the ceiling. "Wait, everyone stop! We can be reasonable! Kyle, please surrender…"

He reached out toward me, and Sofia must have taken it as an act of aggression, for she quickly intercepted him and grabbed his arm, twisting it around. Dr. Noble screamed. For a split second, I saw Sergei's face turn into a mask of fury.

He shot me in the leg.

"STOP!" Dr. Noble cried out, tossing his gun angrily away against a wall. "Stop this madness now!"

But even as he opened his mouth to speak, it was already too late. The instant the first shot rang out, everyone opened fire. Sofia shot Sergei in the shoulder, knocking him to the floor. Don shot one of the USOW guards in the face even as he was firing at Sofia. The soldier's shot hit Sofia in the chest, but it only struck her armor, knocking her off balance. She then angrily mowed down the other guard. Then Don called for reinforcements.

Then all Hell broke loose. I heard the thunder of distant gunfire and explosions as the battle outside resumed. Sofia did not order her men to stop this time. When more USOW guards rushed in, she and Don cut them down in a hail of gunfire. I hefted my own rifle and joined in, until no more guards tried to enter.

For a moment, the room was clear... or so I thought, until I saw the third scientist in the room – the one who had sat beside Dr. Noble and Sergei without saying a word – trying now to sneak up behind Sofia. He had a gun leveled right at the back of her head. Without hesitating, I unloaded my magazine into his chest. I had never seen so much blood. He fell to the ground, his white lab coat now soaked in red.

"*NO!*" Matthew Noble cried in pure anguish, rushing in vain to help his fallen friend.

"Toss your gun, Sergei!" I screamed, my adrenaline pumping hard now.

But he didn't.

With a look of disgust, he just turned... and shot me again.

Then, as if it were planned and perfectly timed, the power to the facility suddenly blinked out, turning the room dark. I felt the familiar sensation of wind swirling around me. I tried to fight it – to shout Sofia's name – but it was no use. The implant had detected a mortal wound.

I was sucked screaming back to Utopia.

T W E L V E
WHEN THEY COME FOR YOU

"Good morning, Kyle Roswell," the sinister voice of Frank Billings said, waking me from my slumber.

I jumped up and looked around the room. I was alone in one of the G4M3 facility's 'simulation' rooms, but this one was emptier than normal. My military gear and weapons were not sitting neatly on the table nearby, though I wasn't wearing them either. Even the bed on which I lay was bare metal, with no cushion.

Once I had gotten my bearings somewhat, I said aloud to the empty room: "You lied to me, Frank."

A glowing yellow hologram of Frank walked into the room, projected from... somewhere. It looked at me and smiled that familiar, disarming smile. But I wasn't convinced.

"I assure you, Kyle," Frank said, "I've only ever told you the truth."

"But not the whole truth!" I exclaimed, interrupting him before he could say more. "You didn't tell me my grandfather came from G4M3! You said he was an employee in the Order's science facility!"

Frank sighed – which sounded like static through his microphone over the speakers. "Oh... that. I was going to tell you about that, Kyle, when I felt you were ready. Yes, Walter Roswell came from that other world, but he also *did* work at the Order's science facility for a short time. He and I worked together to create... this!" Here Frank flung his arms out and looked around the room. "This wonderful facility which has kept us alive for so long! We built it using the information Walter brought back from his homeworld, which he knew was a lost cause long ago..."

"How has G4M3 'kept us alive', Frank? It hasn't kept us alive – it's been killing us!"

"Nonsense. It's only been killing the people in G4M3, and those people were dead anyway. Your grandfather realized that; he cared even less than *me* about the lives that would be destroyed by his invention!"

"I don't care what Walter thought!" I shouted. "This machine has caused the deaths of countless men and women whose blood is on *your* hands!"

Frank rolled his eyes. "Haven't you been listening? They were dead anyway. That *whole world* is dead! And I'm not lying – G4M3 *has* kept us alive. It has kept the *Order* alive! You don't know how close we were to true chaos, until your grandfather brought us this gift, allowing humans an outlet for their baser instincts, rather than bottling them up..."

I gave a laugh full of scorn. "Maybe the Order could use a little shaking up. I care about the people of Utopia, Frank, but do you really think I give a rat's ass about the *Order?*"

"You've spent too much time in there, Kyle. You're starting to get a dirty mouth."

"That's all you have to say? Not going to warn me about speaking ill of the precious Order this time?"

"The Order is what keeps the people of Utopia safe, Kyle. You can't have one without the other. Watch how you talk about it, and not just because you should fear it – but because of all the hard work and spilled blood that has gone into building it. Generations of–"

I spat on the ground at the feet of Frank's flickering hologram. "*Damn* the Order."

I couldn't believe my own mouth. I was high on adrenaline now, as terrified as I was angry. I fully expected a squad of robots to come bursting into the room that very second and drag me off to 'disappear' somewhere. But to my surprise, none came.

Instead, Frank said something that surprised me far more: "Kyle... I *am* the Order."

I did a double take, not believing him. "Wh... what?" I laughed. "Do you really expect me to believe that?"

He shook his head, smiling in a new way, a way I had never seen him smile before. He seemed to have thousands of ways of smiling, each one different than the last. This one was a knowing and sinister one, the smug smile of a powerful man as he sentences his enemies to execution.

"I never *quit* working for the Order, Kyle," Frank said. "Even when your grandfather, Walter Roswell, thought he was passing secret information about his new G4M3 project to a trusted friend and confidant, he was actually passing it to the Order – to *us*. Nothing can escape our notice in Utopia – we see and hear *everything*. Your grandfather thought he could build this facility under our very *nose* and get away with it. But instead, the Order handed the project to me."

My eyes went wide as a realization struck me. "Frank, you… Don't tell me it was you who…"

Frank smiled his darkest and most disturbing smile yet. "Poisoned your grandfather? Yes, it was me. Once every secret of the facility's functionality was revealed to me, I invented an excuse to rid myself of that bothersome Walter Roswell. He was about to tell your idiot father about the truth behind G4M3, and we simply couldn't have that… so I concocted a little 'disease' that would put him out of work. It kept him silent, or so I thought, while still making your family believe that it was a normal occurrence. That way, his mental faculties would still be available if I needed them, but under my control. At least, I thought so until…"

"Until the day I visited him…"

"Indeed, Mr. Roswell. I was watching your entire conversation with that raving old man. He almost told you our dirty little secret… So, a while after that, I finally ended his suffering. I think even *you* will agree it was no worse a fate than he deserved."

I had to sit back down on the bed, my head swirling. "Why are you telling me all of this now? Are you done using me like a tool? Ready to throw me away just like you threw away my grandfather?"

Frank frowned. "Well, since you clearly failed in your mission to kill Dr. Noble, you aren't much use, are you? But no, I'm not going to kill you, Kyle. I *should* have killed you a long time ago, after ruining your transceiver to leave you stuck in G4M3 didn't work… That day you returned in the wrong simulation room, I should have exacted justice for poor William Byrd by pumping in some poison gas while you were sleeping."

I glared up the hologram. "So, the transceiver really *was* empty... because of you!"

"That's right, my boy. But don't worry; the Order never kills unless it absolutely has to. For nearly every being, no matter how insubordinate, has their usefulness. Now you'll get to see what you were so curious about, Kyle. Now you'll get to see the other side of Utopia... the dark side."

Instantly, my vision began to swim. I wasn't sure if he was pumping gas into the room like he'd mentioned before, or if he was using some other method, but I quickly began to lose consciousness. I tried to shout one last curse at 'Uncle' Frank, but I couldn't get the words out before I toppled to the ground...

===

I awoke with the realization that I was not in the world of G4M3. I'm not sure why I'd expected to wake up there; perhaps I'd just gotten used to always waking up in another world. But I was still in Utopia this time – just not a part of Utopia I had ever seen before. I was in a small, featureless holding cell. I had the sensation that the room was moving. Was I inside a transport? They were taking me somewhere...

"Hello!" I exclaimed aloud. "What's going on here?"

A mechanical voice answered me from speakers built into the blank metal walls around me: "Subject displays unfamiliarity with environment. Slight agitation and fear. Please remain calm, Citizen 4069AU. The situation will be explained to you. You have been placed under arrest for disobeying orders given to you by an officer of the Order, for disturbing the peace by being up too late after appropriate hours, for missing your work for too many cycles consecutively, and for the murder of Citizen 1032AU, also known as William Joseph Byrd. You are being taken to a rehabilitation facility outside Utopia. There, you will be given manual labor to perform so that you, as a healthy young male, can still contribute to society."

"Wait!" I exclaimed. "Don't I get to argue in my own defense? What proof do you have of any of this?"

"Ample evidence was provided by Employee 0951WA: Frank Billings. Evidence provided includes video and audio recordings of yourself confessing to the crimes of which you stand accused, as well as other photographic evidence and data files. All evidence was scrutinized and found to be reliable, accurate, and not artificial. Subject was judged guilty of all crimes accused. Subject has been sentenced to manual labor until rehabilitation is judged complete by a licensed official. Subject will then be allowed back into Utopian society under stricter monitoring as outlined in the Utopian Citizen's Bill of Privileges, section 3, subsection F."

I fought back a wave of disgust. I wished I was back in the war-torn world of G4M3. G4M3 was a horrible place – certainly more horrible on the surface than Utopia – but at least the evil there was plain for all to see and fight against. Here in Utopia, the evil hid itself under a pretty and polished layer of plastic, claiming to be benevolent and then ridding itself of its enemies in secret, offering them no chance to resist. It was a single plotting, truth-twisting, iron-fisted evil, as opposed to G4M3's many destructive, violent, and obvious ones.

"So," I said aloud, "I'm being taken to the… 'other side' of Utopia? The other side of the planet?"

"That is correct. You are being taken to the Other Side to join those who must work. Subject is displaying signs of agitation; continuing conversation sequence. You see, early in the development of the experimental self-supporting ecosystem known as Utopia, those in charge of the project realized a perfect society could not function, due to a lack of motivation for the citizens to perform their labors. Even though eliminating capitalist markets improved equality, it also made the citizens less inspired to work hard to improve the community as a whole, because they themselves would receive no immediate personal advantage. Humans are, sadly, as selfish by nature as they are violent. So, a caste system was created, in which those judged unfit for the community of Utopia were sent to the Other Side to perform manual labor for the good of all, including their own. The situation has improved since then. Fewer laborers are needed, as robots do most of the work. But worry not, Citizen – there will still be plenty for you to do!"

I closed my eyes and tried to absorb it all. "But how can you do this to people? Wasn't the Order created to serve and uplift mankind, not enslave and destroy it?"

"No humans are ever destroyed by the Order," the voice replied. "We end no human lives. Sometimes humans die, and sometimes their relatives are told they are dead while they are actually moved to a more suitable location."

I sighed, but since this computer seemed eager to talk, I wanted to ask it all I could. "Who did this? How did the Order come to be? What *is* the Order?"

The machine paused before answering. "I... can't say. The Order arose from humanity's desire to better themselves and their society. That is either all I know or all I have access to."

"Who started it? Can you tell me that?"

"I can't say," was the only reply.

"So, you don't know where you came from."

"I did not say I did not know," the machine responded. "I only said: I can't say."

Before I could stop myself, I had spat out the question: "What happens if I try to escape?"

"We will activate your Citizen Control Implant, and you will be rendered unconscious for recovery."

"My Citizen Control Implant?"

"Subject displays unfamiliarity to installed regulations and control procedures. Explanation will be provided: As dictated by the Founding Document of the Order of Utopia, Section C, Subsection 3, all citizens are implanted with a Citizen Control Implant, or CCI, upon birth. The CCI aids the Order in the location, identification, and apprehension of every Citizen, if necessary."

"So that was how Frank knocked me out..." I muttered to myself.

But the machine heard me and quickly replied, "Impossible. Employee 0951WA, Frank Billings, does not have access to any control over the CCI of Utopian citizens. The incapacitation to which you refer was applied by your G4M3 Transceiver."

I closed my eyes, but kept talking to keep myself from thinking about my situation. "Oh, so now I have two implants inside me? Wonderful."

To my surprise, the machine answered, "Negative. Sensors detect only one implant located in the subject's biological matrix."

"Only one? But, according to what you've said, I should have two implants..."

This actually gave the artificial intelligence unit pause for thought. "Processing... It is possible that E0951WA Frank Billings has equipped you with the experimental implant unit designated CCGTI, or Citizen Control and G4M3 Transceiver Implant. This prototype implant was created to have the capabilities of a standard CCI and G4M3 Transceiver in a single unit. E0951WA Frank Billings was given permission by the Order to use the experimental implant on a single Citizen unit. He apparently chose you as the test subject."

I unconsciously reached under my shirt and felt of my stomach. "But that means I can..."

It was worth a try. Without wasting a moment, I pressed the button in my navel and held it down for a few seconds, to deactivate it the way Frank had explained. Almost immediately, I felt the vehicle slow to a halt. The doors in front of me opened wide to admit my passage. I stood in shock for a second before the computerized voice explained the situation.

"Subject's signal lost. Possibility of escape. Initializing search-and-recover procedure. Dispatching probes."

As I sat there dumbly, four holes opened in the ceiling above me, and a hovering robot drone dropped out of each one. They flew right past me, out into the street, searching every alley. It had worked: By disabling my implant, I had blinded the machines to my very existence. To them, I had simply disappeared – ceased to exist. As soon as I realized this, I leaped out of the back of the vehicle and darted off down the street. I was not about to waste this opportunity.

It was night, though the streets were bright as day in the light of the streetlamps. This made the dark shadows contrast sharply with everything around them. I had almost never been out at night; it was not a thing encouraged in Utopia. The air was dreadfully cold. The streets were silent, and the blank white walls of the identical buildings stared down at me menacingly as I passed. I felt like they were watching me.

Then I stopped. I'd heard footsteps – metallic ones. There was a security robot approaching, stalking its way along the streets, the light on its head glowing red. I felt terror grip me in its icy fingers; I had nowhere to go, and the Order was everywhere. But as the robot drew closer, I noticed that it was making no move to hinder my progress. As I stood there, waiting for the end, the patrolman passed me by.

I was appalled. Did these machines even have visual sensors – or motion sensors, or heat sensors? It was hard to believe they relied so completely upon the unknown implants hidden in each citizen. Hadn't anyone ever thought to fix this? It was strange: I had been told since the day I was born that the Order was always watching, but now it was utterly blind to me. I suddenly felt that familiar sensation of true freedom – the feeling I got whenever I entered the G4M3.

Unfortunately, I was not given long to enjoy my freedom. The Order, as Frank had told me before, was not stupid. Apparently, they somehow figured out what had happened, for as I jogged down the street, I heard a metallic voice shout behind me, nearly giving me a heart attack:

"Halt! Halt now, or this unit will resort to force!"

I dodged into a nearby alley, and I heard the air sizzle behind me. I turned to look, and a beam of blue-white energy flashed past my eyes. The Patrolmen were armed after all! I glanced back out, looking both ways down the sidewalk, and saw two robots: one approaching from each direction.

I knew I would be cornered soon, so I resorted to a dangerous plan. I simply dashed out from the alley and ran across the street. As I'd hoped, the two androids fired immediately, with pinpoint accuracy… but I was out of the way just in time. The two blasts streaked right past each other and into the opposite patrolman. There were two explosions, and then all that could be heard was the crackling of electrical fires and the clatter of falling metal.

This surprised me more than anything. Had the robots actually been using lethal force? I turned to see both units blown to pieces, as if they had overloaded with energy when shot. But I didn't have time to think about it; I knew more patrolmen would be coming.

Quickly, I ran to where the arm of the nearest robot had landed. I was hoping I could use the laser weapon, but it seemed to be built into the arm itself, with no external trigger for the use of a human. I tinkered with the various switches and buttons, but with no luck. They all seemed to just open various access panels for repair purposes, or else they did nothing.

But I was not going to leave this useful object lying there. I picked the heavy arm up by one end… and it slid apart in my grasp. I was now holding only half of the arm, while the rest was lying on the ground, with a mechanical hand now revealed on the end of it. I shoved my arm into the piece I was holding and felt a handle deep inside, with a trigger.

I was astonished. Obviously, at one point, these robots actually *had* been made by humans, and they had installed safety features to make sure their weapons were not useable by only the bots themselves. To test the device, I pointed it at the ground and pulled the hidden trigger. A burst of blue-white light lit the area and, with an echoing blast, blew a black hole in the asphalt.

Satisfied, I continued my run down the street. The night seemed so calm and peaceful, the buildings so tranquil and silent… but I knew that more androids could come from nowhere at any minute. The Patrolmen always kept their silent vigil. So, on I ran, until I came to the foot of a Builder statue. The blank face of the 'man' stared down at me, and I suddenly imagined him coming to life and smashing me with his hammer. I kept getting the awful sensation that the statue was watching me menacingly.

But he was a marker; I was on the right track. Or was I? There were hundreds of Builder statues in Utopia, probably thousands or even millions. In truth, I could be anywhere; even miles from home, since everything in Utopia looked the same. There was only one way to know: I had to call a transport. So, I pressed the button on the nearest lamppost and slid into the shadows, sitting and watching patiently.

It wasn't long before I saw a group of five Patrolmen pass by down the street. Two of them broke off to search the alleys on either side, their bright red eyes leaving trails of light behind them when they turned. I watched and waited, steadying my gun arm. Then, when the one nearing my hiding place was close enough, I fired. The robot's head was blown completely off, but its body kept coming, now firing randomly in my general direction, unable to aim but still sensing my presence somehow. I shot it again, this time in the chest, and it exploded. Apparently, its weak spot was not in the head.

The other robots had detected this commotion and were now approaching... along with the trolley I had called. The little bus just peacefully rolled along its designated path as the four machines of battle stomped by on either side of it. Each one was carrying out its own programmed task, only noticing the other robot enough to stay out of its way.

I'll blast apart every stupid robot in Utopia if I have to, I thought, trying to build up my confidence. Then I rolled out of the alley and opened fire on the patrolmen. The first two fell beneath my onslaught, but the remaining pair caught on quickly. Flashes of white light blinked through the air. I felt terrible pain as a blast skimmed the side of my arm, burning my skin.

I returned fire, taking out the leg of one of the robots. It fell over, toppling onto its companion. This caused enough confusion for me to take out both units with a few more well-placed shots. Their explosions lit up the streets, sending debris bouncing in all directions.

I ran as fast as I could and jumped into the transport trolley. Then I stopped for a moment to catch my breath. The tram stopped as well.

"Identify yourself," said the pilot bot, where it sat in the driver's seat of the taxi.

"I'm... Frank Billings," I lied. "Employee number 09... uh... 51WA I'm using an experimental CCI and G4M3 transceiver implant. That's why your scanners aren't picking me up. Take me back to the G4M3 facility and I'll get to work on fixing this right away."

The thought struck me that the robot would detect my deception as soon as it noticed Frank's CCI signal on its scanners. It would know Frank was somewhere else and that I was not who I claimed to be. I was trying to think of what to do next when the robot's friendly voice surprised me with a positive answer:

"Yes Sir, Employee 0951WA. Anything you say. Please take your seat, and we will begin immediately."

I sat down, and the vehicle began its rapid journey down the road. I lay back in the chair, exhausted and relieved. Apparently, Frank held considerable sway in the hierarchy of the Order, or at least was important enough to not be questioned by the robots.

I recalled what he had said: "I *AM* the Order." Had he simply been raving, or had he actually meant that? What exactly did it mean? At any rate, I could hardly believe my luck. But I was not about to be inattentive because of it, so I stayed on the alert, sitting up and looking out all the windows, my laser cannon at the ready.

Thankfully, I had little to worry about. We were approaching the G4M3 facility. It loomed ahead, tall and quiet against the dull, dark sky of Utopia. Soon, we slowed to a stop, and the doors opened. I walked out, looking around for any patrol bots. There were none, and I slipped inside unmolested.

"Hello?" said the friendly, silver-hulled, blue-eyed robot behind the admissions window. "I assume you are here for the tournament. I regret to inform you that all the slots have been filled, and all Players are already in the arena."

"What tournament?" I asked, confused. I had never heard of a G4M3 tournament before.

The bot blinked its lights at me. "The first ever G4M3 Tournament Mission is being held today. In this mission, twenty of Utopia's most elite Players begin a G4M3 session in the same virtual world instance. They then follow their leader with the objective of destroying two important boss characters. Since this is the first Tournament ever, Frank Billings himself, the owner of the G4M3 facility, is leading the Players into battle."

My eyes went wide. "You mean… Frank is in G4M3?"

"Yes, sir, along with all nineteen other Players. We regret that there is no more room for you to join, so you will have to return tomorrow."

I licked my lips nervously, not even wanting to know the answer to my next question: "Where are… What simulation are they running? What… characters were they sent to kill?"

"The location is Saltpit City. Their targets are known as Doctor Matthew Noble of the USOW and Commander Sofia Tyler of the Eagles. It should be quite a difficult fight. There may be a holographic video of it available for your enjoyment tomorrow, if you return."

I swallowed hard. "I… I have to get in there! I know there are more than twenty rooms here; start up a session for me!"

"I have specific instructions not to let any more Players join the game. I am sorry, sir. Do come back tomorrow at regular visiting hours."

"But… I'm Frank Billings! Employee 0951WA! I got kicked out of the simulation, and I need to get back. My implant malfunctioned. Show me into my office, immediately!" I said all of this quickly, hardly thinking.

The robot did not respond. Its friendly blue eyes began to glow brighter and brighter, until they were intense and white. I quickly leapt aside, just in time, as a pair of white lasers blasted a hole through the wall behind me. I hefted my own rifle and pulled the trigger. The little secretary robot was blown apart. I actually felt a twinge of sadness for the friendly little bot, but then I remembered it was just a mindless digit of the great machine that was the Order. And I had work to do.

With some difficulty, I slid through the admissions window and landed on the other side, the pieces of the bot I had destroyed crunching under my shoes. There was the door to Frank's office: the 'Commander's Room'. I walked up and put my hand on the control panel. There was no response.

For a moment I looked around the room, wondering what to do, and then an idea struck me. I stepped back and blasted the controls. There was a small explosion, and sparks flew across the room, but still the door did not open. I muttered a foul curse I had learned in G4M3. How stupid was I to expect the door to open just because I shot the controls, anyway?

So, I lifted my gun and blasted the door itself. I fired again and again, until the white-hot lasers finally started melting their way through the structure. As soon as I'd made a hole big enough, I stopped, not wanting to damage anything inside. The gun was extremely hot. It shook and beeped, venting hot steam. I ignored it and slipped into Frank's office.

Upon looking around, the first thing that caught my eye was a book: a simple, white paper book, lying open on Frank's desk. I was surprised; I thought books were non-existent in Utopia, since everything was on computers. I sat down in Frank's luxurious, cushioned chair and felt it automatically adjust to my height and the shape of my body, even growing warm to keep me comfortable. I blew out a sigh of contentment, though I couldn't help thinking of all the people of G4M3 who never had a chance to live in such luxury.

Because they destroyed their own world, I heard a voice in my head say. It was almost like I had Frank right there inside my brain. Perhaps he was right about G4M3 and Utopia, or perhaps Doctor Noble was right, but at that moment I didn't care about either one of them, or anyone else in either world. I only cared about one thing: Sofia. I had to find her... or at least stop Frank from finding her. And I had to do it fast.

But nothing in the room seemed useful. There was no holographic computer screen active. The surface of the desk was just flat, polished wood, and all of the drawers were locked. The only thing accessible seemed to be the book, lying there open and inviting. I leaned over and scanned the letters. It was obviously a journal. Right below today's date there was an entry:

Kyle Roswell is no longer a threat. It pained me somewhat that I was unable to get him to see reason, but at least he will live on, working away the rest of his days on the Other Side. Matthew Noble and this Sofia Tyler will not be so fortunate.

I will soon be leading a group of Players into the G4M3 world to hunt down and exterminate Miss Tyler and Dr. Noble. My companions will not realize that they are doing anything other than killing 'bosses' in a game, and I will equip them with the finest Utopian technology to make this all the simpler. There will be no stopping us.

I considered simply sending the Players in alone, but that was the mistake I made last time with Kyle. I'm not about to make it again. As much as I hate to set foot in that god-forsaken wasteland, I have to see this through personally. Then, and only then, can I rest easy, knowing that there are no further threats to the Order.

Unable to contain my curiosity, and hoping to find some information that might help me stop him, I began flipping backwards through Frank's journal. Every page surprised me more than the last, until finally I grasped the whole heap of pages and flipped them to the other side, turning back to the very beginning. The first entry was as follows:

Note: I am writing this on actual paper, because the Order has access to all information on computer, and I cannot risk them discovering my plans.

I, Frank Edward Billings, also known as Employee of the Order of Utopia 0951WA, am writing this journal as I begin taking steps toward acquiring what could be considered complete world domination. It seems silly and naïve to term it such, but in a way, it is true: I may in fact be able to secure for myself a position of complete control over the Order.

I have studied deep into the Order's past, and I have finally come to a conclusion: The Order was not created all at once; it is the result of years of government planning, to build the perfect society. It all started with a global alliance – a council of nations – called the United States of the World. This name is the same as the one that my friend Walter Roswell heard in the alternate dimension that we discovered. Could this mean that we have actually discovered a time machine?

Day 2: I sifted through the records some more today. When the USOW attempted to assert world domination, there was a war. But it was nowhere as long or catastrophic as the one that is now occurring in the alternate dimension. Either the Order's records, old and seemingly untouched as they are, are inaccurate, or my time machine theory was incorrect. I will research more into this tomorrow.

Day 3: Success! I have come across the most important records of all today. They detail how the USOW created an army of robots and coded them with a program called 'The Order of Utopia'. There are not many records after that point, and all of them are frightening. They tell of how the Order became autonomous, thinking for itself. It turned on its creators, killing those that could threaten its existence.

Then the records cease. Perhaps the USOW did not help themselves; they destroyed themselves. Or perhaps they – some of them, at least – actually meant for this to happen, to remove human error and human greed and ambition from their perfect government. Either way, this could mean that there truly are no humans controlling Utopia – that the Order is nothing but a robotic hive mind, carrying out its programming! If this is true, then I could find a way to bring my plan for power into reality…

Day 4: Walter told me the truth today – something I never could have expected. He told me how this dimension he 'discovered' was actually his home. He is actually <u>from</u> this other world! I have been wondering about his strange accent and manner of speaking for some time now, and I wondered all the more when I heard the people of the *other dimension speaking similarly. Now I know the truth. It seems that Walter...*

I already knew this story, so I flipped through the book some more until I reached another interesting spot:

I've done it! Through extensive research, hacking, and espionage, I have made my way into the bowels of the Order's brain. I have elevated myself in status from a mere "Employee" to a person of real rank. I will continue to hold the same name, number, and title, but now the Order and its minions will obey my every command.

I have carefully covered my tracks so that none may follow me. My experiment shall never be repeated. None other than I shall hold this much power and influence, for only few other than I have enough intelligence and sense of responsibility to exercise it properly. But there is still one man who may find me out: Walter Roswell. I will have to take care of that.

I closed my eyes tight and balled up the page in my fist. Frantically, I kept flipping through the journal. I found all sorts of strange, cryptic notes scribbled on the corners of some pages, most of which meant nothing to me. But one set of four numbers caught my eye, for some reason. The numbers were 12, 25, 19, and 91. Above them was written the word 'REMEMBER', in capital letters and underlined. I tried to commit the numbers to memory quickly, without wasting too much time. Then I kept going.

At last, I stumbled upon something relevant: a page detailing the construction of the first G4M3 facility for use by the general public. Frank rambled a bit about how useful G4M3 would be for letting the citizens of Utopia express their violent urges 'safely'... but then he actually said something interesting:

According to Frank's journal, the implants could work *anywhere* in a G4M3 facility. The 'simulation rooms' were nothing more than boxes. They contained no actual technology that enabled one to enter G4M3. All of that was in the transceiver… and all one had to do was press the button while standing inside a designated G4M3 building.

Without further delay or hesitation, I reached down under my shirt and pressed the button on the device in my stomach. Right there, in the middle of Frank's personal office, I felt the world begin to spin, and the sensation of blowing wind surrounded me, carrying me through the fabric of space…

T H I R T E E N
WORLDS COLLIDE

The streets of G4M3 looked even worse than usual... because they were littered with bodies. I stared at them in astonishment – corpses scattered along the sidewalk, burned and blasted, just like the buildings around them – covered in blackened holes created by energy weapons. Frank's men had been here, and they had left no one alive.

I felt a wave of nausea. Only then did I realize I had another small problem: I was completely naked. I hadn't even considered the fact that my regular clothes would not be transported with me into G4M3, since they were not counted as part of my bio-matrix like Frank's special uniforms.

There was nothing to do but take from the dead. Feeling sick and ashamed, I scanned about for a person approximately my size, wearing good gear in decent condition. I tried not to look at the man's face as I stripped him of his clothing and equipment. His leather jacket was missing one sleeve – it seemed to be a local style – but I didn't mind, since it had armor attached.

Once I was no longer naked, I found the best long-range rifle, submachine gun, pistol, and any other weapons I could carry. I wasn't the only one doing it; one or two other vultures eventually appeared – poor Saltpit City citizens always eager for scraps. I pitied them as much as the dead.

Once I was fully equipped, I headed for the hidden garage where the Eagle named Scott and I had found that old truck and taken it for a ride to the Eagles' base. It was a long shot to hope there would be more working vehicles there, but it felt like my only hope. Frank and his men were probably headed either to the Eagles or the USOW base, and I had to catch up with them.

Once again, luck was on my side. Before I'd even left the street, I ran across a vehicle, though not a truck. Lying on the sidewalk, its rider killed by Frank and his men, was a motorcycle. I had ridden one in a simulation once, so I knew how to work the strange controls. I stood it back up, sat down, and tried to figure out the bizarre device someone had rigged to the engine to repair it. Eventually I found the fuel valve and ignition.

My heart nearly leapt into my throat when I turned the handle, and the vehicle almost shot out from under me. It was a lot faster than the one in the sim. And extremely loud. But I didn't care – speed was exactly what I needed. I felt a rush of exhilaration as I kicked it into high gear and sped out across the desert. I knew in what direction my destination lay, but it would be a while before I would reach the mountains. All I could do now was ride... and hope I had enough gas.

As my motorcycle cut its way across the vast, flat desert wasteland, a storm began gathering over the land around the Saltpit, its clouds casting a black shadow over the already darkened earth. The rain made the trail muddy and the going slow, and the streaks of lightning that split the black sky of G4M3 terrified me. I had never before experienced a thunderstorm, but I knew what they were. So, I ignored the flash of the lightning and the peel of the thunder, gradually growing used to them, even anticipating them, in wonder at their majesty.

At last, I reached the hidden USOW base. As I'd expected, it was now a ruined battlefield. The trucks that Sofia had positioned around the outside of the science facility were mostly just gone, but there were three lying in a heap of slag, completely destroyed. Bodies littered the area, and smoke was rising from a gaping black hole blown in the front of the science facility. As I walked about the wreckage, checking each body for signs of life, I started noticing unusual wounds: blast marks, not left by bullets, but by lasers. Some of the USOW and Eagle soldiers even looked like they had been fighting side-by-side.

There was only one possible explanation: Frank's men had gotten here before me. He and his elite G4M3 players had the advantage of Utopia's advanced technology, along with no remorse, and no fear of death. It was So, a bloodbath. I remembered what Dr. Noble had said: *Lord, forgive them, for they know not what they do.*

I understood now what he'd meant, and he was right. I could forgive them. But I was not going to forgive Frank Billings, for he knew quite well what he was doing, and what he still planned to do. As I jogged along, I became more frantic. My pace quickened, along with my pulse. I stopped checking for wounded men and instead only checked each dead Eagle to make sure they were not Sofia.

I ran through the base's crumbling doors, my feet spattering through mud puddles, the thunder roaring behind me. Signs of battle were everywhere: on the walls and scattered over the floor. Everything confirmed it: the USOW and the Eagles had dropped their quarrel and fought together against Frank and his boys. It was quite a twist of fate: the only thing that could unite them was a common enemy.

As I checked the bodies, my heart skipped a beat. There was Sofia Tyler, lying against the blackened wall like any other dead soldier. I ran to her and kneeled down. She was lying on her side, her eyes shut tight, her breathing shallow. But she was alive. I let out a deep breath in relief.

Then I saw the wound: the burn wound. It was bad.

"Sofia?" I whispered, gently touching her shoulder.

"K-kyle!" she gasped, smiling faintly, lifting her pale face to look at me. "You... you came back..."

Her voice was strange. It sounded far away, sad and happy at the same time, in pain but also... relieved. The fire in her green eyes seemed dim, and she could barely keep them open. Her breathing was shallow – so shallow.

"I... I knew you would come back," she said. "Thank you."

"Sofia, you're hurt. There's a burn..." my voice cracked as I inspected the hole in her side. "You... Let me help you..."

Sofia softly pushed me away, gasping: "It's okay, Kyle. I... knew this day would come. The pain is... fading now. Don't... ruin it."

I started to rise, looking around the room for anyone or anything that could aid Sofia. But there was nothing. Never before – not even in the midst of my first real battle – had I felt so completely helpless. The crack of thunder split my ears, shaking me out of self-pity.

"I… I'll look for a first aid kit," I said. "There's got to be one…"

But Sofia grabbed my leg. "D-don't leave me, Kyle! It's too late for me now… You… just stay here… a moment. I have to… tell you something."

My vision blurred as tears filled my eyes, and I fell to the floor, sobbing. I couldn't form words. When I tried, they caught in my throat and hung there painfully.

Her breathing was slowing now, so that every word she spoke sounded soft, like a sigh. "Oh, Kyle… Don't… crack up like that. I want to believe… you're stronger than that. I… care about you, Kyle. I want… you… to live. I only… wish…"

And then, in mid-sentence, she died. I knew it instinctively, even before I checked for breathing and checked her pulse. I felt more heartbroken than I had ever imagined I could feel. I wanted to go with her – to die with her. I wanted to go wherever she went.

Go wherever she went…

There *was* something I could do. I frantically grabbed at the hilt of my knife and slid it out of its sheath. I dropped it in my nervous hurry but quickly picked it back up again. Then, without even pausing to think, I made a tiny cut in the skin above my navel… and pulled out the transceiver device. Then I pushed it into the wound on Sofia's chest and pressed the button.

For a second, it seemed it would do nothing. Perhaps, I thought, I had been too late, and Sofia was truly lost forever. Then I heard a very faint sound, like the rushing of air… and without flash or fanfare, Sofia's body disappeared, like it had simply ceased to exist. Her empty clothes sank slowly down into a pile on the floor, like something I'd once seen in a movie.

So, that was it. I had sacrificed my ability to return to my home in Utopia – my ability to come back from the dead – for a hope: a faint glimmer of hope that perhaps Sofia could be saved. It was enough to keep me going – to make me rise back to my feet. But now I knew for certain that I was stuck here. There would be no going back, probably not for a long time. And I could die. If I were shot here again and wounded mortally, I would die.

I thought about death then, as I had seldom done before, wondering what lay beyond life. But I had no answers. All I knew was that my Utopian immortality was gone. With determination that surprised even myself, I hefted my gun with one hand, keeping pressure on the tiny cut on my stomach with the other. No need to bandage it – it wouldn't bleed for long. I knew now what I had to do: I had to find Matthew Noble, and save him if I could… and stop Frank Billings.

I wandered the halls of the dead and dying, searching each room methodically for sign of the USOW scientist. I didn't find Noble, but I did find another one. He was in a round room with dark walls, darker than any of the other walls in the building. Tools hung on racks all around the room, and a research computer, powerless and broken, lay on the floor… along with a wounded USOW researcher, his white coat burned on the side.

He heard me enter the room and looked up. "You… are one of the Eagles?"

"I am," I said.

"Then… take the weapon. I'll open the way. There's no way I could use it, but you can. You can follow that monster and kill him."

"What weapon?" I asked. I didn't feel like talking much.

He looked around. "This place was a research room. I stayed in here to guard it… and the secret weapon we'd been working on. Now I'll open the door for you."

With that, he reached up and pressed a button on the wall that he was leaning against. I heard a sound behind me and turned to see a section of the dark metal wall recede about an inch and then slide away to one side. I turned back to the scientist, and he nodded to the hidden door.

"Go in there and take what you see. If it's still working, you'll know how to use it."

Before entering the door, I asked, "Where is Doctor Noble?"

"I don't know if he made it out… but if he did, he'll be at our secret research base in the old sports stadium." Seeing my expression, the scientist continued, "You may not know where that is… It's been a long time since anyone in the Pit played any games there… Wait, I'll find a map of the city… I know there was one here earlier."

While the scientist rummaged around in a pile of papers on the floor, I took a peek inside the secret door he had opened. It led to a small room with a table in the middle, on which lay one of the strangest-looking weapons I had ever seen. It was obviously a gun, but it was made out of a shining, silvery metal and had blue lights glowing all along the sides. A faint green glow came from what looked to be the gun's ammunition magazine. It looked almost Utopian, but still slightly too primitive and utilitarian.

"What… is it?" I asked.

The scientist stood up, slowly and painfully, and handed me the map as he answered, "It's a particle projector cannon – PPC, which… But that doesn't matter. It's a gun. Works like all the ones you're familiar with. But this particular gun is very powerful. Make sure you know what you're shooting at."

I nodded, picked up the gun, and slung it over my shoulder, securing the strap as comfortably as I could. "It's heavy. Is it loaded?"

"The charge will be expended after about a hundred shots, give or take a few. You have plenty to work with. But here: take these glasses. They'll protect you from the flash."

"All right," I said, slipping on the silvery eyewear. "I'll make good use of it."

The scientist nodded, with a serious expression. "I'm sure you will. Make those bastards pay."

I was surprised: he actually seemed confident in my abilities, not treating me like a greenhorn at all. I glanced at my reflection in a reflective metal cabinet nearby. It was like looking at a stranger. Clad in my torn leather jacket and battle-scarred armor, carrying a small arsenal of different weapons, with my eyes hidden behind the reflective visor... I really looked like a warrior of the wastelands of G4M3. I wonder what Frank Billings would think when he saw me coming... right before I killed him and took his transceiver, in order to return to Sofia. That was my mission now – my only mission.

I nodded to the scientist. "I trust you can find your own way out of here?"

"Oh, don't worry about me. I'll be fine. I'm not going with you, that's for sure."

"All right then... Thanks for your help."

"Good luck," he said. "You're definitely going to need it, considering who you're up against."

I made my way back out to my motorcycle. Thankfully, it was still where I'd left it. I fired it up and took off across the desert. The gloomy and foreboding sight of Saltpit City loomed in the distance, its bleak and abandoned black towers jabbing like teeth into the grey-black sky. The bolts of yellow lightning streaking down from the clouds to strike the pinnacles of the tallest spires were truly a sight to behold.

Once I reached the outer limits of the city, I stopped my bike and pulled out the map the scientist had given me. It was difficult to tell where I was, since there were no longer any signs marking the names of the streets in this desolate ghost town, but the scientist had denoted a few prominent landmarks. I rode slowly through the streets, following the map's prescribed route, ignoring the stares of the vagabonds I passed. One man tried to rush me, but I fired a warning shot with my pistol, and he backed away.

Finally, I came upon my destination. It rose before me, dark and imposing. The outer rim of the giant sports stadium was crumbling in disrepair, now as much a ruin of the past as the Colosseum of ancient Rome.

I stopped my bike at the door and dismounted, taking the keys with me. I hefted my bulky prototype weapon and readied it, using the strap across my shoulder to hold the awkward thing steady.

The weapon emitted a soft blue glow and a faint hum as my finger slipped behind the trigger guard.

As I approached the stadium, I heard gunshots ring out from inside. I hurried through the halls, following the sounds of battle, which were growing stronger and stronger. Finally, I reached a pair of large doors leading out to the main arena. They had been blasted off their hinges.

Streaks of light blinked across what had once, perhaps, been a sports field of some kind – now just some hard dirt. Flashes of yellow and blue-white gunshots lit the night, mingling with the lightning above, blasting apart the stadium seats and railings like a fireworks show.

I looked up and saw Frank's forces moving about in the grandstands, clad in suits of metallic bluish armor, like the armor plating of the robotic patrolmen. There were USOW and Eagles defenders in the opposite stands, answering the energy blasts with hot lead. But the defenders were losing. This was clear from the bodies that littered the seats and the playing field alike – none of which were Frank's men.

In that moment, I felt a righteous anger the like of which I had never experienced before in the almost emotionless world of Utopia. The rage overwhelmed any thoughts of caution – any thoughts at all, in fact. With a cry of fury, I raised my gun, aimed for the first soldier of Frank's group that showed himself, and pulled the trigger…

A bright, violet-blue flash seemed to illuminate the entire arena like a lightning bolt. The kick of the gun nearly threw me off balance, and I didn't even get to see the streak of angry blue energy as it spanned the distance between myself and the target. When I looked, all I saw were the charred remains of the man I had shot.

He was dead. Not just temporarily dead, but permanently. Because the gun had blown a blackened hole right through his stomach – blasting right through his armor and then obliterating the part of his body containing his transceiver. There was no way this man would be returning to Utopia.

I had a brief second of hesitation then. I had no desire to kill my fellow Utopians, who were completely ignorant of the fact that all of this was real. To them, this was just a game. Yet my anger at seeing all of the dead Eagles quickly overrode my hesitation.

But I didn't have time to fire again before Frank's forces returned fire, sending me running for cover. I felt one laser graze my shoulder and another my leg as I slid behind some kind of huge metal device sitting on the dusty stadium field.

Fortunately, my killing of the Utopian had rallied the defenders. I heard at least a dozen rifles sound off behind me: covering fire from the Eagles and USOW soldiers. I was their only hope, I realized.

With that thought, I rose up to my feet and took aim once again, even as blue-white enemy lasers cut through the air nearby. It was a frightening thing, risking my life like that. Before, I had always been assured of my survival because of my transceiver. Now I felt vulnerable. But I wasn't going to let that stop me.

After gunning down another of Frank's boys, I ran and climbed up into the stadium seating, quickly dropping back out of sight as lasers sizzled overhead. Then I walked between the seats, crouched low and out of sight, slowly making my way around to where Frank and his men were positioned.

I stood up and fired again. The flash of the gun was blindingly intense, even with the goggles the scientist had given me shielding my eyes. I hoped that my being wet from the rain would not cause the electrical-looking energy bolts to shock me.

After two more of the Utopians fell before my onslaught, they retreated, darting into the doors that led under the stadium. As soon as they were gone, the remaining Eagles and USOW troops slid out of their hiding places to come greet me. One of them was Don, towering above the others.

"Where's Sofia?" was the first thing he asked.

"Gone," I replied. "If you want to help kill these assholes, follow me!"

"No, you follow me," Don said, waving me back. "They'll be headed for the scientists. We gotta protect 'em!"

I nodded. Don led us back between the bleachers, splashing through rain puddles. A few laser beams lit the air above our heads, but they missed their targets. I followed the Eagles down the staircase, through a locked door, across a hallway, and into a room full of benches and lockers.

There was the bald USOW scientist, Sergei, shuffling around and scrounging through the items in the lockers. And there was Dr. Matthew Noble, carefully piecing together a strange machine on an operating table. He looked up at me and lifted his spectacles.

"You're back?" he said.

"I'm here to help you," I replied.

"Not to murder us?" Sergei put in, his voice full of hate. "Are you sure?"

"I'm willing to forgive you," said Dr. Noble, "for what happened before, if you just hand me your transceiver."

I shrugged, resting the barrel of my enormous weapon on the floor. "Sorry, Doc. Transceiver's gone. I found Sofia, dying... so I gave it to her and sent her to Utopia for healing."

"Oh, you stupid child..." I heard Sergei mutter.

I felt Don put a heavy hand on my shoulder. "Thank you."

I nodded to him. "I did what I could... I just hope it worked."

Dr. Noble sighed. "I... understand. But how can you help us with no transceiver?"

"I know where we can get one. Those soldiers outside are from my world – from Utopia. A man named Frank Billings, who runs the G4M3 program, led them here to kill you. If we can take one alive..."

"Take one alive?" Sergei shook his head. "We'll be lucky to even survive their next attack."

Right on queue, a bolt of white-hot energy cut through the door, blasting a blackened hole in the far wall. The Eagles immediately ducked for cover, while the USOW soldiers ran to herd the scientists to safety. Dr. Noble ran to throw a cover over the strange device lying on an operating table.

"Everyone, get down!" I cried.

Once the path was clear of my allies, at least those alive, I leveled my PPC gun and opened fire. The flashes of the powerful weapon lit the corridor from one end to the other, and lightning sizzled and crackled through the air until I could feel my scalp prickling. Frank's soldiers screamed for mercy, but I just kept firing, once, twice, three times. I was in a mad rage now, angered by the unfair advantage that Frank's group held over the Eagles and the USOW soldiers.

Finally, I remembered that we had to take at least one soldier alive. So, I took my finger out of the trigger guard, and the blue glow of my weapon gradually faded away. Blue smoke rose from cooling vents on the sides, hissing angrily.

Don cleared his throat behind me. "Nice job."

I didn't respond. I was checking the corpses of my fallen enemies, hoping I hadn't killed them all in those few bursts of fire. The bodies were charred and contorted, their faces stuck in expressions of surprise and pain. I could not look at them for long. But there was sure proof that I hadn't slain them all: Frank was nowhere to be seen. I wondered if he had even actually come... or if he had left.

But wondering would not help in this situation, so I swallowed my doubts and sprinted off down the hall, completely forgetting about my fellow soldiers. I heard footsteps echoing through the corridor ahead of me. When I turned another corner, I saw someone's heels retreating through a doorway. I followed quickly, moving as silently as I could, for fear that my target would panic and activate his transceiver. I had to get this one alive.

The door led to a narrow passage containing nothing but a ladder. I could see the man above me, retreating upwards until he disappeared out of the top. I clambered up after him, well aware that he could hear the racket I was making in my haste. As I reached the top, I slowed down, moving more silently. Cautiously, I poked my head out of the top of the passage and peered outside.

There was my target, standing on the very edge of the outer rim of the stadium, his form silhouetted against the red and black sky. Then, when a bolt of lightning lit the area and the crack of thunder resounded in the deep sports stadium… I saw my target's face. It was Frank Billings himself, wet and miserable, but wearing battle armor and loading an advanced laser rifle. As I watched, he dropped down onto one knee and aimed at the stadium below.

I climbed up and out of the ladder shaft and turned to see what he was aiming at. What I saw was Dr. Matthew Noble. He and the remaining scientists and soldiers were rolling out the bed on which his machine rested. He was issuing orders as to how it should be placed, and he seemed to want it in the very center of the muddy playing field. Why he was doing all this, in the middle of a battle and a storm, I didn't know. But I was not about to let Frank Billings stop him.

"Frank!" I cried out, my voice echoing in the ring below.

Frank started and turned to look at me, with wide eyes full of fright. By then I was rushing at him. He whipped his rifle around to fire, but he was too slow. Before he could shoot, I had kicked the rifle out of his hands and sent it flying into the stadium below. I could see that I had an audience now. Dr. Noble and the others were looking up at us.

"Kyle…" Frank hissed, breathing hard. "Wait."

I kicked him in the stomach, sending him rolling backwards on the narrow edge of the outer stadium wall. He got up to his feet with surprising speed, however, and reached for a pistol on his side. I lunged forward and grabbed his hand, forcing the pistol barrel upwards. He fired several times, his shots flying off into the clouds overhead, and then I managed to wrench the weapon from his grasp and toss it too over the edge into the abyss.

"It's all over now, Frank," I said menacingly.

"Kyle, now *really*… are *you* going to kill *me*?" he asked mockingly, reaching for his belt.

No, not his belt, I realized: he was reaching for his transceiver. He was trying to go home. I grabbed his hands and jerked them away from his body. He snapped his knee forward, right into my gut. I reeled and released my hold on him. Then, with surprising quickness for a man his age, he whipped out a long combat knife.

I managed to take a step back just in time, though the blade flashed right past my face. I then drew my own knife and closed in. Frank anticipated this, however, and he still had a few tricks up his sleeve. He raised his knife and pressed a button on the hilt. A dart-like projectile whizzed past my ear. Frank cursed at his miss, turning to retreat.

I chased after him, running precariously along the wet and slippery, narrow surface. I was taller, younger, and faster than Frank though, and soon caught up with him. Once I was close enough, I made a desperate leap and grabbed Frank's pants. He stumbled and fell. With a cry, he slipped over the edge. I held on tight to his pants, and looked down to see him dangling by my grip. But he had fallen off on the side that faced inwards, over the stadium seating, so the fall was not very great. He struggled, trying to free himself from my grasp. He was heavy in all that combat armor, so I was forced to let go. I heard him give a little cry and fall to the floor below with a thud.

"Hah!" he laughed, limping off away from me.

I looked down at him, but I was hesitant to make the jump after him. "Frank! I don't want to have to kill you, Frank!"

Frank gave a laugh that sounded almost insane. He was fumbling with the bottom of his shirt now. I could see it clearly because he was standing with his side facing me. I needed Frank alive, but I could not let him go. He had killed Sofia once, and, if he found her in the G4M3 facility in Utopia, he would probably not hesitate to kill her again. I could not let that happen; I would kill him first!

So, I hefted my glowing PPC lightning-gun and leveled it at Frank's head. He saw me, and his eyes went wide. I knew that in a moment, he would be reaching down for his transceiver button. I saw him from the side, with his arms both clearly visible... Acting on a sudden thought, I turned my barrel down just a bit and fired.

The flash of light lit the arena in an alien blue glow, acting in tandem with the loudest, deepest roll of thunder I had yet heard...

and Frank Billings's scream of pain. I stood up and looked down upon my handiwork. There was Frank, falling to his knees and screaming, with both of his hands blown off at the wrists, leaving only charred and smoking stubs behind.

He was on the ground now, writhing in agony. I wondered if the shot had electrocuted him to death, and if it had shorted out his transceiver. I was not sure exactly how the gun worked, and I had taken a great risk by using it in such a way, but to my surprise, my plan seemed to have succeeded. Frank was stuck in G4M3 now, with no way to go back.

"That was for Sofia!" I exclaimed, jumping down to join him.

"No! No, you can't k-kill me, Kyle!" he wailed, ceasing his screaming, his arms apparently numb from the burns. His breath came in quick, ragged gasps.

"No!" I exclaimed, grabbing him by the collar of his shirt and hoisting him up to his feet. "I'm not going to kill you, you scheming, murdering liar! That would be too good for you!"

"Kyle…" he wheezed, "I beg you…"

"Oh, shut up, Frank Billings!" I snarled. "Don't beg anything of me! Get out into the field!"

I jabbed the end of my gun at Frank, but he didn't move. So, I gritted my teeth and pointed the barrel at his leg. He gave a cry and stumbled back. I turned him forcibly around and led him off into the field of mud where Dr. Noble was waiting for me. I tossed Frank down at the doctor's very feet. He looked at me and nodded grimly.

"Doctor Matthew Noble," I said, "meet Frank Billings."

"Thank you, Kyle," the scientist said.

Frank looked up and whimpered, "Don't… don't do it! You can't take my transceiver! I… I'll be stuck here! I'll be stuck here like this, with my… my arms blown off!"

"It must be done," was all that Matthew Noble said.

"How did you know where they were, Frank?" I demanded, jerking him to his feet once again. "How did you know where to look for Dr. Noble?"

"You think I didn't keep tabs on you?" Frank wheezed, still breathing hard. "Your transceiver was acting as a tracking device... and I know more about what goes on in G4M3 than you think."

"It doesn't matter anyway," Dr. Noble said. "Not anymore..."

Frank, suddenly terrified again, shot a frantic look at the back of Dr. Noble's head, and then he turned back to me. "Kyle, I am telling you: We have to stop this madman! I've heard his crazy plan! He's going to declare war on Utopia!"

"Shut up, Frank!" I snapped. "All you've ever told me is one lie right after the other, all fashioned for your own gain and for the Order! Why should I believe anything you say?"

"Because if you don't, you'll regret it for the rest of your life... if you live long enough!"

"Do silence your howling, Mr. Billings," Matthew Noble said in his usual calm, soft voice as he inspected his device and hooked in a wire that was running along the ground. Then he picked up a knife that was lying on the table next to his machine.

Frank gasped. "If you shove that scalpel into me, you'll be shoving a sword into the throat of every being in Utopia! You'll be destroying your own paradise!"

Dr. Noble turned and shot a look of utter contempt at Frank. "If the machine doesn't work... If the beings I am trying to transport die in the process, by accident... then at least they'll be going to a better place than this."

Frank Billings laughed, a wheezing, almost mad laugh, and launched into a rapid speech. "Listen to him blather, Kyle! He's insane! He thinks if he kills us all, it's just fine!"

Dr. Noble shook his head. "I do what I do to save my world, because I *care* about its people!"

"Then what about mine?" Frank shouted. "People live in my world too! If you bring your soldiers to Utopia, you will ruin what mankind has striven toward for millions of years!"

Dr. Noble looked at me, but then turned away. "I feel sorry for you, Mr. Billings."

Frank looked both angry and terrified, and even somewhat pitiable, lying on his knees in the rain, with his arms reduced to charred stubs, wailing. "Oh, save me your lofty pity! If you're so benevolent then why are you about to destroy my world with the flick of a switch?! Why are you letting me lie here, injured, cold, and wet..."

"I am not destroying *any* worlds!" Dr. Noble roared, louder than I had ever heard him. "I am *saving* them! *Both* of them!"

"Don't let him pull that switch, Kyle!" Frank screamed, looking frantically at me.

"Enough of this! Restrain him!" Dr. Noble commanded.

The nearby soldiers advanced and grabbed Frank's shoulders. He struggled and spat in their faces, cursing all the while, but they ignored him. And Matthew Noble advanced, scalpel in hand.

And then Frank Billings looked at me, and his face turned suddenly calm. He closed his eyes and sighed. He looked terrible, and I suddenly felt sorry for him, in a way. For a moment, I stood on the brink of hesitation. The terrible expression plastered on the face of the old man that I had once thought of as a father, combined with something frighteningly sincere in his tone of voice, made my confidence waver.

But then I remembered Sofia's broken body and the look on her face as she had died, and I closed my eyes. I heard Frank Billings hiss in pain. Then, when I opened my eyes, I saw him fall in the mud as the two soldiers released him. And Dr. Noble turned around, holding Frank's bloody transceiver. He dashed over to his machine, thrust the device into a compartment, and slammed the door shut.

"There... that should keep it from self-destructing," he muttered. "Now, begin gathering the soldiers and the refugees. We're moving."

F O U R T E E N
WAR OF THE WORLDS

Frank Billings had to watch as Dr. Noble went about preparing for what he called the Exodus. The USOW, the United States of the World, was no small organization. They had claim over less and less land as the wars dragged on, but their numbers were many. As word spread from Dr. Noble, they began to gather in the stadium. The Eagles were fewer in number, but they too gathered for the Exodus.

Under the oppressive sky of G4M3, I saw hope on the faces of its people. As they met in the stadium, former enemies shook hands and spoke with each other like good friends. A row of the USOW's old but well-constructed tanks drove in and lined up on the playing field, and behind them came a row of dilapidated yet effective Eagles trucks. I wondered if all this firepower was really necessary, but then, I had no idea what kind of secret weapons the Order might have in store.

I sat for hours, watching the vehicles roll in, followed by wave after wave of infantry, until I grew tired of waiting. When I noticed the influx of refugees beginning to dwindle, I grew restless. I walked back to the center of the field and found Dr. Noble seated there in front of his device, now with two other desks beside him containing radar screens and communication equipment. He had, I noticed, donned a suit of battle armor under his white lab coat. He sat with one hand under his chin, inspecting the computers in front of him.

"Dr. Noble," I said, "is it time yet? How long must we wait here?"

The Doctor looked up and turned around. He was his calm and peaceful self again, but there was something too cool about his manner now. It bothered me.

"Kyle," he said, looking at me over his glasses, "I wanted to ask you something. What kind of defenses do you have in Utopia? Tell me about the security forces you spoke of earlier."

I nodded. "Well, there are robots that patrol the streets, like I said. They have guns that can be used by humans, just like the ones Frank's goons were armed with. It looks like the same armor too. But the patrolmen are the only threats I know of. Though, you should probably shoot every robot you see. Even the little ones seem to have hidden guns..."

Dr. Noble nodded, looking pensive. "I wish I had time to make armor like this for our own soldiers. It seems to have some kind of mesh on the back that protects the wearer from energy blasts. But the few intact suits we've gathered will just have to be enough."

I looked him in the eyes, gazing through his glasses, as I asked, "You sound like you're going to war, Dr. Noble. Do you really want this to be a war?"

"Mr. Roswell, all my life, I have seen nothing but war. I have no desire to fight another one... but if there is a security force, we will deal with it. And if it is robotic, all the better. We will not be killing anyone."

I sighed. "I don't know if it'll be that easy. Utopia probably has other weapons I'm not even aware of..."

"We'll have to deal with these problems as they arise. I'll be as prepared as I can. The gathering is almost done, Kyle. Then we can begin the Exodus."

I shook my head. "Sofia might not have that long..."

"I hope we find Sofia; I really do. But if she were here, Kyle, don't you think she would lay her life down to achieve what we are doing now – to save her people?"

"How would you know?" I muttered.

"Hmm? What? I couldn't hear that."

I didn't reply. I just walked away.

===

At some point, I was so tired that I accidentally fell asleep there in the stadium. When I awoke, at first I thought I was back in my house in Utopia, and everything I have thus far written about had just been a long nightmare. But the feeling passed quickly, and reality dawned on me all too soon. I sat up, rubbed my eyes, and walked back out into the playing field.

What I saw amazed me. The field was packed with vehicles now, mostly tanks, but also some trucks, armored cars, and even motorcycles. The stadium benches were full of people – not a single seat empty. There must be hundreds of thousands of them, I thought. Most were fidgeting in their seats in anticipation, as if they were waiting for a game to start. How ironic, I thought. It was like Dr. Noble had invented his own version of G4M3, working in the opposite direction.

As I walked between the vehicles, I saw members of the different, previously warring factions talking with one another and making plans. As I passed them, they shouted greetings to me. I remember them pointing to me and talking about my lightning gun, whispering my name.

Suddenly, I was famous. Yet another irony came to mind: All this time, I had wanted to be the hero of Utopia, and now here I was: the hero of G4M3. After walking a good distance, I finally ran into Dr. Noble. He was still seated in the middle of the stadium, at his computer, now surrounded by guards clad in Utopian armor stolen from Frank's squad.

"Dr. Noble," I said once again.

The good Doctor did not even turn to look at me this time. "You're just in time, Kyle. We're about to bring him back. Wait."

"Bring who back?" I asked.

Sergei Ivanovich, who was standing behind Dr. Noble, explained, "We sent in a scout, to see if the landing zone was clear or not. He should be back soon. If he isn't…"

"Here he comes now," Dr. Noble interrupted.

There was a flash of light, and a gust of wind blew over all of us as the soldier re-entered our dimension. This was the first time I had ever seen someone else coming in from the other side. It was Don, also now wearing Utopian armor.

"It's just like you thought it would be, Doc," Don said. "There's row after row of buildings. Don't know why you didn't trust the camera; the picture was accurate. Anyway, there's no stadium there. Guess that means if you brought us all through like you said, those in the stands would fall on their ass from a mighty tall height."

Dr. Noble nodded. "That's just what I was thinking. I haven't learned how to pinpoint exact locations yet. I was actually afraid the elevation level might be different on the other side. We had that happen one time... We teleported a camera when it was lying on the ground, and it ended up merging with solid rock on the other side. The camera came back as dust."

I said, "But doesn't that mean some of our people could... merge with the buildings?"

"That'd be an ugly sight..." Don muttered.

"I wondered about that myself, Kyle," Dr. Noble replied. "We... interrogated Mr. Billings about it, but he passed out. We tried some convincing, you see... but I actually think he was faking it somehow. His body should have been able to stand that much voltage easily."

My eyes widened. "You... tortured him?"

Dr. Noble sighed, and I noticed his hands shaking. "They assured me it was nothing much... Just a little sting, they said."

"And you didn't learn anything?"

"Not much. He wouldn't say much. But I think I've formed a plan on my own," the Doctor stood up and gestured around him. "We can teleport this entire structure through, and then simultaneously teleport whatever is on the other side back here."

I stared at him incredulously. "You can do that? Isn't that a bit much?"

"It's the only way to transport this many people, Kyle. That's where you come in. You and a few others will go to the other side, to

Utopia, and plant these devices in the right places. I'll set it all up for you. Try to be exact. Here; take this."

The Doctor handed me a palm computer. It had a large, black screen with a grid of green lines on it. Looking more closely, I saw that it was a map of the streets of Utopia. There were red dots flashing at certain points, forming a sort of elongated oval shape.

"Once you've placed all the twenty markers, activate the transceiver in the computer to come back here. To activate it, just press right here. It should bring you all back..."

His voice sounded tired. Only now did I realize how worn-out he looked. His eyelids were drooping, and he continually stopped to lift his glasses and rub his eyes.

"I won't fail you," I said, "but it could take a while. Try to get some rest, Doctor."

"I will, Kyle. Scott and Don will go with you."

"Are you sure we shouldn't bring more?"

"I don't think we should send too big a group. Besides, we only have one transceiver. And I don't even know for sure if it will work at all with a group this size... but that's a risk we have to take. I can't spend any longer working on it, or we'll run out of time."

"But, Doctor... isn't this all kind of pointless now? Look around you: there's peace between the USOW, the Eagles, the other gangs..."

"But not the rest of the world. And need I remind you this planet is dying? This is just the first stage of the Exodus. There will be more to come, as you will see."

I shook my head slowly. "I hope you're right about all this, Doctor..."

"We're ready, Doc," Don said, with determination.

I turned and saw Don, Scott, and a USOW soldier standing behind me. Scott had a sniper rifle, while the other two were armed with Utopian patrolman cannons, and all wore Utopian armor – the USOW soldier was only recognizable as such by emblem on his collar.

I had never thought about it before, but USOW armor looked a lot like Utopian patrolman armor anyway...

The USOW soldier spoke up: "I'm going too, sir. My commander told me I had to go to represent the United States of the World. You can call me Ian."

Don nodded. "Who's in charge here, Dr. Noble? Surely I'm still in command of the group?"

"No," Dr. Noble said, shaking his head.

"Not the USOW son of a..." Don muttered.

Ian shot him a hostile glare, but Dr. Noble shook his head again. "No; Kyle Roswell is in charge of the mission. He knows the lay of the land, he's proven that he can fight, and he has the device that will tell you where to plant the beacons and to bring you all back. You will follow his orders. The computer is programmed to transport all of you, your clothing, and your weapons."

I swallowed. "Okay, when do we go?"

"Now, if you're ready."

I nodded, fortifying my determination. "I am."

I looked back at the others, and they nodded. Without further delay, Dr. Noble pressed a button on the keyboard in front of him. An orb atop a rod of metal that was mounted on the back of the computer began to glow brightly. Then came the same feeling of air blowing against my skin from all sides. I wondered how many more times I would get to feel this sensation...

I had no idea at the time, but the answer was only once.

===

We all reappeared on the other side at precisely the same moment. I landed right on my feet this time, with my lightning gun – the PPC – at the ready. I was used to the transition by now, possibly more than anyone else alive. I immediately noticed a patrol robot, and was about to blast it just because I could, when I thought better about alerting it to my presence and ducked behind a building instead. Don, Scott, and Ian soon joined me.

Don waited for the patrolman to move on before asking, "So, where to… Sir?"

"The first beacon location is just ahead."

"How many are there?" Ian asked.

"Twenty. There are twenty beacons. Avoid contact with the patrolmen if possible."

"What the hell kind of a place is this…?" Scott was muttering, looking around as if dazed.

"Keep it together, soldier," Don reprimanded him. "Focus on the mission."

I too was having trouble concentrating on the task at hand; I was thinking about Sofia. I had given her my transceiver and sent her to Utopia. That meant she should be in the G4M3 facility here. For a moment, I considered telling the others about her. I knew Don and probably Scott would come with me to try to find her, but Ian was a different story. I knew he would want to complete his mission. I decided it would be best to keep them all in the dark.

"This way," I said.

Glancing at my map computer, I raced along the Utopian streets, the others following close behind. I was actually headed toward the G4M3 facility. I had no idea where it was, since all of Utopia looked the same, but the map on the computer had a building marked as 'tall', so I thought I would try that first. I knew well that the G4M3 facility was the tallest building in this residential sector. It wasn't long before I saw it on the horizon. I stopped for a moment to look at it, and I could sense my companions growing suspicious.

I kept moving. It seemed to me that I could hear a strange buzzing in the air – a very high-pitched sound that could barely be registered. I looked up at the unnatural, yellowish sky of Utopia, but I saw nothing. The dreary clouds of smog floated lazily overhead, and the white sun shone past them like a dim and dying lamp. It was only when I reached the door of the G4M3 facility that we met resistance. Two security bots were waiting there in front of the door. Scott shot one with his sniper rifle, right through the chest, and it instantly exploded. The second one shot Ian, but the blast didn't penetrate his armor. He and the robot exchanged a few shots before I blew it apart with the PPC.

"This doesn't feel right..." Ian said uneasily. "Where are you leading us, Roswell?"

"I'm doing exactly what the Doctor ordered," I replied calmly. "I'm saving everyone I can."

With that, I blasted open the door to the G4M3 building. Stepping inside over the wreckage, I found a new robot sitting behind Frank's front desk. It turned to regard me, but showed no sign of hostility. I was on the ready, however. The last time had taught me a lesson about these altogether innocent-looking bots.

"Oh, back so soon?" it squeaked. "But where is Master Billings?"

"He hasn't come back yet," I said.

"And he's not going to," laughed Scott.

The android didn't reply, but its eyes began to glow.

"Shoot it!" I shouted.

Scott leveled his rifle and fired. The android's head was blown clean off, and it flew back into a far corner of the office.

"You idiot!" Ian shouted at Scott.

Scott raised his hands. "It's not my fault!"

"Let's move," I said, running for the elevator.

Once we were all in the lift, I pressed the button for the next floor. The others wondered at my impatience; I stood directly in front of the door as we rose upward, and I darted out once the doors slid open. My men followed more cautiously. Hurriedly checking room after room, I found all of the doors closed.

"Sofia!" I called out, banging on the nearest door.

"I'm in here!" came a muffled voice.

I ran to the door and knocked. "Here?"

Don ran up behind me. "What? Sofia?"

I fumbled about, trying to figure out a way to open the door. The control panel wouldn't respond to anything I tried.

"Sofia, can you stand away from the door, off to one side?" I asked. "I'm going to blast through."

"Okay," she said.

"Close your eyes!"

I waited for a moment, and then lifted the PPC, resting it against my shoulder. Bracing myself, I pulled the trigger. The door was blown away, smashing into the far side of the room, blackened and burnt, with a gaping hole in the center of it. I started to rush inside, then Sofia stepped out in front of me.

She was a spectacular sight. It was actually the first time I had seen her *clean*. The workers here had tended to her wounds and fixed her up fabulously. Her hair was long and flowing, her face bright and healthy. She looked more feminine than she ever had before, in the simple white shirt and pants she was wearing.

"Kyle..." she said. "What's going on?"

I lowered my gun and stepped closer. "Are you all right, Sofia? I thought you were..."

"So did I," she interrupted, looking into my eyes. "I always knew it was going to happen. But I'm glad it didn't."

"Sofia..." I said, "I came back to rescue you, but we also have a mission to complete. We still have to place these markers before Utopian security forces come down on our heads..."

"Commander?" Don said behind me. "You might want this."

He pulled the pistol out of his holster and flipped it over in his hand, handing it to Sofia. She took it and looked it over. Then she reached for my gun and jerked it out of its holster.

Sofia twirled the two pistols around on her fingers, smiling. "Let's go."

"Take this ammo belt," Don said, taking off his own and handing it to her. "And... Ian, give her your armor!"

"Oh, cut it out," Ian said. "Give her *your* armor, Eagle."

"Just forget it; I'll be fine," Sofia said.

"We don't have time anyway," Scott interrupted. "Do you hear that?"

We all stopped to listen. A strange muffled buzzing sound was coming from outside. The building had no windows, so we couldn't see what it was, but it grew louder as we rode down the elevator. We all checked our weapons and stood at the ready for whatever might come when the doors slid aside. The elevator stopped suddenly, giving a beep, and the portal opened wide. Floating in the hallway were two flying robots with swiveling guns, inspecting the scrap heap that had been Frank's greeting bot.

We blasted them. The drones were blasted apart instantly, but more came buzzing into the room, their wing-engines swiveling. They opened fire, but so did we. We killed drone after drone, their broken parts littering the hallway, but each time, more came to replace those that had fallen. After we had destroyed about two dozen of the little bots, we cautiously approached the exit. I peered out, looking up and down the street. All of the lights were off, all of the windows on the houses had tinted to an opaque color of the same shade as the walls, and a voice blared out throughout the city. It was a calm female voice saying: "All citizens, remain in your homes. This disturbance will be taken care of shortly. For your own safety and protection, the Order asks that all citizens please remain in their homes…"

As the others followed me into the street, I heard a deep humming sound.

"More of them," I said. "Run!"

A swarm of drones swooped down upon us like vultures, raining fire. We skipped and dodged, firing back, sending more and more of them falling out of the air. Scott got hit in the leg, but he managed to limp along behind us. We all tried to protect both him and Sofia as we headed to the first marker location. Patrolmen came from all sides now, filing out of the alleys between the buildings and firing flashing blades of white energy through the air.

Suddenly, I realized that I was at the first marker location. I reached into the pouch Dr. Noble had given me and pulled out one of the small metal cylinders. Pressing the button on the side of it caused four feet to pop out. I dropped it on the ground feet first. Tiny claws grasped the earth, and the feet sucked in until the device was secure. A light on top began to blink.

"That's one down!" I yelled. "Only nineteen left to go!"

My comrades were fighting off the security bots as well as they could, using what they could find, usually the square trash bins, for cover. I noticed something headed down the street: one of the Utopia trams. The driver bot, as usual, was paying no attention to the world around it. It drove right past the flying lasers, even as they blew open the windows of the small bus.

"Get in the bus!" I shouted. "Everyone get in!"

They comprehended my orders immediately, and we all dashed for the vehicle. Since it was headed in my direction, I was the first to reach the door. I ran for the opening, but the little pilot bot's head swiveled in my direction, and the door slammed shut in my face. Apparently, this one was paying more attention than the last one had been. I leveled my PPC and blew the door away, along with the robot behind it. Sofia climbed in right behind me, followed by Don.

"Flyboys at twelve o'clock!" Ian called out, as he ran to catch up with the moving tram.

I leaned out to look. A swarm of drones was headed our way. Turning back to check on Ian and Scott, I saw that things seemed hopeless. Scott was lagging way behind.

"Can we slow this thing down?" I asked.

Sofia looked around the driver's seat. "It's got no controls! The robots must be plugged in directly. Wait a minute; I recognize this circuitry! Maybe I can hotwire it…"

"Hurry up!" I shouted.

The buzzing was growing louder now, as the flock of metal killers drew nearer. A shower of blasts peppered the pavement outside. Drawing my head back in immediately, I heard the lasers pound down upon the roof of the car like a deadly rain. Small orange spots glowed hot on the ceiling above us, but none of the blasts got through. We also heard a scream come from behind us, but it was quickly drowned out by the buzzing as the drones passed by overhead.

I stuck my head out of the window again and scanned the streets. Scott lay in the road, dragging himself toward the sidewalk, his body covered in burn marks. Ian was nowhere to be seen, but the metallic buzzards were turning in a circle above their prey, flocking around for another pass. I was not about to let them come at us again. Hefting my lightning gun, I pointed the barrel out the window and watched it begin to charge. The kick of the weapon threw me back as the thunderclap of the blast split the air. Most of the drones fell to the ground, fried, and the others flew off into the yellow sky.

"Ian?" I shouted outside, looking around.

Suddenly a pair of booted feet swung around off the top of the tram and landed on the edge of the window in front of me. I stepped back, allowing Ian to enter the vehicle. His armor was burnt in a few places, but mostly he had escaped unscathed.

"Scott's down," he said.

"I saw," I replied.

"Go get him," Don grunted. "We don't leave a man behind."

"We don't have time–"

"*Go get him!*" Sofia snapped. "I'll drive."

Ian shut his mouth and climbed back out. Don followed after him to help, as Sofia slid into the driver's seat and grabbed the control stick, slowing the vehicle down and then reversing it. The half-destroyed robot pilot lay thrown to the floor, and she was seated in its place.

"I thought there were no controls," I said.

"I thought so too," Sofia replied, "but once Don knocked the robot out of the seat, this control stick just popped right up."

"I see…"

That was the second fail-safe mechanism I'd seen in Utopia. The first had been the removable arm guns from the security robots, with their built-in triggers made for human hands. Perhaps there was a fail-safe mechanism for the entire Order itself, to shut down the whole program? I could only hope. I would have to tell Dr. Noble about it.

Sofia must have seen my pensive expression, for she put a reassuring hand on my shoulder. "Don't worry about Scott. We'll get him help – find a medical facility…"

The tram buckled as Don and Ian loaded Scott on board. I heard him groaning, but didn't turn to look. If he was alive, Utopian medicine could heal him. Once we finished the mission.

"Sofia," I said, "get this can moving as fast as it'll go. We have to keep setting up the markers. You drive by the spots on this computer, and I'll drop the marker out the door. Make it fast."

I looked out the window. It was strange to see a transport bus hovering off its tracks. Were the tracks just for show? Up ahead stood a statue of the Builder, staring emotionlessly down at us as we passed. It was so tall, stern, strong... and inhuman. But it *was* shaped like a human, if only vaguely. The Order had been constructed by humans. Perhaps, I thought, the Builder's hammer was not only for creation; maybe it worked both ways. Perhaps there was a fail-safe for the Order itself... a way to destroy it.

"We're at the second location," Don said, looking at my palm computer. "Drop it."

The vehicle slowed to a halt. I leaned over and placed the metal rod on the ground. The feet popped out, and the light began to blink. Checking my computer again, I now saw that two of the dots had turned green. The giant oval looked intimidating.

"Ahead full speed," I said, handing Sofia the computer. "Only eighteen more waypoints to go."

===

For a while, the security forces left us alone. We drove from waypoint to waypoint, stopping at each one for only a second to drop the marker out the door. It seemed like no time before we had over half of the lights green. We rounded another corner, stopped, and I dropped out the device. The sixteenth light winked online. I turned to give the order to step on it, but something caught my eye.

There were two vehicles heading up the street. They were huge, rounded metal things, the same blue-grey color as the hull of a Utopian security bot. They were low and wide, and each had white numbers painted on the front. As I watched, turrets with hidden cannons slowly rose out of the back of each one and rotated to face us.

Don had already spotted them, and he grabbed my arm. "Shoot 'em with that damn gun of yours!"

I raised the PPC and pointed it at the first tank. My sight ran along the hull until it reached the point where the turrets had emerged, which I hoped was a weak spot in their armor. I fired, and the bolt flew true. Arcs of bluish energy reached out and caressed the vehicle's hull from the point where the gun had hit it. These increased in number until flames erupted from the crevice. I started charging my gun for a second shot when the first vehicle exploded... and the second tank fired its main cannons.

A pinkish beam of energy erupted from the vehicle's cannon and struck the ground beneath our bus. The earth glowed brightly and exploded in a rain of molten asphalt. Our transport was thrown into the air, and I fell out of the door onto my face. Looking up quickly, I saw the bus twirling over and over, until it landed upside-down on the sidewalk. The metal seemed to make a screaming noise as it bent and contorted, and shattered glass covered the concrete like snow.

But my gun was recharged now, so I stood and fired a bolt at the second tank. This one missed its mark. The weak spot was a hard target to hit; I had gotten lucky the first time. The tank rolled – or hovered, I'm not sure which – forward, until it was almost on top of me. Then it rotated around, and a hatch on the back fell open. Two rows of folded-up security androids were inside, and, one by one, they unfolded and stood up. As they raised their gun arms, I rolled into the crater that the tank had created. The robots' lasers flew through the air overhead and all around me.

Then Sofia ran out from behind the crashed bus and lobbed two grenades in my direction. They flew over my head and landed on the other side of the crater, at the androids' feet. There was a resounding boom, and various metallic pieces of junk rained down around me. Sofia leapt into the pit with me just as the tank fired another blast where she had been standing. Another crater was blown into the street. Sofia grabbed a grenade from my own belt and activated it, pitching it over the edge. It rolled under the tank.

"Duck!" she yelled.

We both crouched down low as the second tank exploded. Once the smoke had cleared, we stood up and made a run for it, back toward the trolley. Ian was just crawling out, dragging Don by his arm. Don stood up, his face contorted in pain. Sofia moved to help him.

"Where's Scott?" she said.

"I don't know," Don replied. "I'll find him. The rest of you, go. There's only four more waypoints to go. You can make it."

There was no time to argue. Don turned back to the wreckage as Sofia, Ian, and I made our way down the street, running as fast as we could. But we planted the next marker without interruption and started toward the second one. Just then, I heard the now-familiar buzzing sound in the distance behind us. More flying drones.

"Not good," Ian said.

We were all beginning to tire, and the buzzing behind us grew louder as we went. I wanted to glance back and see how Don was faring, but I didn't dare. Sofia shouted that we had reached the second marker. I quickly fumbled with one of the devices in my pouch and dropped it on the ground. It lit up and activated.

"Two more to go!" I laughed excitedly.

But as I looked back at the others, I saw a dark cloud on the horizon. It was a much, much bigger swarm of drones than the last one. When they all fired, there was no way we could avoid that many blasts.

"RUN!" I screamed. "Faster!"

Around the next bend in the street, we saw another unfriendly sight: a row of security androids, spanning from one side of the road to another, marching in exact formation toward us, completely blocking our path. Still running, I turned to look behind. The cloud was growing nearer, throwing its shadow over the buildings it passed.

I heard Sofia's computer beep. I stopped and dropped the device I'd been holding. It planted its feet in firmly and lit up, online.

Ian came up beside me and fell over forwards, breathing heavily. I looked at his injuries – the burns from the drones; they were worse than I'd thought at first glance. Sofia looked at him and then me with a panic-stricken expression.

"Stay here," I said, with surprising calm, glancing at the computer to confirm the last location. "If I don't make it back, run back to Don and use the controller to get out of here!"

"No, we won't leave without you!" Sofia replied.

But it was too late. I was already off. I dropped my PPC and charged blindly ahead, unarmed, carrying only the pouch that contained the final signal device. When I estimated I was at the right spot, I fell to my knees and poured out the bag's contents. The instrument rolled out. I grasped at it. Looking up, I saw the army of security bots marching forward. Their feet stomping in unison sounded like the thunderstorms in G4M3, I thought. Suddenly, I wished I was back there. I fumbled with the marker device, clumsily, or so it seemed to me, until finally I was able to activate it. The thing rooted itself down, and its light flashed online. It blinked for a second and then turned a steady green. All of the markers were active.

"We did it!" I shouted. "We did–"

My jubilation was cut short as I found myself flying through the air. There was a bright white light all around me – so bright I couldn't see – and a wind so loud I couldn't hear. I was thrown headlong against the far wall, the breath knocked right out of my lungs. Then, the blindingly white world faded to black.

FIFTEEN
THE LAW OF THE CONCRETE JUNGLE

"Oh, Kyle… Kyle Roswell…" a familiar voice echoed tauntingly in my head. "Can you hear me?"

I was still in a half-dreaming state, and at first, I thought it was my father speaking. I coughed and whispered, "Father…?"

"You are dead, Mister Roswell…" the voice said, in a more sinister tone. "You are officially registered as dead, and your family has been informed. Is it a lie? No, no. You truly are dead… or at least, you will be… So, wake up, Mister Roswell… wake up and beg for mercy."

I opened my eyes. Of course, I already knew what I would see… and I was right. There was Frank Billings, in the flesh… mostly. I noticed his hair was even greyer than before, and the lines on his face seemed deeper. But there was a light in his eyes: a spark of some energy, some force driving him, and he seemed more active and alert than ever before.

In fact, he looked like he'd gone mad. As he stared wide-eyed at me, the muscles in his face twitched now and again, in spasms. He was wearing his dark grey suit, but the sleeves were rolled up, revealing his arms. His skin ended abruptly just below the elbows, giving way to cold metal. His lost hands had been replaced by twisted steel machines, their mechanical fingers twitching like greedy talons.

"How did you survive?" I asked. "How did you get here?"

"I came here with your 'good Doctor'," he replied, pacing back and forth. "I was trapped in that stadium when he brought it here. I never knew something that large could even be sent between worlds. It caused quite a reaction – destroyed a great portion of the city. But who cares about Utopia and its people, yes? Fortunately, Utopia retaliated. My robots attacked, rescued me… what was left of me…"

He reached out and put one metallic finger on my forehead. It felt cold – so cold it was almost painful. Then, slowly, it began to grow warm. There was a flash, a sharp crack, and a sharper pain in my head. The air hissed. Frank stepped away and laughed.

"Just a little sting…" he muttered. "Look at my hands, Kyle. Look what you did to me. They are cold. They feel nothing. They sense no pain or pleasure. Don't you feel bad about what you did? You should."

I knew that he was going to kill me, so I answered him directly. "Sounds like they fit you perfectly, Frank Billings."

He looked furious for a second, but then he laughed aloud, turning around and pacing back toward the wall. I struggled to get my bearings, looking around the room. We were standing on a raised platform in the middle of a huge room surrounded by many windows, overlooking the city of Utopia far below. There were three huge, towering computer terminals surrounding me, covered in screens and control panels. They emitted a deep hum that reverberated in the air, and the very atmosphere seemed to be glowing with their power. There were four security robots in the room, bigger than any I had ever seen, with metallic red armor instead of the usual bluish grey. They each had shields of energy on one arm and giant guns on the other.

I tried to move, but my arms and legs were bound to a metallic bed that was turned upright. I couldn't budge them, or even turn my head to look at them. I knew the bed was metal though, and I was almost naked, because I could feel the cold steel against my skin. Then I felt Frank's chilly claw, colder by far than the bed, clutch at my chest. I heard the sound of electricity, and pain coursed through my body. My muscles convulsed, but I could not move at all due to my restraints, which only increased the pain.

"Welcome, Kyle Roswell!" Frank cackled. "Welcome to SPIRE!"

"Spire?" I echoed, coughing.

"Yes," Frank went on, nodding and gesturing at the room around him. "This is the computer database that operates almost all of Utopia. This tower is the central hub of the worldwide network that is the Order's very nerve system. The tower itself is usually cloaked so that it's invisible to most citizens. Is this place the brain of the Order? No, it is merely the spine. The Order is not in these computer terminals you see here. Only its base functions are designated in these. The Order is a higher form of life than a simple program. It thinks. Its creators designed it here, programmed this building to control their robot army, programmed the army to protect all of mankind... but the androids formed a hive mind, a collective consciousness. As they computed the damage they saw humans doing to themselves and their own world, they decided that, for their own best interests, humans should not be allowed control society. They were too greedy, too violent. But they could not simply seize power in a day. No, it was a far subtler task..."

"And now you've become a robot just like them; is that it?" I snapped. "Is that why you got those hands? Now *you're* their brain; the queen of the hive. What a powerful position... lord of a bunch of mindless drones."

Frank laughed. "Kyle, Kyle... You're a true soldier now, a follower on the field of battle – a tool of whoever wishes to control you. It's no use arguing with you. I could probably turn you to my side again, if I wished, as I did countless times in the past when you doubted me. As I said, you're just a tool, not a mover and a pusher – just a pawn. No... more useful than a pawn, and more naïve about the world, deluded into thinking what you are doing is 'right'... perhaps you're a knight. Either way, I could easily have changed your colors after bringing you here, making you my knight again. And you're too stupid to realize it. You never realize when you're being used, because you have no thoughts of your own."

I was growing tired of this rant, so I broke in: "Then why do you care what I think? Why are you even talking to me at all? Just kill me and be done with it."

Frank grabbed me by the throat, his clammy fingers clutching at my skin, and sent another jolt of electricity through me, making me scream as the pain nearly blinded me. When it had subsided a bit, he let go and went on talking.

"That's where you're wrong; I care about Utopia. I care about its people, and I wish to protect them and the society that we have formed. I wish to keep the results of human progress that you would help destroy."

"Then kill me…" I gasped. "Just… kill me… and be done with it…"

Frank smiled. I had seen him smile so much in the past, and this smile was not so different from those smiles of old. But now I knew it for what it truly was: the smile of a lying, manipulative dictator.

"The Order doesn't kill," he said. "It uses… and when a person tries to cause trouble, it breaks them. It makes them see the light; the way things truly are. It makes them give in and act as they should. The Order doesn't kill… unless I tell it to."

"You'll have to kill me then," I said, "because you *won't* break me. I've seen too much. I know too much."

He gave a short laugh. "What, you don't think you can escape? What about your *friends*?"

"Haven't you killed them by now?" I knew that was what he was leading up to, but why he wanted to torture me so, I had no idea.

"It's too late, Kyle," he said, nodding. "I've finished my plan. Right now, poison gas is seeping through the streets of Utopia. All of the citizens who are following orders as they were told are locked inside their houses, safe from the toxin. Those who did not obey, and your rebel friends in the streets, are going to die. I've even un-tinted all of the windows on the houses, so that the citizens of Utopia can see what happens to those who fight the Order."

I knew he was telling the truth. I let my head drop. My entire mission had been for nothing. The last ray of hope had left my body, and all I yearned for at that moment was death. There was nothing left to go back to now.

I said nothing more.

So, at length, Frank broke the silence himself: "They tortured me, Kyle…" he whispered. "I had never truly felt pain before, but they fed it to me in abundance. I told them everything I knew. I remember what that Doctor said, when he told them to shock me: 'Just a little sting...'"

Still I did not reply. I just didn't care anymore.

"You're no fun anymore, Kyle," Frank scolded me. "But still, I'm not going to kill you. There's plenty of room for you in the rehabilitation centers on the Other Side. Eventually, you'll forget everything you've ever seen – all your friends, all this conflict. You'll only remember what the Order wants you to remember, think what we want you to think. And you'll be happy! So, buck up, old boy."

And then, suddenly, everything went yellow – dark and yellow. The blue-white illumination of the lights and computers winked out, leaving only the sickly sunlight of Utopia, filtering in through the windows. Frank stood aghast. The power had gone out. The echoing, almost deafening roar of the vast computer systems in this place he called Spire... had fallen silent.

"Guards!" Frank shouted.

The red robots were still active. They backed up to Frank's position, protecting him on all sides, and surveyed the room for hostiles.

Frank turned to me and pointed an accusing finger. "This is your doing somehow! But I'll have you know this: The Order does not die with the death of one communications tower, even one as important as Spire. The collective consciousness of the computer systems all over Utopia will still run."

"Target all life forms except us, and let none enter the room alive," Frank instructed his guards. "Give me a status report on all patrols, now!"

The nearest robot's monotone voice, sounding as if it echoed from within the monstrous creation's steel frame, responded, "Contact with several more patrols has been lost."

"What about the scouts we sent to inspect the dead soldiers in that... arena that appeared?"

"Scout party M302, dispatched to survey arena structure, sent back word of the discovery of thousands of dead humans, but could not confirm their complete extermination. Survivors possible. Contact with the scout party has been lost. Additional patrols have been dispatched."

"If any humans escaped, then why haven't the regular patrols spotted them and killed them?"

"Patrol units have not sent word of contact with live humans after the release of the poison. Hold – new information incoming – Sir, additional units that were dispatched to the arena structure have confirmed that no life forms were found in the vicinity."

"Then what…"

There was a loud explosion from across the room, and then another. Frank cowered in fear. "What is going on here, guards?!"

"Scanning…"

But the answer came soon enough. There was another explosion, and this one blew a hole in the wall. In stepped three soldiers, all dressed from head to toe in the metallic blue armor of the Utopian patrol bots, their faces obscured behind black-masked helmets. As they entered the room, the giant red guard units made no move to stop them. It was as if they didn't even see them.

"Guards!" Frank snapped. "Switch to motion sensors and fire!"

The red guards lined up in a row along one edge of the platform, their shields forming an impenetrable barrier… until, that is, one of the enemy soldiers swung a huge weapon around and fired. A bolt of lightning split the air, along with the shields and bodies of two of the red robots. It was my PPC.

Then the battle began in earnest, with blue and red lasers setting the air ablaze in a deadly light show. I saw Frank hide behind the edge of the table to which I was bound. The soldiers coming to my rescue fought well, dodging enemy fire and returning it with lethal accuracy, but two of them eventually went down, leaving only the one with my PPC gun still fighting. He took out the last robot and then advanced up the ramp to the top of the platform.

Then Frank Billings rushed at him. The soldier fired the PPC right at him. I expected to see Frank charred to a crisp or blown apart, but the lightning blast split into two separate fingers of electricity, and each one was absorbed by one of Frank's hands. I now noticed some sort of battery pack on Frank's back, which started to smoke as he performed this daring move.

Frank reached out with his hands and sparks leapt forth, grasping at the soldier, arcing over his body. The soldier did not cry out, but he fell to his knees, dropping the PPC. He grasped futilely for the sidearm holstered on his belt, but his arms twitched and spasmed, until his whole body began to convulse. Frank walked closer and closer, still sending out electricity with one hand, as he drew a pistol from under his coat with the other.

"Enough of this child's play..." Frank hissed, leveling his gun at the soldier's head.

"Stop!" came another voice.

Frank turned to see another soldier standing at the top of the ramp, holding a pistol in one hand and clutching a wound on his side with the other. Simultaneously, he and Frank both opened fire. But Frank's aim was better. The soldier took three bullets to the chest, sending him to the ground.

But this gave enough time for the first soldier, still lying on the floor, to finally draw his sidearm and shoot Frank Billings. He unloaded his entire magazine into Frank's back... and the man who had claimed to rule the world finally fell dead into a pool of his own blood. He didn't get back up.

I stared at the two soldiers who had saved me. Both struggled to rise again. The one Frank had shot in the chest pulled himself to his feet and stumbled closer to me, clearly struggling for breath.

The other soldier reached out as he passed, saying, "Don't... Doctor..."

"Doctor?" I gasped.

The wounded soldier threw off his helmet. It was Dr. Matthew Noble. His glasses were gone, and his eyes were growing dim. He fell to a kneeling position on the floor in front of me.

"Kyle," he said, "I have failed."

"H-hang on, Doc," said the other soldier, struggling to his feet. "I'll find a med-kit..."

"Too late," mumbled Dr. Noble, gazing out the window behind me, at the sea of identical houses beneath a dim, yellow sun. "This place... is not what I imagined," he whispered. "You were right, Kyle... I can only hope... that I will be forgiven... for what I've done."

"You did nothing but what you thought was right," I said.

"Is... He... out there?" Dr. Noble whispered, and then he fell over onto his side.

He had stopped breathing. The other soldier finally found the strength to walk to where Dr. Noble lay and check his pulse. Then he stood up and shook his head.

"Dead," he said grimly, but I heard his voice crack with emotion.

Then he walked up to me, pulled a device off his belt, and started cutting through my shackles with it. It was some kind of torch; I felt the heat from it, and sparks flew. After a moment, I felt my arm come free, as a piece of metal clattered to the floor. He repeated this process for my legs and my other arm, and then my body fell limply forward. I could barely move my limbs. The soldier caught me in his arms.

I looked up at my reflection in the dark visor of the helmet above me. "Who are you?"

A hand reached up and removed the metallic mask, shaking free a mass of long, dark hair. Sofia looked down at me and smiled. "What would you do without me, Kyle?"

I can't describe the feeling I felt then. I had thought I'd lost her more than once before, but always she'd returned. I had felt with such certainly that she was truly gone this time... but here she was, in the flesh.

I laughed and coughed simultaneously as I replied, "I'd... be a content Utopian citizen... living a normal, boring life."

Sofia gave a short laugh. "Somehow I can't see you as ever being a content citizen."

"Sofia, you have no idea... how glad I am to see you... How did you...?"

"I'm just lucky I guess," she replied. "I'm also a lot harder to capture than you are."

I tried to walk, but she still had to catch me and support me. Here I was, shaking and fragile, wearing only a pair of trousers, hanging limply in the arms of Sofia, my rescuer, standing tall in her shining armor. I suddenly felt awkward, to say the least.

"I... think I can walk," I said, and when I was back on my feet again, though wobbly, I went on. "If you're alive... then is what Frank said true? Did he really gas the streets?"

Sofia closed her eyes and nodded. "Yes, Kyle. Most of the soldiers died. Some Utopian people sheltered us in their homes though. That's how I survived until the few soldiers who had grabbed gas masks arrived and found me."

"Wow. I'm surprised Utopians were willing to do that. Maybe the programming doesn't run as deep as Frank thought."

Sofia looked at Doctor Noble's corpse and shook her head. "Do you think he had a plan, for all this? What will we – what will *the world* do now?"

"Go on," I said bitterly, "as it always has."

Sofia strode over to Dr. Noble's body and bent down to inspect it. She closed his eyes, straightened him out, and took his weapon and ammunition. Out of curiosity, I approached Frank's corpse and began searching him as well. I found a square data module, some ammo for his pistol, and a notebook. The notebook was filled with random scribbles and notes, even some drawings. I was surprised at some of the images I saw in there: sketches of the evenly rowed houses of Utopia set ablaze, pictures of the robot kill squads murdering screaming people. Were these, I thought, Frank's plans for the world? Had he gone completely mad? I did not know, and I could not know... but one thing was clear: there had been more going on inside his mind than I had suspected. It certainly showed, at least, that he had doubts.

"I think, in the back of his mind," I said aloud, "Frank wanted to destroy the Order, even if he wouldn't admit it to himself."

"Who cares what that madman thought or wanted?" Sofia said with a curse.

"Because he might have actually found a way…" I muttered, thinking hard, trying to remember…

I remembered all of the other fail-safes: the android weapons, the driver's seat in the bus… I looked at the disk in my hand. There was a biohazard symbol on it, but nothing else. I wondered what it could be. I turned back and inspected the notebook more carefully. Above one of the sketches, one of the androids shooting everyone in the streets as the city burned behind them, was depicted the same biohazard symbol.

"Sofia, turn the power back on," I said, rising. "I have to see what's on this disk. It might be the answer to everything."

Sofia stared at me. "But, with the power back on, the security systems in the building might finally detect us, figure out what happened, and bring the guards down on our heads."

I nodded. "But they'll find us eventually anyway, somehow. This world is still swarming with them, all part of the hive-mind. We have to risk it."

"I guess you're right." Lifting her helmet, she spoke into its communicator. "Ian, this is Sofia. Restore power to the building… I don't have time to discuss this, soldier! I gave you an order! Do it."

There was a loud humming sound as all the systems in the tower came back online. One by one, the computer screens on the wall in front of me lit up, illuminating the room in their artificial glow once again. I immediately ran to the nearest control panel and inserted Frank's biohazard disk into the slot. The computer read it instantly, and two options appeared on the screen.

The first option was a shortcut to some program deep in the memory cores of the computer. The program was entitled "failsafe." The other program was on the disk itself, and it was entitled "biohazard." For a moment, my finger hovered between the two, not sure which to pick. But as the images of the dying world that Frank had drawn in his notebook came back to mind, I veered away from the "biohazard" program and pressed the one entitled "failsafe." Four text boxes instantly appeared on screen. At the top were the words "Failsafe Protocol – Input Passcodes." I swallowed and bit my lip. I flipped through Frank's notebook but could find no codes.

Then I remembered: the four numbers scribbled in the corner of Frank's journal. What were they again? I tried desperately to recall. The first was 12, I knew that. And the second was 25, I suddenly remembered. Both were common numbers. What was special about the last two? They had been reverse images of each other: 91 and 19. Which had come first? The smaller one, I thought...

"Kyle," Sofia said urgently, "I don't know what you're doing, but Ian says there's a cloud of drones in the sky, flocking this way. So please, hurry."

I said the numbers aloud as I input them: "Twelve... twenty-five... nineteen... ninety-one."

But when I got ready to push the 'submit' button, I wavered. My determination shook. To fortify myself, I turned back around to look at what lay behind me. I saw the bodies of Dr. Matthew Noble and Frank Billings, the two men who had been most influential in my life. I saw Sofia, standing there and wondering what I would do next, but trusting me to do it.

Sofia was the only thing I had done right my whole life, I thought. Everything else had been pointless – just destruction, destruction, and more destruction. And now I was getting ready to destroy even more. But it was all I could do. I had to make all of the fighting and death worth *something*. Even if what I did was catastrophic in its results, I at least had to try...

I pressed the button.

For a moment, it seemed like nothing had happened. Then, suddenly, I heard a loud metallic groan, and the floor began to shake.

"Run!" I shouted, and together we dashed down the ramp on the side of the platform.

Ian ran to meet us at the bottom. He removed his helmet, staring wide-eyed at something behind us. I glanced back to see. The huge cloud of drones was visible outside the window – so vast it blocked out the sun. My heart jumped into my throat. My program had failed. Soon, we would be dead.

And then, without flash or fanfare, they all fell from the sky. I hoped no one was standing below, because that shower of deactivated metal bots must have been destructive when it hit the earth. The lights in the room around us started to blink out, going dark once again. The building stopped shaking, and we all relaxed a bit.

"Wait," Ian said. "Does that say… USOW? There, on the wall. I… I don't believe it…"

"Believe it," I said. "Frank's journal confirmed it. The United States of the World also existed in Utopia's past, but in this world, they were not stopped by rebellion and broken by war. They united the world and created the Order."

"So, this is the answer to history's greatest question," Ian said, shaking his head. "This is how it would have all turned out if we'd united the globe… Amazing. It's not exactly how I dreamed it would be."

"Let's just get out of here," Sofia said.

"Wait…" I said. "Let me go look at the computers one more time."

I ran up the long, tall ramp, with Sofia and Ian close behind me. The sun was setting behind the low, flat horizon of Utopia now. It was not a beautiful sight by any means… the sun and the sky were still pale and sickly, but the twilight had a somewhat enchanting effect nonetheless, as it always does. I looked at the computer screens in confusion; each one only showed one thing…

"Connection lost," I read. "Connection lost…"

"The network…" Sofia breathed. "You destroyed it."

"It worked…" I muttered, hardly able to believe it.

Sofia shrugged. "Well, there's only one thing we can do: go outside and see what happened. Suit up in one of the armor outfits and let's go."

===

On our ride in the elevator down to the lower levels of Spire, we were surprisingly silent, each lost in our own thoughts. I didn't ask how they had infiltrated the facility and figured out how to cut the power. I was too tired to ask, nor did I really care at the moment. We continued our ride down and left the building. The streets of Utopia looked the same as ever, though they were bathed in the eerie twilight glow of the setting Utopian sun.

We walked along, looking silently around. All that could be heard was the slow, measured tapping of our feet as they hit the pavement. There were no sounds of animals or people – not even the wind. We seemed to walk forever together, our shadows stretched out before us like tall, thin giants on the road. Finally, after walking for nearly an hour, we noticed a small gathering of civilians in the street. They were all inspecting something. I walked up and looked over their shoulders. It was a security bot. It was deactivated.

One of the Utopians noticed me and turned around. "W-who are you three? What's going on with all the patrolmen? Where did that huge tower come from?"

"This is revolution," I said. "The Order is gone. The androids are dead. You're free."

There was no excitement, no exclamations of joy, no gratitude; nor was there anger, resentment, or hatred. There was only astonishment and confusion. The civilians stared blankly and looked around. We did too. There were robots standing in groups on the sidewalk up and down the street, all deactivated, all dead where they stood. There was a bus as well, stopped dead, with the driver's head lying on the steering wheel. In one fell swoop, the Order was gone. The civilians who gathered their wits enough to speak began asking us questions, but I waved my hand in mock impatience and pressed on.

"We have to investigate," I said, assuming an air of importance. "Stand aside."

The crowd parted for us immediately. We looked so much like security bots, wearing armor of the same color as their protective hulls, that the citizens obviously thought of us the same way. It was in their programming, I thought. Sofia led us the way they had come, back down the street toward the location where all the fighting had taken place – where I had been sucked up into the aircraft.

There was something different now though… On one half of the street, the rows of identical houses were gone, and a huge crumbling stadium stood in their place: the stadium from G4M3. It was a strange sight to see a piece of that other world stuck so awkwardly in this one. The two places contrasted so sharply that it seemed they could not be, should not be, side-by-side like this. I stared in wonder, while Sofia's eyes were downcast. I looked down. There in the road and on the sidewalk lay several dozen dead soldiers… Eagles and USOW and some factions I did not recognize.

"This is where we saw you abducted," she said in a low voice. "The stadium appeared and blew everything away, including you. Then the robots attacked. We couldn't find you in the chaos, but I guess Frank Billings did, after the bots freed him. The fight lasted a while. It seemed to be going well, but it ended when… the poison gas came. I heard it venting and held my breath. Some of the others weren't so quick. Most of them didn't make it, except for the ones with masks."

"Tens of thousands of people died here," said a deep voice from a nearby alley, "because of Matthew Noble's stupidity."

Don appeared, still clad in Utopian armor, which was now covered in burn marks. Despite his grim comment, a bright smile cracked his dark face when he saw us all alive and well. He and Sofia clasped each other's arms. Then Don noticed Ian and scowled.

"Don't blame him, Don," Sofia said. "We can't do that to each other. Doctor Noble is dead. He died saving Kyle and me. He died helping us kill the leader of *this* world – the one who released the gas. They're both gone now. Now, there's only… us."

"What about Scott?" I asked.

"Dragged him with me to safety," Don said. "He's with the survivors. Healing, hopefully…"

I looked around at the bodies and said sorrowfully, "It's all Frank Billings's fault. The Order would never have used lethal force, if not for him. It was programmed never to harm humans. It wouldn't have waged a deadly war. It was created to end war – to change everything."

Sofia snorted. "War never changes, Kyle. People always die. These robots had lethal weapons on their arms for a reason. They would have used them. Anyway... there's no use talking about it. Let's keep going."

Just then, the door to a nearby Utopian house slid open. A man – a Utopian citizen – stood in the doorway and beckoned us inside. We followed him. There in the living room, which was only slightly different from my family's own, were a dozen more Eagles and USOW soldiers.

"I gave these boys and girls shelter from the fighting," said the Utopian homeowner. "I'm glad to see you're alive too, Kyle."

I looked up at the old man's kindly face. He was my next-door neighbor! I barely knew him, but my parents visited him often. I didn't know how to reply to him. It seemed too strange, the two worlds colliding like this. They had remained separate in my mind for so long, and now... A thought suddenly hit me.

"My parents," I said, rising. "I have to go see if they're okay."

The old Utopian put his hand on my shoulder. "Kyle... they're..."

I could read his next words on his face, and I didn't want to hear them, so I brushed him aside and stood up. I ran out the door and into the street. Turning to look at my house, I stopped. There was a hole blasted in the wall... a stray shot from a tank, I thought. I walked slowly inside, in a daze. The house was dark and silent. I walked past the familiar objects, touching them like ancient relics. It felt I like I hadn't seen them in years. The house was dark and silent and dead, like a tomb. I had never, ever seen it like this, with the lights and the holovision turned off. Not even at night. I swallowed as I stepped into the bedroom, already sure of what I would find.

They were both seated on the edge of their bed leaning against each other, holding hands... and not moving. I was right; the blast had let in the poison gas. From the peaceful looks on their faces, they hadn't felt a thing. A few tears ran down my face as I approached them, but part of me was glad to find them like this. They looked so calm, so at peace. They had always been satisfied with their life under the Order. Perhaps it was better this way; they would never have to face life without it.

I wondered how in the world the other citizens would survive. They would have to build their own city infrastructure, their own government, and figure out how to do all the tasks that normally fell to the robots. Thinking about it made my head hurt, so I pushed the thoughts out of my mind, all thoughts... and walked numbly out of the house. Sofia was waiting for me outside. She put her arm around my shoulders. It did make me feel better, but not much.

"Don," Sofia said, in charge of the situation as always, "do you still have the palm computer?"

The Eagle nodded and unclipped the device from his belt. All of the lights that we had tried so hard to light up were now black, but the map was still there, glowing green.

"It'll still work," Don said, "I think... It's still on, anyway... still has power."

"I want to go see something," I said on a whim. "I'm going to the G4M3 facility."

I started leading the way immediately, not waiting for a reply. The others had noticed the determination in my voice, and seeing no reason to tarry there, they fell into step behind me. Sofia stopped to thank the family that had sheltered the soldiers, but for some reason I could not.

It seemed like my life had become a series of instabilities ever since I had first started playing G4M3. My emotions were always on edge, and whenever I thought things were understandable, they turned upside-down again. I could deal with it no longer. I just wanted to run, to get away from it all, to take a break.

At length, we reached the G4M3 facility. The door was gone, so we walked right in. The debris of the flying sentry robots that we had destroyed still lay scattered around, and the walls were covered in blast marks. No friendly greeter bot sat behind the desk to say hello. Frank was not there smiling and welcoming me. No other players were there to talk to or train with. There was only death and silence… debris, destruction, ashes, dust, and echoes…

I walked around to the computer behind the front desk. I was surprised it was still working. It seemed that the power in the city was not dead, just the network and the Order's androids. And along with them, the security on the computer. I could access everything. I dug deeper and deeper through the files. I found what I was looking for… and something that I wasn't.

"Amazing…" I muttered.

"What is it?" Sofia whispered, as if she was afraid to break the stillness and silence in the room.

"I came here to destroy this building," I said. "I was planning to make sure no one from G4M3 came to Utopia like we did, or vice-versa… but look here… Frank found something that he never expected: a *third* world."

Sofia looked over my shoulder. There was one picture there: one unclear, fuzzy picture of the signal that the facility had locked onto – of the dimension Frank had found. It showed plants, green foliage, a shining lake, and a bright blue sky. To all of us there, the picture looked like heaven.

"I'm going there…" I muttered, speaking my thoughts aloud.

"You can't be serious," Ian scoffed behind me.

But Sofia's sharp green eyes looked at my face and saw my determination. She knew that I had made up my mind, and she seemed… pleased about it. I could see it on her face as well. Could it be possible, I wondered…?

"Will you come with me?" I asked her, almost in a whisper, a confidential tone, yet still a pleading one.

A smile formed upon her lips. I could tell right away that the answer was yes. It seemed as if she had been wishing for the same thing as I – a way to get away from everything. I truly hoped that was the case. We had both been born in worlds we had grown to hate, and now we had both left them… but we had to go somewhere. Now a third choice was presented to us. I could not speak for her, but to me the choice was clear. I couldn't stay here any longer.

"Yes," Sofia said, still smiling. "Yes, I will."

Don stared at her. Sofia looked away.

"There's nothing left for me here," I said to her, though I was looking at Don while I said it, "but if you want to return to your world, Sofia, then I'll go with you. I hate the thought of remaining in Utopia. I never want to see this forsaken place again."

"No, no," Sofia said, with a sort of regretful determination. "I can't go back now either, Kyle. Back to Saltpit City, now that I've finally escaped that hell? Why would I even consider that?"

I breathed a deep sigh of relief.

"So, this is goodbye then," Don said, with disapproval clear in his voice. "I guess this makes me leader of the Saltpit Eagles... probably all the Eagles. I'm going back there if you're not, Sofia. I'm gonna set things right."

"I'm going back too," Ian said, stepping forward. "You'll need my help keeping the peace between the Eagles and USOW. And the USOW need to know what I've seen here."

Ian extended his hand, and surprisingly, Don immediately shook it. Sofia breathed a sigh of relief, smiling happily. At least some good had apparently come of all this death.

"Don," I said, "you still have the device. You take everyone out of here."

"You sure you want to do this?" he asked, looking at Sofia.

"Yes," she replied. "I'm sure."

"Godspeed then, Commander. It's been an honor."

"Good luck," Ian said, "wherever you're going."

Sofia and I watched as they left, heading back to gather the other survivors from G4M3. Sofia gazed out the window in silence for some time after they had gone. I didn't interrupt her. After a while, however, we heard something moving around outside. It was probably just a wandering Utopian, but it broke Sofia from her reverie.

"Let's go," she said.

SIXTEEN
THE THIRD WORLD

Can you imagine, dear reader, having everything you know turned upside down, with fantasy suddenly turned into reality? Can you imagine having your entire world destroyed? Can you imagine having almost everyone important in your life suddenly gone, in an instant? And then can you imagine taking a leap of faith into the unknown, in order to escape from all of it?

And then, finally, can you imagine ending up lying in a grassy field with a beautiful woman you have come to love... all alone, beneath a clear blue sky and wholesome yellow sun the likes of which you never dreamed you would see in your lifetime... and both of you completely naked?

That's what happened to Sofia and me. We had locked the doors to the G4M3 facility soon after hearing the approaching footsteps and then hurried to find a transceiver. It turned out that one was still implanted in Sofia, from when I sent her back to be saved, but I had to find a new one. It was surprisingly easy to tell the computer to program the transceivers to take us to this third world. We also found all of the other transceivers that we could and destroyed them, to keep others from following us. And then we slipped into the other dimension... but since they weren't part of our bio-matrix, none of our clothes came with us.

"W-what happened?" Sofia asked. "Why the hell are we naked?"

I laughed and threw a pile of clothes at her. "Don't worry – I brought some gear that was programmed into our bio-matrix."

She caught the clothes and glared at me. "And you didn't tell me to, you know, put these on?"

I shrugged. "Must have slipped my mind. Hey, I hadn't seen that tattoo there before."

She actually blushed at that. "Yeah, that's... a story for later, I guess. Couldn't you have packed more than this?"

"I wanted to travel light... and preferably not bring an arsenal of weapons to a place that looks like the Garden of Eden."

For a moment, we sat in silence, contemplating the beauty of all the green nature surrounding us. There was so much *noise!* It was almost terrifying. Birds flitted through the tree branches, and insects buzzed over our heads. I regarded Sofia, looking so different now, with her hair down and an expression of hopeful curiosity in her eyes. Such eyes...

She caught me looking at her and laughed. "So, what now? Should we build a camp, hunt for some food...?"

"No! I brought some survival supplies in a crate here. They'll last us quite a while. Let's just suit up and look around."

"Let's not suit up," she said, standing up and dropping her clothes in the grass. "You don't wear *clothes* in the Garden of Eden."

I laughed and followed her lead; I wasn't about to complain.

We started exploring the forest in a perimeter around our supply crate, but everywhere we looked, we saw only trees. There was nothing anywhere except tall, bright green trees, some covered in vines, a few bearing fruit or flowers, with the sun sending rays of light piercing through their dense boughs. The ground was covered in a carpet of damp fallen leaves and occasional patches of grass, and the air smelled of vegetation... and nothing else. Every breath felt crisp and clean.

We were in a world that was alien to the both of us: a world of nature, with not a building to be seen in any direction. As we walked together in this strange third world, careful to keep in mind where we'd left our supplies, I felt a sense of both awe and peace. It was as if we had died and passed into paradise. I half-wondered if we would find Matthew Noble here, waiting for us.

"It's all so beautiful..." Sofia said. "It's like a dream. I've only seen pictures of places like this... ancient pictures from a time long gone."

"Me too," I said. "Even in Utopia, the trees were grown in neat little rows in the parks, and the leaves of all the plants were clipped daily by the androids that patrolled the place. Here, everything is running wild. The Order used to teach us that a place like this would be terrible…"

"Do you think we've slipped into the past?" Sofia asked, her voice losing its awestricken tone all in an instant as another thought struck her. "Do you think… that we might find a city soon? Or a village?"

"I don't think so," I said. "But maybe we can find a high place to look from. Maybe a tall tree…"

"There's an open space with no trees up ahead."

We walked together through the dense foliage to a place where the light shone with blinding brightness. As we stepped out into the clearing, we saw the sun shining down upon a huge lake, which looked as big as an ocean. It stretched out to the horizon, where sky and sea met in a thin, perfectly flat line. Between us and the water stretched an expanse of glittering white sand. Swarms of little gnats buzzed around the water's edge, and a flock of birds passed low over the waves, their graceful forms reflecting on the water's surface.

"It's a paradise," Sofia sighed airily, walking out onto the shore and running her toes through the sand.

Actually, though the land behind us seemed quite attractive, as I walked out toward the shore of the lake, I began to feel a strange creeping sensation. Something wasn't right. I did not like this lake, though I had no idea why. Out of curiosity, I approached the shore and put my hand in the water. The water seemed… wrong… unclean, somehow. I lifted my finger to my mouth and touched my tongue. The water was salty.

"Sofia…" I almost whispered. "It's the Saltpit."

Sofia squinted, staring off into the distance. "Those mountains… I think you're right. Let's go bring our supplies here and then look around some more."

"If you insist," I said.

We brought our supply crate to the shore of the lake, and then, since it was growing late, we finally put on some clothes and even strapped on our sidearms. After all, there could be wild animals here. Since it was getting dark, we brought flashlights too.

Then we walked along the shore as the sun set over the horizon, casting its long red reflection upon the glittering waters. Something happened then that I will never forget: I saw the stars, for the first time in my life. In G4M3, the sky had always been overcast with clouds of smoke and ash... and in Utopia, there had been too much ground light and pollution. But here, in this third world, the stars shone true. I had never dreamed there could be so *many*.

Sofia felt the same way, apparently. She walked up beside me, and we put our arms around each other, staring at the night sky as we strode along the shore together. We didn't even need our flashlights. The stars and moon lit the area in a beautiful, soft light, unlike the harsh artificial street lamps of Utopia. I felt like I was walking – no, floating – through a dream.

So, it came as a complete surprise when something hit my toe.

I stopped and looked down. It was a stone, but it didn't feel natural. It was too flat on the side. I took a step back. I could see now that it was a large slab of concrete, sticking up out of the sand... and that frightened me. Sofia stood beside me and stared at it wordlessly. We exchanged glances, but could find no words to say. Summoning up my courage, I advanced toward the ancient, cracked object and brushed aside some of the salty sand covering it. Staring at the ground, I beheld a sight that took my breath away.

"Sofia..." was all I managed to say.

When she came to my side, she was surprised to see a statue of a human man, worn and cracked, lying in the sand, covered in the dark grime of many years. She stared at it and felt of its surface, wondering, trying to find an inscription, but there was none.

I didn't need one. I knew exactly what it was.

"It's the Builder."

E P I L O G U E

Well, it would seem that I have finished my book. And it would seem that you have read it. I will now try to explain how it came to be in your possession. We still do not know the story behind this dimension or why we found the statue of the Builder here, but Sofia says she thinks there are other humans here, and we should find them eventually. At the moment, however, we are perfectly content to stay apart from them, if there are any here.

After we arrived here in this world and were done exploring the immediate area, Sofia and I began sorting through all of the gear that we had managed to bring with us. Among the other belongings, we were surprised to find a blank book. Exactly what purpose the book was to serve on a G4M3 expedition I do not know. Perhaps either Walter or Frank intended to use it as a journal while exploring another dimension, to put words on paper instead of a computer, as Frank had said in his own journal, in order to keep such information off the Order's computer networks.

Well, that is what I have used it for. I wrote down every word you have just read in that book. Once I was done recording my story, I formed a plan. Since the book came with us on the journey, that means that the transceivers must have considered it a part of our bio-matrix. Which means, I hope, that if I remove Sofia's transceiver, put it in-between the pages of this book, and then press the activation button, it will send it to another dimension: either one of our own unfortunate worlds, or some other. Only you, the reader, will ever know exactly where.

Sofia and I have found peace in this new world and do not wish to ever leave. I will keep further details about this place to myself. I wish not to lure in any further travelers. Are we alone here, or did we find other humans living amidst the ruins? I leave that for you to conjecture. But if the transceiver is still in the pages of this book when you find it, and if you now have in your possession the transceiver that was once in the body of my beloved Sofia... then please read my story before you try to use it. It is now up to your discretion what you are going to do with it. I hope you can make the right choice.

For that is why I am sending you this book: so that you can make the right choice. So that you can learn whatever lessons might be gleaned from my story. I could not save my world, but maybe you can save yours. Maybe you can have the wisdom that I did not have...

Before I played the G4M3.

THE END

www.ingramcontent.com/pod-product-compliance
Lightning Source LLC
Chambersburg PA
CBHW071237260626
47159CB00005BA/1762

* 9 7 8 0 9 7 2 7 3 4 1 0 3 *